GLASS
WATER

Cover Design: *Infixgraph Designs*

Copy Editing: *Jen Boles*

Copy Editing: *Lisa Fox*

Interior Formatting: *Fox Formatting*

ISBN (paperback): 979-8-9880450-2-1

For my husband Stephen—your love knows no bounds.

ONE

I free-fell in lonely silence, blinded, struggling for a grip, arms flailing. Nothing. It was as if there were no physical substance in this place. Nefarious whistling, distant at first, crescendoed into hurricane-like winds, blasting me from all sides, tossing me like a rag doll. An invisible force punched me square in the stomach, and I doubled over. Another gust pummeled my side next, and I reeled. This was nothing like what I'd experienced inside P6's alluron. This was hell.

Just as I was about to give up and let the tempest tear me to shreds, luminescent ribbons floated toward me, unaffected by the welter. They sizzled, extending one side toward me, their ends swallowed in the darkness. My instinct told me to choose one, but which? About twelve of them hovered in front of me, each a different color, yet that revealed nothing. What if the fate awaiting me on the other side was far worse than the death in this void? What if it led to Invicta's underground cells?

Tremors shook my body. Another freight train gust knocked me sideways, spinning me in the empty darkness.

The ribbons were now out of my reach, and panic set in. My foot snagged on something as I awkwardly maneuvered with my new set of wings. Searing pain shot up my leg, and then I saw *it:* two laser-red eyes stared at me from below. I kicked at the thing, connecting with something hard, and the grip on my leg loosened.

The screeching below intensified, and legions of red eyes popped open everywhere. As I fought the winds and wriggled closer to the ribbons, sharp claws tore into my abdomen. My wings protected my back, effectively blocking attackers there, but I was weaponless. My punches and kicks weakened their grip. The red-eyed creatures navigated the maelstrom with ease, while I continued to flounder, losing my sense of direction.

I let one of the small demons grip my thigh, using it as a springboard to launch myself away after landing a fierce punch on its head. The gamble paid off. I drifted into a current that whisked me by the ribbons. As I zoomed past, I grasped the first ribbon shimmering in electric blue. A jolt of electricity shot through me, the blue light crackling and twisting its way up my arm. My wings recoiled inside me with a painful snap.

Before I could blink, the ribbon pulled me into a tube of blue rings. A blazing bright light rushed at me next. Shielding my eyes with my arms, I braced myself. Then the tunnel spat me out.

TWO

I hit a hard surface, and the impact sent a sharp jolt of pain through me. Blurred faces stared at me. My gaze fixated on pairs of red orb-like eyes. The tunnel had dumped a few of the void creatures along with me. In the light, the creatures resembled hunched-over goblins—the non-friendly ones. Saliva dripped from their jagged teeth as they snarled. I only had time to blink once before they charged me. Scooting away on my butt, my hands brushed over slick metal—utensils, and by the feel, I was lucky to come across a knife. As the first one sprang on me, I plunged the knife into its chest and shoved the body off. The second goblin leaped on my right arm, knocking the knife out of my grip.

The entire situation infuriated me. Why couldn't anything end well for me for once? Why couldn't the tunnel dump me on a paradise island with dolphins hopping in the water against a backdrop of a picturesque sunset? I yanked a feather stuck in my shirt and stabbed the needle point into the closest goblin's grotesque eye. I must have applied a great deal of force because the feather punctured the creature's head. It was an instant kill.

I roared in pain as another bit into my thigh. Then someone lifted it off and dispatched it with what appeared to be a sword. My vision blurred again, obscuring the frenzied scene. I tensed, readying for another attack, but nothing came. I gave into the dizziness and collapsed onto my back. As my head hit the surface, I felt the sensation of landing in a liquid substance, accompanied by the unmistakable sound of a delicate dish breaking. My eyes snapped open. Blurriness danced around the edges, but the view above me was clear. King Cygnus's face, a permanent mask of disapproval, betrayed no emotion.

"I was planning to eat that." The king's words dripped with scorn. I had encountered King Cygnus, the formidable ruler of the Andromeda Fae, on two occasions in the Earth realm. The first time he'd used me; the second time he'd abandoned me on the battlefield. Always watching, never engaging in Earthly matters.

"The goblins?" I managed with a labored breath.

He took a second to consider my words, then a minuscule smile tugged the corners of his lips upward. He picked up an embroidered-edge cloth napkin from his lap and dabbed at the bits of soup trickling down his tight, black shirt. When he lifted his eyes to mine, the saffron in them fired into vibrant yellow. I averted my gaze, propped myself up on my elbows, and surveyed the gathering of twelve fae warriors seated at this section of the expansive wooden oval table. Crystal clear bowls holding their green liquid meals sat in front of them untouched.

The warriors scrutinized me with hard stares of their own. The one closest to my right rested a sizable clear blue sword on his shoulder with bits of dark green goo stuck to it.

He must have killed the goblin that bit me. I scanned the table for the creatures' bodies, but they were nowhere to be seen. I attempted to swivel my legs to the left to get off the immense table. There I faced a rather pissed-off fae. He crossed his bulging arms, which were covered in the same unfamiliar soup I had plopped my head into. My eyes widened, and I scrambled away, hissing from the excruciating pain in my right thigh that my shocked brain hadn't registered until now.

Vice-like fingers wrapped around my left bicep and spun me around. I gritted my teeth against the pain, fighting the urge to black out. The king roughly picked up my right leg to inspect the injury, and I yelped. His saffron eyes lacked compassion.

"Gollum venom," he said. He glanced at one of his men. A chair scraped.

"Wha-what's...a gollum?" My tongue quit working.

"The heinous creatures you brought into my realm," he replied, yanking at my leg with displeasure. I reached a hand to swat at him but swayed instead and fell to my elbows on one side.

"The...venom?" I struggled to speak.

"It kills weaker beings which we now know you're not. But you're at risk of paralysis."

What?

I had to get out of there. There was no way I'd stick around the enigmatic fae king while unconscious. I pushed off, attempting to slide down the table. The king released my leg, and I flopped to my belly, unable to stand. Shit! I was too late. If the king ever rolled his eyes, I sensed that would've been the moment. Instead, two fae flipped me over and laid me on my back again, pressing my shoulders into the table.

"What—?" I tried to kick with my good leg, but someone

had pinned it down too. Through blurry vision, I saw King Cygnus standing over me with a wicked gleam in his eyes, brandishing a fiery hot blade. "No..." I begged.

In slow motion, the king lowered the knife to my thigh. He pressed it firmly to the wound. I waited with trepidation for the oncoming pain. It gripped me soon enough. I arched my back off the table, cursing them all, screaming. But that was only the beginning. Waves of excruciating pain surged through every fiber of my being, causing my body to convulse uncontrollably until I drifted into oblivion.

Moans escaped me as I rolled to the side. I felt like I'd slept on a flat board. My whole body ached, and *ohmagod,* was I drooling? I ran the back of my hand across my chin and blinked my eyes open. Blue fire danced and crackled in the large hearth in the fae's dining hall. Apart from the crackling, an eerie silence filled the room. Someone had cleaned the table; even the hardwood floors sparkled, absent any evidence of my messy arrival.

Gingerly, I pushed myself to a sitting position, scanning the vast room. King Cygnus faced the arched windows, gazing out at the picturesque fields, rolling valleys, and serpentine lazy river, all bathed in the soft glow of dusk. Wherever this place was, it was captivating.

Surprisingly, my right leg seemed to be working now. Pulling it up, I inspected the damage inflicted by those deranged supernaturals. The area had a wide leaf resembling a palm frond wrapped around it. My fingers trembled as I prodded, looking for a way to unwind the leafy bandage.

"It only responds to magic." The king's voice diverted my attention. His gaze locked on the leaf, which unfurled itself and floated toward the fire, disintegrating in an instant.

Someone had cut off my pant leg a few inches above a now faint scar on my thigh. I traced it with my fingers. It didn't even feel puffy or angry as it should have been after being torn apart by this gollum creature and then singed shut.

"How?" I asked.

"The leaf draws the venom out," he replied.

"Venom?"

If the king grew exasperated with my ignorance, he concealed it well. He appeared at ease in his domain, though any semblance of friendliness was absent. His saffron eyes flared with emotion, then dimmed as he struggled for composure. He strode over, his black silk attire fitting snugly without a crease and his golden circlet adorned with a yellow stone sitting atop his head. His pants resembled jeans, but the material was unlike anything I'd ever seen. The same disapproving frown he had given me in the human realm appeared slightly less pronounced. He folded his arms over his chest and cocked his head to the side, scrutinizing me anew.

"I'm sure there's a good story behind your abrupt appearance," he said.

I fought the fog in my head and the ringing in my ears, remnants of my own ear-splitting screams, no doubt.

"I crossed into Invicta's allura."

"Obviously," the king drawled. "Why are you here?" He ran his fingers through his slick hair, his eyes flashing with intensity. Shivers rippled over my skin.

"What are gollums?" I asked meekly.

"Gollums rule the in-between. Only inexperienced travelers linger there long enough to encounter them," he explained, raising an eyebrow. "Most don't survive."

The mere thought of turning into a gollum snack made my blood run cold.

"You survived, crashed my dinner party, and even hauled a

few gollums along." The king's eyes flashed with anger. I stiffened.

"I-I'm sorry?" I stammered, unsure what else to say. I scooted to the edge of the table, feeling vulnerable sitting there. The king's eyes traced my movements. As I cautiously hopped down, landing on both legs, I expected pain but felt none. It was as if my injury had healed months ago. Yeah, the scar was still there, and I'd probably always have it, but this was close to miraculous. I spun around to face the king.

"Why?" I asked, trying to mask my desperation. "Why the torture?"

"The gollum venom has anti-clotting properties," he said, emotionless. "You would have bled to death without our intervention."

"Why did you help me? You didn't care if I lived before." Was it only today that the Earthbounders had faced Bezekah in battle?

"I may have found you useful," the king said. He turned and strolled toward the open double doors. I hesitated, then followed, scanning the room for any signs of portal energy. A beautifully adorned wreath, filled with the fresh, woody fragrance of evergreen branches and adorned with sturdy pinecones and shimmering golden beads, lay in the middle of the table. I glided my hand over it but sensed nothing unusual. I straightened, contemplating my next move. Black velvety wallpaper adorned the walls, with golden symbols embroidered into it. The hearth was broad enough to fit ten people. A heavy crystal chandelier hung above. Carved wooden chairs rested tucked under the tabletop. Nothing here exuded magical properties. Resigned, I crept to the open door and peeked outside.

At the end of the hall, guarded by two faeries, another set of double doors awaited. The guards' uncanny eyes dared me to deviate from the course. I strolled over and when they didn't stop me, I crossed the threshold to find the king and a few of his men around a low table brimming with fruit, cheeses, and pitchers filled with some kind of drink. The king reclined in a high-backed black leather chair, a crystal cup in hand.

"Sit," he commanded, pointing a long finger to a floor cushion by his chair. Out of options, I complied. The fire caressed my back, and tingles spread across my shoulder blades, reminding me of my retracted wings. I kind of missed them. I didn't understand why they had retracted in the void, or the in-between, as the fae called it.

"You'd like to return to your world," he stated.

I glanced at him, nodding. Based on the prelude in the dining hall, the king needed me for something. The question was whether I could provide what he wanted. My life essence was out of the question. Definitely. Maybe. It depended.

He swirled the vibrant pinkish-purple liquid and sipped it. The rich aroma filled my nostrils and I jolted, suddenly craving it. I curled my fingers around the cushion. Swallowing hard, I forced my gaze to the floor.

"I have a proposition for you," he said, leaning over the armrest. "I have a portal you can use to return to your world, but I require you to take a few of my men with you."

"I've never transported anyone before," I said, cautiously. Hadn't he seen how bad I was at portal jumping? I'd nearly gotten myself killed.

The king reclined in his chair, resting his head against it.

"My men have not been to Earth in millennia. With the banishment came a binding that prevents me from creating potent magic. Until I break the bind, I'm unable to take them with me even though I can portal by myself."

He spoke the truth—the fae couldn't lie. Although the

Earthbounder books did not mention the details of the banishment, they only stated that they were banished for breaking the edicts. I twisted my lips and weighed his words.

"What will your men do while on Earth?" I asked. The king rubbed his forehead with apathy. I studied his men. Their faces showed clear signs of restrained anticipation, their movements becoming jerky and restless.

"I've spoken enough," he said. "It will be done." The king swirled his electric drink and sipped it again. I squared my shoulders and met his gaze directly.

"I can't do that," I said defiantly, bracing for the worst.

Iron fingers dug into my neck, and suddenly, my feet dangled in the air. Then I was tumbling over the table. Crystal glasses crashed to the polished floor, vibrant liquids spilling around me. I blinked up at the king, his face red and eyes brimming with fury. He bared his pointy teeth at me.

"You never go back on your word," he growled. I stared at him, struggling to catch my breath. He read into my obedience as a sign of agreement between us. The fae ways were a mystery to me. I bit my lip, considering my options. Maybe I could restrain them once we made it over there before they caused any damage to the human world.

Before I could correct my mistake, the king flung me across the room as if I were a toy he was done with. I crashed against the top edge of the couch and tumbled over it. My heart pounded, and my ears rang. Elegant shoes approached from the other side of the couch. I rolled over and scrambled away.

"No," I whispered, my back against the wall, pulling myself up. The king's face twisted into a demonic visage, his ears elongating. This was the end of me. A sharp crack reverberated through me, and I folded over from the pain. He lifted my head by my hair as warm liquid trickled down my back.

"It appears you scared the wings out of her, my sire," one of his men quipped. I trembled as the king took a minute to eye my wings. His mood lightened and features molded into the image I was familiar with—of a handsome dark fae. He released my hair, then ran the tips of his fingers over one wing as bile rose in my stomach. My wings shook with agitation, fending him off. There was one thing we agreed on—*we didn't like the king's touch*. He harrumphed.

"I haven't seen such wings in ages," he mused, his eyes lingering on my frightened ones. He ogled as if he wanted to get inside me and fish for answers there.

He stalked off in the direction of the dining hall. Two of his men guided me behind him, stealing enamored glances at my wings. What was with this fascination with wings?

The king swiped his hand over the centerpiece, revealing a small blue circle shimmering on the table's surface. This must have been my portal. He had sealed it off from detection with his magic. He called four of his men by their names, and they stepped up onto the table, hauling me with them.

"Angel, pick your destination wisely. You only have one chance at avoiding gollums and certain death." He leveled his eyes at me. "My men have a destination of their own, so don't expect to see them on the other side."

In tandem, the fae placed their hands on my shoulders. I didn't like the idea of losing track of them. But withdrawing from the deal at this point meant certain death, fae-style. And the king would bring his men to Earth eventually. I was better off warning the Earthbounders about King Cygnus's plans and seeing how much wrath awaited me from the Magister's hands.

I chewed on my inner cheek, considering my options. The error I'd made the last time was not setting a destination in my mind, not mentally mapping out where I was heading. Before, when I created a portal myself, I had thought of

Xavier, and the portal dumped me outside the fissure site where he was at the time. I couldn't go there, obviously. That place had to be swarmed by furious warriors. An idea popped into my mind. I closed my eyes, focusing on a destination, and stepped into the portal, hoping for the best.

THREE

Shelves stocked with jars, tinted glass bottles, and baskets of dried herbs rushed at me. The tunnel curved at the last second and spit me out onto Malcolm's Persian carpet. Underneath, the floor heated, and wisps of blue flames rolled from the center to the frayed edges, singing some of the exquisite material in the process. I rushed to one corner of the carpet, which surprisingly lit up, and I swatted at the tiny flames with the palm of my hand, extinguishing them. I laid my forehead against the floor, my body rocking with laughter. *Holy shit, I made it!*

The sound of bubble gum popping alerted me to someone's presence. I leaped to my feet, spinning around. The gothic girl who had managed the front desk when I came into this dry cleaning shop with Paulie weeks ago leaned against the doorway, her arms crossed, an amused expression curving her thin, black-painted lips.

"No one's ever entered the shop this way before," she said, her eyes sparkling with amusement.

"Er... I put out the fire." I shrugged, feeling awkward.

Geez, I was so bad at small talk, chatting, and people in general.

"Come on." She beckoned me to follow. I stepped off the carpet and into the back room filled with rows of bars and hanging clothes in plastic bags. I focused on the girl's black hair with red highlights pulled into a bun atop her head to navigate this sea of clothes. We crossed into a small, enclosed kitchen. She filled a plastic cup with tap water and handed it to me.

"Portal travel always makes me thirsty," she said. I took a sip, then another, until I'd gulped it all. Wiping drips off my chin, I thanked her. I guess I never paid attention to my body's physical needs when I jumped portals before.

"I'm Daria, by the way," she chirped. Her tone didn't match her gothic-inspired attire. I studied her, intrigued by her prior statement.

"So, you jump portals?" I asked.

"Kinda. My uncle can do portal magic, and I picked up a few tricks." Why did it sound like her uncle wasn't aware and probably wouldn't have approved? She was maybe fifteen, sixteen? "I'm actually the best at what I do." *Oh?*

"What can you do?" I asked.

She stepped closer, glancing over my shoulder into the hall.

"I can break into places. Warded places," she whispered. I narrowed my eyes, debating whether to push for more information. Something in my gut told me this conversation was important.

"Where?" I whispered back, infusing my tone with urgency.

"The Emporium," she squealed, bringing her knuckles to her mouth and biting into one. Her confession had the desired effect; my mouth fell open. It couldn't be. Paulie, my homeless elderly friend who had turned out to be a druid, would've never... She was still a child.

"That's dangerous. You didn't...take anything while you were there, did you?"

The girl's eyes rounded, and she nodded.

"What did you take?"

"The soleil," she said, detailing how Paulie had approached her a few months ago, training her to avoid detection inside the Emporium. "No one's ever stolen from there before." She giggled. I seethed. Paulie had attempted to remove his own soleil from the Emporium, but to use a child for such a dangerous task? No wonder she'd filched the wrong one.

"Would you happen to know where Paulie is now?" Paulie and I were bound to have a few words. Stat.

"Oh, I don't. I haven't seen him since he was last here with you." I was afraid of that. "But he comes often to see my uncle."

I plucked a feather from my back pocket that I'd picked up off the floor after King Cygnus made my wings explode out of my back. They'd retreated again during the portal jump.

"I need you to alert me when he comes. Or if you see him anywhere. Are you familiar with how this works?"

She accepted the feather, wide-eyed.

"No one's ever gifted me a feather before. But I know what to do." She stashed it in her skinny jeans' back pocket. I had a vague idea of mechanics, but when crushed, my gifted feather would guide me to Daria. That was as good as a DM on social media plus GPS. "Everyone's been looking for you. I mean *everyone*. Where will you go?"

I winced. Landing in the middle of New Seattle put me in a vulnerable position, but my list of portals was short. I had hoped to get in touch with Paulie, but that was no longer an option. At least, not for now. I turned hopeful eyes to Daria.

"I'll need new clothes."

FOUR

The over-the-door bell jingled as we entered a palm reader's shop, two buildings down. The scent of a mélange of incense combined turned my stomach, and I held my breath while passing the main table display. Daria pranced toward a glass counter holding crystal skulls and tapped the bell there. A tall rectangular mirror in the corner by a carousel of colorful dresses caught my attention, and I gazed at my reflection. I was wearing black washed-out jeans and a dark purple long-sleeved shirt with some punkish band on it. I braided my hair and put on a dark denim-wash baseball cap to obscure my face. *I should've cut my hair short.*

The beaded curtain rattled as a heavyset woman in a ruffled paisley dress entered the shop from the employee-only area. She smiled at Daria and slanted her gaze at me.

"What trouble are you in now, Dee?" the shop owner asked Daria.

"No trouble. I'm helping a friend who needs a protection item."

The woman's gaze bored into mine, unblinking.

"Hand," she instructed, placing her palm up on the

display separating us. Daria nodded, and I offered my palm. The shop owner pulled a pair of glasses tucked into her curls down to the tip of her nose. She traced one thick finger pad over my palm lines and retraced her finger over the one curving downward.

"You have a twin?" she asked.

"No?" The question caught me off guard. Was there a chance I had siblings? Yeah, sure. The thought had crossed my mind. But a twin? No, the lady was on something. Maybe all this incense messed with her brain?

"This line here"—she pressed it for emphasis—"looks like a single line, but it's not. I see two distinct lines intertwined. Perhaps if you don't have a twin, you're living a parallel life somewhere, out there." She released my hand and gestured skyward, her eyes turning dreamy.

I raised an eyebrow at Daria, who pinched her lips to one side and shrugged. The shop owner crouched and pulled out a tray filled with bracelets and amulets from beneath the crystal skulls. She beckoned me closer with her fingers and instructed me to run my hand over the items. I did so slowly. The woman frowned at me.

"These are powerful amulets I've collected over the years. If they're not able to protect you—"

The bell at the door jingled harshly from a kicked-in door. I glanced over my shoulder. Four men in black shirts with matching striking designs of blood-red roses with thorns strode in, carrying baseball bats.

"Leave, or I'm calling the police. And this time, they will tear your gang apart. I've seen it in the cards." The woman rose to her full height.

The lead man pointed a bat at me. "Lady Aurelia, relax. We've come here for her." He smirked.

"She's my client. You will leave her alone," the shop owner said firmly.

I scrutinized the men. They were locals, judging by the conversation. Daria scooted closer to the shop owner. Heart pounding, I reached for a tray of blue powder on the counter and tossed its contents at the approaching men. The substance cracked in the air, generating micro explosions. The men howled in pain.

I bolted for the back room, grabbing a stunned Daria's arm and pulling her along. Shouts erupted, and the bead curtain rattled like a snake about to strike. We ran into a small kitchen and darted for the back door. Lady Aurelia had the damn thing locked with four different locks. Before we could file outside, the first man reached the kitchen. I took off into a small courtyard, crossing it quickly and checking doors in the alley.

"Over here!" Daria called out from behind me, standing inside an entryway she had opened. I stepped toward her but froze when two men, covered in blue powder and sporting angry red blisters on their faces and arms, reached the alley. Without taking my eyes off them, I shook my head at Daria. She was better off without me. They wanted me, not her.

I spun on my heel and sprinted through the end of the alley and onto the sidewalk. Turning right, I weaved through pedestrians. As I was about to cross another alley, a dark van pulled up in front of me, and I bounced off its side door, falling on my behind. Not losing a second, I leaped to my feet, but the two men were upon me. They lifted me off the ground before I could scream and tossed me into the van, into the hands of another man who clasped his oversized hand across my face. With my arms pinned, I couldn't defend myself. He covered my nose as well as my mouth, and I struggled to breathe. My eyes flicked wildly. There were four men in total, one driver and three men in the back with me. The back of the van had a bench on one side and shelved crates with items on the other. One of the men flicked open his pocket knife.

"Bitch, you will pay for this little stunt. Let's cut her up," he said with deranged euphoria. I began blacking out, going limp in the man's arms. He tossed me onto the bench, and I gulped for air. The van turned, and I landed on all fours on the floor, then scrambled to put my back against the back door, eyeing the men. The one with the knife lunged at me. Scowling, I kicked his knee straight on and it bent backward. He dropped the knife and fell to the bench, stunned. The second man gripped my shirt and hauled me up, his sneer broad and jeering.

"Put her down," commanded the last man in the back. He was larger than the others and judging by lack of red welts on his forearms and face, he'd waited outside the shop. "She's no good to us damaged. We had explicit instructions."

The man pinning me to the back unfurled his fingers in a show of displeasure and stepped back.

"Instructions from whom?" I asked. The leader joined the driver in the front. The man beside me sneered.

"Go on. Ask another question. He won't stop me from shutting you up," he taunted.

I scowled and gazed forward. My heart raced. My only consolation was that whoever had ordered my capture had also ordered me unharmed. The van took a sharp turn, and the first man cried out, clutching his injured knee. A tiny smirk lifted the corner of my mouth. Maybe that wasn't my only consolation.

FIVE

We drove deeper into the industrial district, passing manufacturing plants and machinery and heading toward the loading docks by the train tracks. Stacked a few stories high, shipping containers loomed over us, with a crane parked below. A black SUV peeked out from between the containers. So, that was it. I'd soon learn who had ordered my kidnapping and whether they planned to return me to Invicta, presumably for a fee. No one would go through this much trouble without expecting substantial gain from the ordeal. The van stopped, leaving room for two more cars between it and the SUV. The man in charge clasped my arm and escorted me out.

A single man dressed in a dark V-neck, cargo pants, and combat boots stepped out. He wore highly polarized glasses that reflected his surroundings. He had short, dark brown hair and a square jaw that showed signs of tension.

"Who's this?" the new guy asked.

"Your bounty."

"She doesn't have wings."

My kidnapper pulled a folded piece of paper from his

back pocket, unfolded it, and handed over a picture of me taken after a training session at Invicta. I swallowed a lump. The unmarked SUV and the guard in front of me were not from Invicta, but they were no minor players in the New Seattle supernatural world either. I hadn't considered that my kidnapper might have no connection to Invicta, nor any intention of returning me there. Big effing mistake! There were evils out there that paled compared to the Magister's wrath.

I wrenched my arm free and managed one step before the guard caught my wrist with exceptional speed, squeezing with crushing force. I gritted my teeth as he scrutinized my face.

"Are you Arien Blair?" he asked.

I bit my lip, refusing to answer.

"You're coming with me." He tugged me toward him, and I swung my free fist. In a blur, the guard pinned my elbow to his side and headbutted me. I collapsed to the ground, seeing stars.

"Stop fighting and your trip will be more pleasant," he said into my ear as he cradled my body. Someone else had paid the gang leader and his bat-wielding men. My captor strapped me into the middle seat in the back of the SUV, then sat to my left. Another guard sat behind us, with two more up front, all in the same tactical gear.

"Where are you taking me?" I touched my fingertips to my forehead; they came away with blood.

"Your arrival is quite anticipated at the Fringe."

I turned to face him, a chill running down my spine. The Fringe had always unnerved me. I stared into his sunglasses, which reflected my stunned face. Lowering my gaze, I noticed a tattoo peeking from behind the V in his T-shirt. *Brie.* How did my best friend's name end up on this freak's collarbone. I gasped and faced the front.

"What?" he demanded.

I glanced askance at his tattoo, disbelieving my eyes, and this time, he noticed. He readjusted his collar. That was Ashton, Brie's fiancé. He must have known about me and Brie. How could he continue carrying out his duties, knowing that? Nothing pleasant awaited me at the Fringe. And he'd headbutted me, the bastard.

I remembered now he had been with Brie when she visited me during a class break to say goodbye. He had worn a baseball hat and avoided eye contact, but I recognized his physique.

The barren fields outside the northern city border stretched for miles. I mulled over plausible reasons why the reclusive shifters wanted me but came up with nothing. The unmistakable wall of the Fringe rose into view, towering higher than most buildings inside. We pulled up to the gate and a guard approached the SUV.

Suddenly, the man behind me yanked my hair, exposing my neck, and stuck me with a needle. I jerked in response, too late to stop him.

My head spun, and it seemed as if the car was tilting, a dizzy sensation engulfing me as I tried to sit up on my own.

"Outsiders aren't allowed to venture inside the Fringe. Not conscious, anyway," Ashton said.

"Too late" hung heavily on my tongue. Ashton didn't know I had sneaked inside these walls once before. My eyes drooped, and I began to succumb to unconsciousness.

"Tell Brie I said hello," I croaked before collapsing forward.

SIX

The sound of a baton running over metal bars startled me awake. I sprang to my feet. Someone leered at me from behind those bars. An unsettling sensation crawled across my skin. The rattling of the baton ceased near the lock, and then the lock pad pinged as my visitor punched in the code. Sweat broke out above my lip as I curled shaking hands into fists. The hinges squeak-rasped in slow motion as he took his time entering, reveling in my disorientation. And just like that, the identity of my visitor became clear.

I masked my expression as the Soaz stepped into the murky light, his face alight with dark desire. A memory of his madness-tinged gaze after he bit my neck flashed in front of my eyes, and a chilling sense of dread swarmed me.

My vision cleared, but my reflexes lagged. He strode across the cell and slapped my cheek. My body twisted, and I fell to the ground, coughing up blood. I glowered at him.

"Ahh, my little secondborn," he drawled.

"Not a secondborn," I wheezed, using the wall to get back to my feet. He grinned, tilting his head from side to side.

"I don't see wings. I've heard the rumor, of course—"

"Why are you here?" One good thing that came out of his greeting was the lifting of my brain fog. They had brought me to the Fringe, the outlawed territory now also known as shifter town. A place Earthbounders officially ignored. Maybe the Soaz hadn't gotten the memo.

The Soaz flicked imaginary dirt from underneath his nail.

"Shouldn't you be asking why *you* are here? At my mercy, again."

"Are you here to take me to Invicta?"

He tsked. "I don't answer to anyone. I'm an enforcer." He shrugged one shoulder. "I put Earthbounders in their place, especially those who defy the council." I swallowed. "That can take as long as needed to encourage cooperation. Some times weeks or even months. Sadly, some don't survive a week." He rolled his head back up, then jerked. I squinted at his spasmodic movements. When his eyes opened, total blackness stared back at me, and I flattened against the wall, my nails digging into the stone. Blood drained from my face.

The Soaz blinked and the blackness receded to the edges of his eyes, lurking there.

"Someone wants to play." His voice came out harsher and more guttural. He sneered, showing off lengthened teeth. No Earthbounders possessed that ability. It wasn't an angelic gift passed down through the generations. Was he possessed?

I widened my stance, legs quivering. I didn't want to face him, but what choice did I have, trapped in a cell with a possessed psycho? He stalked me all around the cell like a lion playing with his food. I shuffled against the bars, keeping my eyes on his. If only I had some kind of weapon to even out my chances.

His deranged grin widened, sending a cautionary signal to my panicked mind. I tensed. In a blur, he rushed me, catching my wrists easily and pulling them high above my head. My shoulders ached. I grimaced. He enjoyed my suffering, dragging my arms higher. Instead of resisting, I pulled my knees up and kicked off, hitting his stomach just below the rib cage. He staggered back, glee shining in his eyes, the blackness threatening to return. Wings shot out of his back, black and leathery, without feathers. He stretched his neck, reveling in the transformation, his incisors lengthening like a vampire's.

"What are you?" I whispered.

He struck faster than before. Four sharp points pierced the skin near my collarbone. His hand muffled my scream, pressing my head against the bars. The venom he injected before drawing blood rendered my body useless. My arms went limp, and my legs buckled under his weight. The crushing force with which he pressed my body to the bars behind me was the only reason I remained upright.

He removed his hand from my mouth, sliding it under my shirt. My lips quit working, and my gaze glazed over, seeing nothing but spots of light. I was a prisoner in my own body, completely withdrawn. My core heated, and an invisible force plucked my soul out. My new vision sharpened, looking at a petrified statue of myself and feeling her wildly beating heart.

Stop!

STOP!

Stoooooop!

I wanted to pry this monster's hands off me, but instead, I drifted further away. My face lost all the color. He was draining me. *No!* My heartbeat stuttered, and I catapulted back into my body, taking a deep, wheezing breath. The leech at my neck hadn't noticed. Anger boiled inside me. I shoved him off with a surprising strength. A sonic boom whooshed from my palms, sending him flying. He crashed into the brick wall across the cell, his head bouncing off. His bewildered gaze narrowed into slits. He straightened, glancing at the indentation in the bricks, then studied me with an intrigued curl of his lips.

"What in the hell are you?" he asked.

I shook my head. How would I know? "A repellent for parasites. You're like a parasite." Ohmagod, I was mumbling. Must have been the blood loss.

The Soaz ran a thumb across his lips, sucking it off.

"You taste nothing like what I'm accustomed to. The first time I tasted you, I thought your blood was poison. It's so potent."

"Potent?"

Soaz smirked in response. He'd guard his secrets. I, apparently, was an open book.

Footsteps sounded. The man who appeared, clad in tactical gear like Ashton's, eyed my bleeding neck and ruffled shirt with wicked intent.

"My momma always told me not to play with my food," he said.

"I killed my momma," the Soaz replied, and the man chuckled.

"Right. Lumeran requests your presence at the meeting," the guard said, eyeing me once more and whistling as he strode away.

I itched to touch my pulsing neck and stanch the bleeding, but I refused to give the Soaz the satisfaction of witnessing my discomfort. Instead, I stared back at him, ice in my eyes, wishing they could turn to icicles and stab his black heart.

He considered me before stalking over. I straightened on my wobbly legs.

"Always so defiant."

He swept a finger across my collarbone, gathering blood. He brought the finger to my lips, and I turned my head. Chuckling softly, he licked the blood off.

"What do you want from me?" I asked again.

"I want to crack your code, nightshade." He pierced me with his enigmatic gaze, then strode to the console and let himself out, leaving me gasping for air.

SEVEN

Nightmares ruled my dreams. Shadows chased me around the city, nowhere was safe. *Tap, tap. Tap, tap.* I moaned, my eyebrows knitting together. The tapping sound persisted, fueling my irritation. I rolled to one side and cracked open my eyelids. A dark hooded figure knelt in front of the lock. The tapping continued until the lock disengaged, and the gate slid open. I closed my eyes, evening out my breathing.

I sensed his stealthy approach.

"Arien—"

I jammed a palm-sized rock into his temple and bolted for the ajar gate, then right down the corridor.

"Wait!" the man hissed, closing in on me. The metal door glinted at the far end. Indecision cost me a stumble, but I righted myself only to be thrown into a small cavern. The man held me tight, his hand over my mouth. The metal door grunted, and two male voices filled the space. I ceased struggling, and we both watched two Fringe guards pass us.

"They will find your cell empty in exactly one minute.

This is our only chance. Will you listen to me when I let go?"
he whispered.

I nodded. He loosened his hold.

"This way." He removed a vent cover embedded in the
bottom section of the wall and signaled for me to proceed. I
stared at it. Shaking his head, he crawled in first. But when a
shrill alarm sounded and footsteps pounded, I lurched into
the opening after him. I mounted the cover from the inside
and anxiously waited as guards went by a moment later. Once
their stomping drifted away, I began crawling, guided by the
soft glow of a device ahead. The man put a finger to his lips
and mimed for me to move faster. I wasn't turning back now,
so I pushed myself to catch up.

The draft picked up as we neared an open shaft with
emergency lights blinking at regular intervals. The man exited
the vent to the left. The shaft extended several stories below
and above. How many levels were in this place? The Fringe
had built a fortress beyond Invicta's imagination.

"We need to get to the ground level," he said, swinging onto a
thick rope. In the flashing light, I could make out his high cheek-
bones and penetrating eyes beneath the hoodie. He extended a
hand to me. I eyed the rope warily but nodded in agreement.

"I need you to go above me. Can you do it?"

Inhaling, I grabbed his hand and climbed onto his back,
then pushed up on his shoulders. *Don't look down. Just don't
look down.* We ascended five levels before exiting into a new
shaft. I caught my breath, leaning against a steel wall while he
climbed the rest of the way. He nodded perfunctorily and led
the way down a narrow walkway. I followed closely, scanning
for danger. A vast space opened, lined with dozens of such
walkways, some leading across and others down below. We
were on the topmost level with the ceiling directly above us.

A strong palm pressed me against the wall. Below, a group

in mechanic gear strolled across, then dispersed. I leaned my head against the wall and exhaled in relief.

"They didn't see us. We need to cross to the other side quietly," he said. Not waiting for my response, he crouched on all fours. I mimicked him. The pressure in my chest eased as we neared the opposite wall.

But then the light filtered in from an open door below. The warrior's eyes snapped to mine. I bobbed my head in understanding, and we scrambled to the wall. Shouts sounded and rushed footsteps filled the space. The Soaz's voice crackled through a guard's comms device.

"Find *her*!" he bellowed.

My adrenaline levels spiked, and spots danced in front of my eyes. He was going to kill me. Once he found me, he was going to end my life in the most excruciating way possible or make me his personal blood bag.

The stranger guided me to another vent. I gritted my teeth and caught up with him as he led us through the labyrinthine vent system. We took turns, sliding down and climbing back up again. As my nerves cooled and rational thinking returned to me, I began wondering about his identity and motives.

He removed a cover from the vent and descended. Laundry baskets and a fresh linen smell greeted me. Washing machines hummed with the sound of rotating tumblers. The man opened the door to an adjacent room and then another door, revealing stacks of black trash bags. The chute at the far end reminded me of another time I'd attempted to leave the Fringe unseen. He ran up to it.

"You're kidding, right?" I asked.

He raised an eyebrow. "After all you've been through, you're afraid of a little stink?"

I growled internally. He didn't know me.

"Let's get out of here." I climbed into the dark chute and pushed off.

***

This ride was smoother than my last. I latched to the rim of the chute and eased into a graceful jump. Then, I worked my way to the bank and heaved myself up. The warrior wasn't as fortunate, judging by the clanking and thrashing sounds.

"Fuuuck... Wait!" he called.

No way. I shot him a glare, signaling to him this was where our paths separated, and dashed for the woods. I'd gotten faster over the last few weeks, thanks to training, and my supernatural speed kicking in. I bounded over fallen tree trunks with ease and dodged dense outcroppings, running faster than I ever had before.

Woosh! Something brushed my left side, and I spun, falling and rolling to a stop by a pair of boots. The warrior cocked his head to the side, staring down at me. Gray wings sprawled behind him. He offered a hand, which I accepted instinctively.

"You're a Power."

"Roan, at your service," he replied with an exaggerated bow and a playful smirk dancing on his lips.

I brushed sticks and leaves off my clothes while he watched, the corners of his lips twitching.

"I'd introduce myself, but I have a feeling you already know who I am," I said.

"Yes, Arien Blair, firstborn of an ancient, long-forgotten order," he said nonchalantly. "Your friends sent me."

At that, my head snapped up. Friends? Did he mean P6, the group of elite warrior descendants of Powers? Kole? No, Kole would've come himself if he knew where I was. If he still cared about me after what I'd done.

"I mean Rae. She's waiting five miles away." Roan handed me a round leaf he picked off the forest floor. "Put this on your wounds. Angelrod helps us heal."

"Angelrod?"

"Yeah, supposedly the first warriors brought it with them to Earth. It recognizes our DNA is all I know," he said.

I placed leaves on my deeper scratches and the throbbing marks the Soaz's teeth had left on my neck as we ambled through the vegetation. With each crack of a twig, I flinched, half expecting the shifters to close in on us at any moment.

"They think you're still inside. We'll be long gone before they extend their search." I glanced at him and then at the silent trees around us, and I had to agree he'd gotten us out of there fast.

Roan chuckled.

"Oh yeah, I'm that good."

"This wasn't your first time in the Fringe," I said. He knew the place intimately.

"I may have been there once or twice before," he mused.

"How come I've never seen you at P6?"

"I don't frequent there. I prefer the *underground*." He wiggled his eyebrows.

I stopped. Was he a rebel?

"Take off your hood."

Roan complied, revealing a familiar face. I gasped.

"I recognize you." He looked much older now, but merely a year ago this boy—this *man*—had gone to high school with me. "Don't lie to me."

"I've no intention to. I was undercover for a few weeks. We were observing you, hoping you were more than the secondborn you turned into on your birthday—I should say false birthday. Funny how things turn out sometimes, huh?"

What?

"Are you always this upbeat?" I didn't expect an answer.

"Yep." His eyes gleamed. "Now, come on, or your friends will get antsy."

Friends? He didn't say Rae. Was it possible Kole was among them? I wouldn't know how to act if I saw him. But I wanted to see him and apologize. And the part of my heart that beat for him hoped he wanted that too.

"Roan?"

"Hmm."

"How long has it been since the Archon attack?"

"Two weeks."

EIGHT

I caught a glint of sun stroked black paint above. Two silhouettes rushed down. I found myself squeezed between two steel-like female bodies, enveloped in a tangle of arms. Sniffling, I closed my teary eyes and gave in to the sensation.

"Damn, you need a shower, girl," Zaira said. I hiccuped with a semblance of laughter. I was well aware of my scent—damp and musky with notes of decay, like the underground where they had kept me. The odor seeped through my clothes and clung to my skin. At least that was what it felt like. And I yearned to strip away every facet of that harrowing experience from my body and mind.

Rae and Zaira, two female P6 members, had grown on me in the few days I'd spent at their headquarters. And, for some crazy reason, they treated me like one of their own. Rae was the more approachable and nurturing one; Zaira had a more direct style. They could never replace my best friend Brie, but I'd do anything for them, without hesitation.

Rae's silence spoke volumes. After assessing me for injuries, she joined Roan, who waited a few steps away.

Zaira slung her arm around me, helping me climb the rest of the way to the road. The single-lane road winded through the foothills of the Evergreen Mountains, marking our location as north of New Seattle and the Fringe. Two black sport bikes leaned, propped up on the side of the road.

"Can you hold on to me?" Zaira straddled her bike.

"Oh, uh." I'd never been on a bike before. How hard could that be, though? "Sure."

Zaira adjusted my foot positioning and my hold on her. To my horror, there were no seat belts, not even a backrest, and I tightened my grip around her waist. I might have grown a pair of wings, but I doubted I was impervious to crashes.

"I forgot." She pulled out a black beanie and handed it me to. "To hide your hair." I twisted my hair in a bun and stuffed it in. I got a nod of approval from Zaira before her attention shifted to the approaching Rae.

"Roan offered us safe passage through the rebellion's tunnels," Rae said.

"Can we trust them?" Zaira asked.

"I don't know. I declined."

"Good. The others will have our throats if we deviate from the plan."

Others? Did that include Kole? I rubbed my forehead.

"Hold on." Zaira interrupted my thoughts. She eased the bike onto the road, for my benefit, and sped up steadily. I didn't even ask where we were going. I was so relieved to be reunited with them. Was P6 safe? Or did Xavier ravage it after I escaped into Invicta's allura?

I hid my face from the wintry winds. We never entered the city, which meant we weren't returning to P6. Unless Zaira and Rae preferred the scenic route. But the constant up and down suggested we traveled deeper into the foothills. About half an hour passed, and we veered onto a dirt road winding left and right to reveal a well-concealed cabin within the wilderness. Stillness greeted us.

"What is this place?" I asked. I took a second to balance on two feet and rolled my neck.

"Vex and I own this place. Only a few trusted warriors know about it," Rae said. Zaira was already bounding up the steps to the cabin and barging in like there was a fire. I furrowed my brow.

"Come on." Rae grabbed my hand. "Don't be alarmed—"

"It's not a good idea," Zaira's raised voice boomed from inside. "She's fine. Kole!" The wooden door swung ominously, and a hulking shadow filled the space.

"Vex?" Rae called out, squeezing my hand.

"Vex may or may not have suffered a broken nose. You may want to check on him." Kole sounded calm, but there was no mistaking the coldness, the fury, the misery underlying his tone. Rae's face blanched.

"Go." I squeezed Rae's hand once and let go. "I'll be fine." She stumbled at first, then ran inside, throwing curses at the Neanderthal standing in the doorway. But then, he stepped out to make way for her, and my breath caught. Angels, this was worse than I'd thought. Kole's hair lay disheveled and plastered around his beautiful face set in a callous grimace. His dilated pupils contrasted with a backdrop of burst blood vessels. If I didn't know any better, I'd have thought him a demon.

Every single cell in my body reacted to him. My heart pitter-pattered from an insane want I couldn't wrap my mind around. The bond that brought us together made me question the intensity of this feeling. Was the emotion even mine to begin with?

The demon strode toward me. Taking his time, confident I couldn't outrun him. Like prey hunted by a hungry wolf, I was at his mercy. Conflicting emotions flickered through his eyes. My back hit the rough bark of a tree. I didn't even realize I had shifted, hypnotized by the creature in front of me. I opened my mouth and closed it. My eyes grew larger as he approached, and I strained against an inane desire to bury myself in his arms.

I lowered my eyes to avoid his scorching gaze. He halted, his neck a mere inch away from my nose. I closed my eyes, allowing myself to breathe in his scent and feel the warmth of his body. *Thud...thud...thud...* Pounding to the side of my head reverberated through the tree trunk and startled me out of my stupor. Tree bark crumpled to my shoulder and down my sleeve.

"Stop!" I ordered, taking hold of his pounding fist. Next, I took hold of his eyes with mine. Dark and merciless, his gaze pierced through me. His body trembled.

"You have no idea how angry I am with you." He averted his gaze. I marveled at the contours of his perfect profile, uncertain what to do or say. I'd betrayed and abandoned him and Rae when I escaped alone. Although I didn't regret it, they would have risked their safety and perhaps even their lives by aiding me.

Gathering his face into my shaky hands, I whispered, "I know... I'm *so* sorry." Our foreheads touched, and breaths mingled between us. Slowly, the trembles abated.

"You're cold," he said.

I didn't expect that to come out of his mouth, or for him to speak to me at all. Thinking about it, chills rippled over my skin. I nodded and withdrew my hands, then yelped when he scooped me up. Kole marched into the cabin, carrying me directly to a living area with a roaring fireplace. He deposited me by the hearth and delicious heat caressed my back. One of Kole's devoted companions, Talen, tossed him a blanket, which was, in an instant, tucked around the front of my body up to my chin. I didn't dare stop Kole when a second blanket appeared. His forehead smoothed, and the grimace melted while he worked.

"Thank you," I said from my cocoon. Kole's expert tucking left me wondering whether I'd be able to move again. When he backed off, I caught a glimpse of the group: Talen sulking with crossed arms, propping a bent leg on a wooden column; Zaira banging something in the kitchen; and Rae holding an ice pack to Vex's nose. The couple occupied a brown leather couch across from me. A grotesque picture of a broken family. I chewed my lip. How much of this mayhem was due to my doing?

"Where's Exiousai Seth?" I asked. I expected to see him here. My stomach churned at the thought of facing him after my omissions nearly cost us an Archon takeover. In hindsight, I was wrong to guard Paulie's secret about him accidentally stealing the wrong *soleil*—a power source belonging to the once formidable great Archon who nearly annihilated the Earthbounders in his attempt to reclaim it. I was blind and naive. I was... Reflecting on the past was like walking through a gallery of my own failures, each moment a painful exhibit of what I couldn't undo, beginning with my mother's death.

"No one knows," Rae said. "The last time any of us saw him was at the fissure site, right after we won the battle."

"You mean after our tame little fledgling decimated Bezekah beyond the ether?" Vex grinned around the ice pack. He gently pulled Rae's hand away, assuring her he was healing just fine. Rae huffed her discontent with him.

"How?" Talen asked. His gaze intensified. If he had the ability to peek into my head, I had no doubt he would search around until he found answers to all his questions.

I knew this moment would come. Friends or temporary allies, they deserved to know how I—*er, her*—defeated the enemy. I began with the dreams of her, her flowing ethereal pale blond hair forever etched into my mind's eye. I described her messages to me. The sky stone I'd got through yet another dream acted as a bridge between us, enabling her energies to enter our dimension and annihilate Bezekah for good.

"Are you sure the stone is called Sky Ice?" Kole asked.

"Yes." I could never forget the name.

"Do you have it?"

I shook my head. "I've never seen it before and the closest I came to it physically was during the battle. But I couldn't touch it. I was paralyzed, first by Bezekah's overpowering presence, then again when the woman appeared. It was as if the stone connected us."

"It's an inter-dimensional vortex simulator. The being grounded you to prevent counter-absorption," Rae said with awe. She stood up, eyes sparkling, and paced a few steps to one side of the couch and back. Vex's lips stretched into a subtle grin as his eyes latched onto Rae's ass.

"You know what this means, right?" Rae scanned faces around her. "We may be on the brink of establishing contact with inter-dimensionals. Maybe even cooperate on new technologies..." She bounced with her index finger pointing upward. "Travel to different realms—"

Vex snatched Rae by the waist and plopped her on the couch.

"Hey." She batted his hands away.

"Before you get too deep into that pretty head of yours, I think we need to establish facts first. For one—"

"We have neither the stone nor can we summon it on demand," Kole said dryly.

"Yes, and two—"

"It's a fancy tale, with no witnesses," Talen chimed in.

Vex pursed his lips. "Can I finish my own sentence?"

"And three—pancakes are ready," Zaira called out from the kitchen. Vex was first on his feet, pulling Rae behind him.

I wiggled but the blanket burrito wouldn't loosen. I begged Kole for help with my best rendition of puppy eyes. The corner of his mouth stretched. He pulled me to my feet and tugged on a corner, sending me into a controlled spin. Controlled by him. He eased up by the end, and my equilibrium caught up with me.

"What's on your mind?" he asked.

"I know what happened. I didn't make this up or hit my head. A few weeks ago, I'd argue otherwise, but now... You believe me, don't you?"

"We all do."

"But Talen—"

"In your layman's terms, Talen's playing devil's advocate. Many Earthbounders will challenge your story. It's important you recount it to the council in the same manner. Nothing more, nothing less. Facts only."

"The council?"

Kole sighed. "Let's discuss later. Hungry?"

My stomach growled at the mention of food. I scrunched my nose up. Kole ran a long finger from the top of my nose down. The gesture seemed to last an eternity. I gaped at him, startled. He studied me, his expression closed off.

"Come." He inclined his head toward the kitchen and fell in step behind me. Goose bumps erupted along my arms, slithering their way up my neck. Strangely, the pull I'd felt toward Kole prior to my allura stunt at the gates of Invicta was no longer there. This sensation was like no other. It felt natural and...exciting. And, for once, promising.

NINE

Rae and Zaira disappeared into the cabin, leaving me all alone on the rooftop outside a window on the second floor. I enjoyed a hot shower and new clean clothes, but being alone got me thinking, questioning if I'd made the right decision to reunite with the P6-ers. I wrapped my arms around my knees. Pinks and bright oranges painted the sky above mountain peaks.

Feet shuffled next to me, and I straightened, following my gaze up the dark jeans to Kole's torso and face. He lowered himself next to me, extending a single cupcake with a candle on his outstretched palm. I eyed it.

"Uh, Rae says that's how mundanes celebrate accumulation in years today." He offered a lopsided smile.

Startled, I sucked in my lips to stop incoming laughter. I took the cupcake, set the unlit candle aside, and bit into the chocolaty cake.

"Mmm, good. Thanks." His eyes glittered. I offered the remaining half to him, and his brows drew together.

"It is also a custom to share your birthday cake with your

friends," I said. "I have no germs, I promise," I added when he didn't move.

"I'm immune to germs and so are you."

I rolled my eyes. Kole lifted the cake from my hand and dropped it into his mouth in one smooth motion. He ground his jaw, and his thick neck bobbed when he swallowed. Our eyes met, and I quickly turned forward, flushing.

"Do you trust me?" Kole asked.

"I do," I said without hesitation, feeling like a layer had flaked off my heart, exposing it. And that scared me.

"Why?"

I faced him slowly. "Because when I'm looking into your eyes, it's as if I'm seeing your soul—and I just know. Bond or no bond." My cheeks pinked, and I averted my eyes from his again. That was the closest I'd ever come to admitting my feelings to a boy. And he wasn't simply a boy. He wasn't even any regular man. I could've been doing this all wrong—not in an Earthbounder fashion.

"Are you afraid to look at me?"

"No. I'm afraid I'm making a total fool out of myself." Seconds passed. *It's your turn, Kole. Say something.* I sighed internally, resigned and, yes, embarrassed. Kole's silence spoke the unspoken. His feelings towards me weakened. I leaned away.

"Wait."

I glanced at him warily, not sure I wanted to hear him out. I regretted my own words. I didn't do vulnerable, but somehow, this brooding Power splintered the shell around my heart.

"I'm an assassin. A killing machine. I live and breathe the hunt. This is who I am and all I am." Rejection hung heavy in the air. Kole inhaled deeply. "I'm no romantic, but for what it's worth, with you I wish I was one."

"What?" The question I asked myself escaped out loud.

A corner of Kole's mouth curved into the sweetest dimple. My chest squeezed. "The truth is—" He swallowed. "—if I felt any less, maybe I could express myself better. But as it stands..." Kole's eyes darkened.

I bit into my lips to stop a silly expression from erupting all over my face. I felt as if clouds had parted and the sun shone down only on me. Giddiness bubbled up in me. Then I deflated.

"It's the bond, isn't it?" I slumped over my knees. "Why does it feel so real?"

Kole leaned forward to capture my eyes again.

"You got my message?" He was referring to the book he'd lent me before the Exiousai had thrown me into a cell. The section on *Ashanti Rosa*—the rare, sacred bond between two Earthbounders—had been highlighted. I nodded.

"How come you didn't tell me this sooner?"

"I fought it. Committing myself to anyone would interfere with my job. The bond would've eventually broken if Seth didn't bring you to P6."

"Oh." I scrunched my forehead. "Why did he?"

"He argued you didn't belong with Invicta. Because of the bond, you should be a Power. But I suspect he did it for me, too. He'd lost his *Ashanti Rosa* several years back, and he wouldn't want anyone to lose the strongest bond Earthbounders can form between each other." A corner of his mouth slid up again. "I fully intended on breaking the bond even when he brought you in. But, with time, being around you, seeing you were so brave, caring, and a warrior at heart, I had to stop deluding myself that what constantly kept me thinking about you was merely the bond."

My chest swelled at his words.

"I used to feel this physical pull whenever you were near," I said.

"But you no longer do."

I squinted at him; the way he spoke the words implied he knew something he wasn't revealing. Kole abruptly got to his feet, extending a hand to me.

"Come. We have a visitor."

I paled at his sudden change of subject and the coldness with which he uttered those words. Whoever the visitor was, they weren't welcome here.

TEN

I followed Kole down the steps to the living room. His neck and back coiled tighter with each step, and he blocked my view by stepping in line with me all the way to the couch. Annoyance began bubbling up to the surface. I needed him to stop coddling me and let me see the threat. Eventually, he let me step beside him, revealing Xavier standing by the window. He wore a white dress shirt with rolled-up sleeves and a few buttons popped off on the top and black slacks over shiny loafers. It appeared he had been in a rush getting over here.

I glanced out the window, curious whether he'd come alone. Xavier, the son of the Magister of the Invicta Institute, and I had had a...strenuous relationship during my stay with the red-winged warrior descendants of Seraphs. Although he had shielded me from the Soaz before, I could never fully grasp Xavier's true intentions. And then there was this minor inconvenience of him being the Magister's—a man whom I despised—son.

Xavier's lapis lazuli eyes locked on me, lips pressed in a rigid line. With his hands in his pockets and windswept hair, he resembled a sexy billionaire from romance book covers. Why was he here? The P6 warriors positioned themselves throughout the room, surrounding him. I glanced at Kole. His jaw clenched tightly as he glowered at Xavier.

"You arrived sooner than expected," Kole said.

"I didn't see a reason to wait." Xavier strolled over to the recliner and sat down with poise, resting his chin on his fist. "I'm being followed; we'd better get to it."

Rae drew nearer and pulled me on the couch with her, while Kole strode to the fireplace, propping his arm on the mantel. The remaining warriors stood at their posts with arms crossed over their chests.

"What's going on?" I asked, flipping my eyes over everyone present.

"Oh, I see I am quite early." Xavier smirked. "You don't know?" He hiked up an eyebrow.

"You have to return to Invicta," Kole said, jaw twitching. "For now." He implored me to understand with his deep charcoal eyes. I swallowed.

"Or for a while." Xavier lifted his shoulder. His blasé statement evoked a growl from Kole.

"Why aren't your wings out?" Xavier asked with scorn underlying his tone. Was it a crime to put the freakish appendages away? He only extended his wings when he needed them.

I shrugged. "Travel in the void makes them retract."

"You unfurl them at will now then."

I shook my head. "The only time they came out was when King Cygnus attacked me. They wanted to shield me, I think." I blew out a breath. Was it weird to talk about my wings this way as if they had a mind of their own? They sure seemed to think for themselves.

Xavier schooled his features and leaned forward on his elbows, his penetrating gaze cast on me.

"We're burning time here. The Archon attack has drawn the attention of the entire Earthbounder world, and they want answers. Our people are agitated, and many wish to hunt you down themselves. Some have accused you of drawing the Archon out in the first place—"

"I didn't." I shook my head.

"We are aware of Kwanezerus's role in this, but not everyone is convinced. That includes the Magister. The only way this ends without you being tortured to death is to put you in front of the Highest Council. Their decision is final and cannot be contested."

I breathed in deeply. Paulie—known as Kwanezerus to everyone else—had to be in hiding since his involvement in Bezekah's reappearance was widely known now. No wonder Daria hadn't heard from him in some time.

"What if they find me guilty?" I asked.

"I evaluated all probable outcomes, and that is not one of them."

I stole a glance at Kole. His face contorted into grim lines, but he did not protest the idea nor oppose Xavier's suggestion. Wait a minute. I narrowed my eyes at him.

"You knew about this—"

"Yes." He cut me off with his harsh words and a cutting glare. "I don't like it, but this appears to be our only chance at keeping you safe. We are warriors, but our adversaries outnumber us a hundredfold. And life on the run is no life. They'll catch up with us eventually."

A chill swept over my body. Returning to Invicta was the last item on my nonexistent bucket list. I'd survived freaking gollums for nothing. For nothing! But that wasn't true, was it? As I stared into Kole's determined eyes and the P6-ers' grimaced faces, I knew I'd have given everything to have this moment with them. These past few hours.

"Do you trust me?" Kole asked. I sucked in a breath. It

wasn't fair for him to pull this card out on me so soon, and he knew it. However, his dive-worthy charcoal eyes showed no signs of apology.

"Can you come with me?" I scanned the room, directing my question at all the gathered P6-ers.

"P6-ers are currently on the no-entry list per my father. Especially her." Xavier pointed his long index finger at Rae.

"Why?" I squeezed my friend's hand reassuringly. Xavier had a tendency to speak gibberish.

"She's madeborn," Xavier said. "She's lucky they didn't discover her status on her last visit."

My head swiveled in Rae's direction.

"What's madeborn?" I whispered.

"It's rare." Kole barked, putting an end to the topic. Rae's cheeks reddened as she stared daggers at Xavier. Vex placed a calming hand on her shoulder.

"Intruders crossed the mountain ridge two miles from here," Talen said, checking his smartwatch. "Your people?" he asked Xavier. The Seraph twisted his lips and rose to his feet.

"We have to go." He pinned me with his gaze. Perhaps he suspected I'd refuse to face those entitled council snobs. I couldn't back away from the challenge, and I couldn't put my family in harm's way. I got to my feet.

Kole cleared his throat. "There is one small matter we need to discuss before we depart," he said. *We?* As in he was going with me and Xavier? I studied him as some sort of eye contact passed between the two Earthbounders. Xavier remained silent. Stretching his collar, Kole exposed a spot above his heart. A tattoo of a single white wing decorated his pec muscle like a painting. It had a sheen of silver and gold streaks to it similar to my wings. I didn't recall seeing this tattoo on him before.

"Alert Invicta and the High Council that Arien now has a Divine Protector."

My knees wobbled and I dropped to the couch, next to a gaping Rae. Vex clapped his hands, each clap spaced farther apart.

"What? Too early to celebrate?" Vex asked, and Rae scowled in his direction.

"The Everlake?" Xavier asked as if he knew what all this was about.

"The Everlake granted this responsibility, this honor, on you?" Zaira asked.

Kole confirmed it, explaining the gift Xavier's mother, Cerah, had left for him and the request that had come with it to take her feather to the Everlake as an offering. No one could deny the mark of a protector, as it was a privilege bestowed only on a select few. It allowed Kole to accompany me everywhere I went and be involved in all matters that concerned me. This meant Invicta couldn't deny him entry. My heart fluttered. I needed an ally inside the Seraph's fortress. I needed *him*.

"So, the bond is then broken between you. I recall a protector can't be one's lover, or the mark will disappear," Xavier said.

"The bond's been absent since Arien escaped into Invicta's allura," Kole said with stoic calm.

That explained why I hadn't sensed the pull when I first saw him. Instead, my heart and body reacted of their own accord, thrumming in absolute chaos. And Kole confirmed he cared about me the same way. Only now, we couldn't be together, and he willingly chose this fate to watch over me and keep me safe. He chose the protector mark over us. A part of me admired him for it. The other part sulked in grief at losing something that never had a chance to even exist.

Anhelm, one of Xavier's devoted warriors, chose this moment to barge in. "We have company."

He shifted sideways to reveal about a dozen armed warriors coming out of the cover of trees.

Talen threw a bandolier at Vex, which he slung onto his shoulder with a smirk. They strode outside with Anhelm. I winced, anticipating a fight. Both Xavier and Kole marched toward the entrance. Kole stopped in the doorway, waiting on me. Rae and then Zaira hugged me, whispering into my ears their support and affirmations of our friendship, wishing to meet again soon.

I joined Kole at the doorstep, briefly scanning his face, and stepped into the daylight.

ELEVEN

"Stay your ground," Xavier bellowed to the score of Earthbounders facing us. "Invicta has recovered Arien, and she is in their custody. Any move against me is a strike against Invicta and the Magister."

I scanned the group opposite us and recognized many of my former classmates, including Paulyna. Stepping to the front of the group, she wore combat gear that only graduates were provided. Donovan must have worked his magic to push her graduation up. She raised her chin a notch.

"We are to believe these lower-order Earthbounders meant to turn her in? It looks to me like they've been keeping her hidden out here," she said.

Zaira's wings snapped and stretched broad to the size of a sedan. I'd never seen her in her true form before. Her wing-span, light gray and captivating, gave off an air of danger. She toyed with a sharp blade on the tip of her finger.

"Bring it, bitch. I'd like to show you how the orders work." Zaira flashed her brilliant whites. Paulyna remained still but her throat bobbed. Anhelm, who was reclining against the SUV with arms crossed and a scowl etched into his tanned face, eyed Zaira with mild interest which in his books might as well have been admiration.

The newcomers did not make a move. Xavier stepped down to the SUV and opened the back door. I followed him in, jumping into the vehicle immediately, Kole on my tail. I met Anhelm inside—the warrior moved fast—and he sandwiched me between him and Kole. Xavier got in the front passenger seat, next to Mezzo, his second trusted warrior. I'd rarely seen Xavier without Anhelm and Mezzo in tow. They were Xavier's personal guard. But I glimpsed a sort of brotherly bond between them too. The centuries together had brought them closer.

We departed without another word. I strained my neck to peered out the tinted back window. The P6-ers stood their ground, bravely facing the intruders. Before we turned a corner, the Seraphs retreated, and I released a puff of air.

Kole's shoulder brushed against mine with reassurance. He scoured the outside as did the other warriors. If the threat to me was so great out here in the middle of the freaking woods, what would it be like at Invicta? I rubbed my wrist, missing my bracelet.

"What did the Fringe want with me?" I broke the silence. I had to. Kole rubbed his jaw.

"We are trying to find out," he said.

"The Fringe has never been our ally. We tolerate each other—I mean my father does," Xavier said. I sensed he didn't agree with the Magister's treatment of the Fringe.

"They're shifters? Most of them?" I asked.

"Yes," both warriors answered at the same time, their eyes snapping to each other's in the rearview mirror. *Why was the Soaz there?* I wanted to ask, but first, I needed to separate my memories from hallucinations. Had he truly transformed into the hideous gargoyle-like creature? Or did my frazzled brain conjure up those images? One thing was for sure. He'd bitten me yet again. The medicinal leaf had closed off the wound and healed the skin, but under the surface, my flesh throbbed as if it were fighting an infection.

"Have you prepared her for questioning by the council?" Xavier's words brought me out of my inner musings.

"We went over the events," Kole said. Xavier tilted his head.

"I'd like to hear it." Xavier turned around in his seat and pored over my face. I had nothing to lose by recounting the events to him. I began with the jump. Kole flexed his fingers resting by my thigh when I reached the part about the gollums' attack and then again when King Cygnus manhandled me.

"We have four unauthorized fae to capture then. Any idea where they traveled to?" Anhelm interjected.

I shook my head. "I wish I knew. I could've refused the king's request. I should've refused it," I admonished myself publicly.

"No," Kole said tersely. "He would've made you do it. Sooner or later. He'd torture you until you cracked. No matter how strong you are, he'd make you do it. It's better this way."

"Agreed," Xavier drawled. My brows drew together. *Since when did these two warriors agree on anything?*

"Where did you transport to?" Anhelm asked.

I explained about the portal circle at the dry cleaners, leaving Daria out of the story, which I'd done with the P6-ers as well. I was unsure of how her role in the heist at the highly protected place in the Earthbounder world would be perceived by the Earthbounders, and the girl had definitely learned her lesson—I hoped. I ended my story recounting the escape with my rescuer who'd brought me to Rae and Zaira.

"He must be one of the rebels," Anhelm said. "Where is he now?" He directed his gaze above my head to Kole.

Kole's shoulder brushed against mine.

"We don't trail rebels. That's Invicta's job." Anhelm's nostrils flared, and hot air warmed my hair. He dropped the subject and turned to the front again.

"In that case, we will overlook P6-ers enlisting a rebel to assist with Arien's recovery, given that the Magister himself invited all supernatural creatures to bring her in. Some less palatable than the rebel problem," Xavier said.

"It wasn't my decision to involve them. Our female warriors tend to take matters into their own hands," Kole said, and I smirked under the curtain of my hair. Rae and Zaira had the P6 men wrapped around their pinkies. "I would've gone myself if I'd known. But, in retrospect, a rebel with extensive knowledge of Fringe's layout was the best choice for this mission. I believe he owed Zaira a favor." At the mention of Zaira's name, Anhelm sat up straight.

Mezzo remained quiet throughout the drive, his eyes constantly scanning the terrain for any danger. Sooner than expected, we exited the highway, and the roads turned familiar. The pit of my stomach tightened in anticipation. There they were—the gates to Invicta. Only two weeks ago, I'd left Invicta knowing and wishing I'd never see it again. The rectangular-shaped iron gates stood twelve feet tall with arches and circles interwoven with the horizontal rods. At the center, a massive metal plate showcased the Invicta emblem —a sword with wings of an angel—divided into two symmetrical halves. I hugged myself, my breath quickening. My judgment day had come. Would they judge me worthy to live?

The Magister's guards waited for us at the entrance to the west wing. I rubbed my hands together to stop the trembling. I couldn't show signs of weakness, defeat. No, I was a Pure now, and I'd done nothing wrong. I had saved them and all of humanity from the ancient Archon, for heaven's sake. The mechanics of what I'd done weren't clear, but facts were facts. I—or the apparition—cindered that horrid demon into ashes.

I stepped out of the car, holding my head high and scowling at the two guards.

"Follow us," one guard said.

"Arien will stay in my suite during her trial," Xavier said.

"We have explicit orders to bring the deserter to a cell and prepare for her interrogation by the council tonight," the same guard declared.

"Well, the orders have changed. The deserter is a high flight risk. I will personally ensure she's delivered to the council meeting." Xavier breezed past the guards before they could respond. Mezzo gently nudged my back to follow. Kole took up the rear. Growling stopped me in my tracks. I turned around, finding both guards with their hands on Kole's shoulders in a tense standoff. The guards apparently had a death wish.

"P6-ers are not permitted on the premises." The guard addressed Xavier. "We cannot allow this override."

"The hell you can't." Heat emanated from Xavier when he strode past me. He tugged Kole's collar down, exposing the protector mark there. "Go report to the Magister that the Everlake blessed Kolerean with the protector mark, and this divine intervention precedes all Earthbounder law." The guards' faces softened with awe. Xavier guided us into the wing, while the guards veered towards a smaller side entrance.

The Magister's son and his guards occupied an entire floor by themselves. A large redwood door with a beveled-square pattern opened into a single room, a dark spacious office. Straight ahead behind a crimson leather couch, a set of double doors opened into his pristine white living space. The exposed whitewashed brick wall, white ceiling, and washed-

out gray hardwood floor elevated the space. I didn't anticipate such elegance from warriors who hunted unsavory creatures at night.

I'd never seen Kole's room at P6 or any other Pure's room
for that matter, so I couldn't make a comparison. The living
area stretched into a well-stocked library. A colorful rug lay
underneath a round coffee table with two lounge chairs. In
the opposite corner, a small kitchen contrasted with the size
of the open space, but it made sense since the Pures were
used to having prepped meals.

"Arien will stay in one of my guest rooms," Xavier said as
he pulled apart two whitewashed barn door panels to reveal a
hallway. A lump formed in my throat. "Kolerean will room
with Mezzo, on the other side of the hall."

Kole clenched his jaw. I scowled at Xavier. If there were
rooms, as in plural, in his suite, why couldn't Kole stay here?
With me. The question hung at the tip of my tongue, but
the door burst open when Nelia, Xavier's half-sister and my
former orientation leader, rushed in. Her pissed-off eyes
held a softness around the edges. She dropped a bag of
clothes on the couch and stomped over to me, getting in my
face.

Kole raised an eyebrow at me, silently asking whether he
should interfere.

"I'm really sorry, Ne—" I squeaked when she engulfed me
in a tight hug. I had injected Nelia with a hefty dose of sleep
agent once we arrived near the battle line. It was a dirty
move, but at that moment I believed it was the right one.

"I get that you are, but that doesn't remove you from my
shit list. At least, not yet."

"I'm fine with that." I stumbled to regain balance and,
well, mental clarity after she released me. Everything was
happening so fast. It gave me a sensation of a mental game of
ping-pong being played in my head.

"The council rescheduled the hearing to five o'clock upon learning that you'd secured Arien," Nelia said.

Mezzo released a low whistle and tension filled the air. I locked my hands behind my back to conceal the shaking. I wasn't ready to face them so soon. We'd only gotten here.

Xavier ticked his head at Nelia.

"Get her ready." He strode off in the opposite direction, opening similar-looking double doors to his own suite. Nelia wrapped her fingers around my bicep, guiding and grounding me. Before I turned around, I caught Kole's gaze, which had turned darker, stormy again. He said nothing; he didn't have to. His presence alone gave me strength. He was my protector now. And my strength.

TWELVE

Nelia brought the bag into my room. I quickly changed into uniform pants, a shirt, and black sneakers. The shirt, with its slits, allowed space for my wings to unfurl without shredding my top. This was a Pure-issue shirt. I let my hair down, brushing out the tangles. Nelia placed her hands on my shoulders.

"Remember—"

"I will avoid making eye contact unless addressed directly by one of them. I will not speak out of turn... Oh, shoulders straight, head held high. Remain calm no matter what BS they spew my way—"

Nelia chuckled. "I think the BS part is your addition."

I sighed. Nelia had preached the proper conduct at formal meetings to me for the last twenty minutes. I had it memorized, but I was prone to misfire.

"You're ready. Let's go." Nelia pulled the barn door open.

At the center of the living room, near the seating area with a fireplace, Xavier and his two men waited, hands stuffed in their dress-pant pockets. I pinched my lips. Why would they dress up for the meeting, while I was wearing a training uniform? Oh, wait, I was a prisoner. Xavier had only saved me from the cell beneath Invicta. My status had not changed.

"Where is Kole?" I asked.

"He can't join us," Xavier said slowly.

I froze, alarms going off in my head. No one stirred. They all observed me as my legs turned rubbery. I perched on the nearest armchair. *That's okay. It will be okay.* I avoided their gazes.

"Guards came in and escorted him away for a meeting with the Soaz." My eyes snapped to Xavier's, which showed no feeling. "They may detain him for a few weeks..."

I heard nothing else coming out of Xavier's mouth. The Soaz? That monster had Kole. My protector. He wouldn't go easy on Kole. No, he'd torture him solely to hurt me. Blood drained from my face. I tried to stand but fell into the chair instead, hyperventilating. Flesh tore under my shoulder blades and bloodied wings snapped out, propelling me off the chair onto the floor. Drip, drip, drip. Drops of blood splashed to the floor around me. Sweat gathered above my lip, and my head spun a few circles before the equilibrium returned.

Gentle but mighty hands righted me, and Kole's burning eyes met mine. I recoiled. What the...?

"You-you're not here... They said they took you in," I stammered, wiping my lip.

"It was either that or inviting the Soaz over," Xavier said.

I stood still. Regret marred Kole's classic dark features.

"What am I missing, damn it?" I said.

"They need to see your wings," Kole whispered. "It helps your case. They have to see them for themselves."

"It's true." Nelia's delicate hand rested against my arm. They were all in on it. I shrugged her hand off and stormed into the kitchenette. I stuck a kitchen towel under running water and covered my face with it. I wanted to scream, but that didn't sound like a thing an Earthbounder would do. So I wiped my face instead, then a few bloody strands of my hair. At some point, Nelia joined me with another towel and helped clean my wings. I sensed a twitch in my right shoulder a millisecond before the wing flexed, knocking Nelia away in the process. Then, it retracted again with a snap. I watched, wide-eyed, as Nelia massaged her jaw.

"Uh...I didn't do that," I said.

"I'm aware." Nelia rolled her eyes. "They have a mind of their own. Just tell them to behave in the council chamber. Wing smiting is a sure ticket to a duel."

I paled. "Maybe we should tie them together?" I asked.

The warriors sniggered. I glared their way. If it weren't for their superior combat skills, I'd walk among them every chance I got and wing-smite them all.

"On that note, it's time to leave." Xavier's eyes glinted. "Relax. You're ready."

THIRTEEN

The Magister's office guards surrounded us as we arrived at the grand staircase. The circular atrium had a glass ceiling that let in an ample amount of sunlight. A Romanesque waterfall trickled water down a plump female angel's naked body into the shallow pool beneath her.

At the top of the staircase, the guards opened the double doors of a chamber with descending crescent-shaped seating. The aisle between rows sloped down towards a raised platform, adorned with seven majestic red chairs that exuded regal splendor. Perched on them were seven Seraphs, each with a look of disdain etched onto their faces.

The occupants quieted upon our entry. Guards led us to a single bench that faced the seven Pures. Xavier and Kole remained by my side. Before I lowered my eyes, as was the custom, I glimpsed Hafthor glowering at his son. The Magister occupied the chair on the dais furthest to the left.

The Pure in the center chair rose to his feet. I peeked from beneath my eyelashes. He was the oldest Earthbounder I'd ever seen. Nelia had explained he was the Oath Keeper—a diviner who oversaw the council. Long strands of pure white hair flowed down to his shoulder blades, giving him an ethereal appearance. His face actually had wrinkles etched into it, and one of his eyes had clouded over. He wore a long white robe with three different emblems patched into it on either side of his chest—Invicta's emblem among them.

The emblems matched those worn by the other six members of the council. Five male and one female Magister of the six regions: Northwest, North, Northeast, Southeast, South, and Southwest.

"Welcome, brothers and sisters. Today, we finally get some answers as to the nature of the latest large-scale security breach." Whispers intensified around the chamber. The Oath Keeper paced from one side of the dais to the other with his hands clasped behind his back. He'd stop and stare at the crowd, which also occupied a wrap-around balcony. Taking a chance, my eyes landed on the widest of the sections and rounded with surprise. I clenched my own hands tighter. Donovan sat there among a few other high-ranking Pures I recognized. Beside him, the Soaz bored his dark pupils down at me and only me. His features tightened, ready to explode. I forced myself to break the eye contact.

"Arien Blair," the Oath Keeper said. My gut wrenched. He approached with a golden breastplate in hand. I gasped. "Do you recognize this artifact?" I nodded numbly.

An ancient Power had supposedly worn the piece of armor, prior to the Seraphs' arrival to Earth. The metal was pure gold or something even beyond the metal known to the human world. A shimmery glint passed through it as if it were alive. One touch would kill a demon. I swallowed. If I had demon genes... I glanced at Kole and Xavier, who had not twitched since we descended into the chamber and continued to stare forward. Were they not going to intervene?

The Oath Keeper extended the armor to me. I longed for

the answer to this question as much as anyone else in this room. Turning my head to the side, I quickly placed both hands on the top. My palms heated. My heart cried out with joy. Wait, what? I opened my eyes and peered down. My palms lit up on contact with the armor, and the sweetest melody filled my ears. A teardrop rolled down my cheek.

"Do you hear it?" I asked the man in front of me, then scanned Kole's and Xavier's faces. I found only a hint of relief in them. The bastards were truly gonna watch me burn alive if I hadn't passed this test.

"I can feel the vibrations. The armor appears to be speaking only to you," the sage man said with awe. I withdrew my hands, and the melody disappeared along with the light.

The charge in the air diminished to tiny tethers. Many warriors had readied themselves for the worst—that I was a demon. And they would've gladly hacked me to pieces. *But I'm not a demon—I'm not.* I closed my eyes briefly to savor this moment.

"*It's not conclusive,*" a masculine timbre sounded in my head. My eyelids flew open, and I raised my head. I recognized his voice, even in my own head. The Soaz smirked down at me from his balcony, and I bristled. He had invaded too much of my life. I sent murderous thoughts back at him, but he never replied. I hoped that meant he couldn't read my thoughts, only project his own.

"That is not definitive." A man in the second chair from the left leaned forward, scowling.

"I concur," the councilmen and councilwomen responded in unison.

The atmosphere charged again. All eyes settled on the Oath Keeper. He ran a hand over the armor.

"The divine armor has not reacted to anyone this way since the last of our forefathers walked among us. Therefore, we must acknowledge ancient blood runs through this fledgling. The wings are a testament to that. The ancients could command the divine devices such as this armor and the allura. And because the armor did not harm the fledgling, she was judged worthy to walk among us again. No matter the stain on her blood, if such can be proved." The Oath Keeper strode to the dais and propped the armor against his chair. Silence followed him. No one objected to his words as if his stance was the word of God.

"Who are the girl's parents?" a redheaded man sitting closest to Hafthor asked, and the entire crowd, including the council, swiveled their heads toward Invicta's Magister. The commanding features of his face tightened.

"We've not been able to trace the parentage. The mother glamoured—or had help glamouring— everyone present at the birth. They placed memory blocks on them. All we know is that the woman gave birth to the fledgling in the southern region of France."

My heart skipped at the mention of my mother. Were they aware that I had her bracelet? I fought back against the desire to glance at Xavier to see if he had kept my secret.

A pregnant minute elapsed between Hafthor's statement and the next question.

"There is a matter of her defeating an ancient Archon. Archons annihilated the original Earthbounders. Are we to believe the fledgling is more powerful than her predecessors?" a woman with blond hair pulled into a tight bun asked. I stared at her a moment too long. I couldn't put my finger on it, but there was something familiar about her.

The Oath Keeper nodded, lowering himself into his chair. He waved his hand in my direction.

"Proceed," he said.

My eyebrows shot to my hairline. I knew I'd have to recount the events of that day, but I wasn't ready. I wet my lips and stumbled with words, blacking out at times, but I believe I stayed faithful to the narrative I'd practiced. The audience remained silent as I described my dreams and the mystical stone, Sky Ice, that boosted my healing, defeated the Archon, and perhaps even caused my transformation. Was I born with ancient Earthbounder blood or simply gifted it by the sapphire stone?

The Oath Keeper rose to his feet again. He closed his eyes and lifted his arms to his side. A column of light traveled through him at a rapid speed.

"The fledgling speaks the truth. They granted me the knowledge of Sky Ice. It remains beyond our realm with our brothers and sisters. Its assistance with Earth matters was of a singular effect. We should not count on its return."

"Where is it, Oath Keeper?" the blond woman asked.

"It is not for us to know." The Oath Keeper shook his head.

"Why was the power of this divine device granted to a fledgling?" A male with an ink-black man-bun pierced me with his laser green eyes.

"That wasn't revealed either." The Oath Keeper meandered the length of the dais and back. When no one else spoke, he stopped and looked each of the council members in the eye.

"The matter of Bezekah's defeat is closed," he announced.

"I concur," the council members sounded at once.

"Power Kolerean, step onto the dais," the Oath Keeper called.

Without hesitation, Kole strode over and faced the audience, hands behind his back. His eyes scoured the crowd with a heated challenge reflected in them I didn't understand. *Is he in danger?*

I glanced at Xavier, who seemed to approve of Kole's behavior.

"The Everlake bestowed a protector's mark," the Oath Keeper said.

In response, Kole removed his shirt in one swift motion. His muscles were more defined than I remembered, sculpted like marble. He hadn't been eating well, if at all, since my disappearance, according to Rae. But he'd never stopped searching, interrogating, and getting into skirmishes hoping to locate me. And that showed in his slimmed-down but formidable figure. With the darkness settling underneath his eyes, he looked savage.

The tattoo gleamed on his left pec, in contrast to his perma-tanned skin.

The Oath Keeper covered the tattoo with his gnarled hand and closed his eyes, tilting his head upward. When he reopened his eyes, faint light settled over them and soon vanished. He stepped away, leaving Kole once again to face the Earthbounders all alone. Although I didn't understand the meaning of this, I didn't like it. My gut urged me to go to him.

"The bond is genuine and deeply rooted. Only the death of its bearer will allow a transfer. Now is the time to step forward or remain silent forever. Are there any challengers among us today?" the Oath Keeper asked.

I choked on a cry.

"Shh." Xavier grasped my arm. "This is the way of Earthbounders. If you intervene, you'll undermine him," he whispered into my ear.

I steeled myself, allowing my heart to fill the wildness inside me with a tune of battle drums. Kole narrowed his eyes to splinters as he impressed upon each skilled warrior in the crowd the promise of pain. I followed his stare around the chamber. Many eyes landed on me, curious, interested...calculating their chances.

Why would they want to become my protectors? I was a

wild card—a crossbreed of the ancient and evil. Yet, I saw it in their assessing eyes wandering between my unusual wings and face. They craved a distinction and—however unimaginable it was to me—glory.

"How much longer?" I asked Xavier.

"Soon. Stop enticing them with your dangerous looks," he reprimanded. I frowned up at him, focusing on his lapis lazuli irises. They grounded me in the moment. My breathing evened out, and I waited. My stomach churned when the Oath Keeper cleared his throat.

"No one has thrown a challenge. Power Kolerean remains the protector for the fledgling."

"I concur," the council members said.

I shifted my gaze to Kole. He picked up his shirt and slipped it on before stalking over to my side with a faint smirk playing on his lips. I expected him to wink at me or to whisper something to me, but his face became blank when he reached my side. The slight brush of his shoulder against mine was the only consolation he gave.

"There is one last matter which must be settled in front of this council tonight," the Oath Keeper said. "Our own excellent Seraph Xavier of Invicta claimed the fledgling as his *Ashanti* prior to her maturation. As we've today recognized her as a Pure Earthbounder and there is no denying her rank, the fledgling must now accept or reject the claim."

All eyes settled on me. I didn't expect to be addressed again tonight or asked to publicly declare my relationship status. I knew the answer, but I still gritted my teeth. My neck and cheeks flashed with heat.

"I reject Xavier's claim."

A collective gasp resonated. Hafthor straightened in his chair, his glacial glare close to the point of shattering.

"Silence," the Oath Keeper called, raising his voice. "The fledgling is young and new to the Earthbounder ways. On this matter, we will allow a twelve-month waiting period and reassess the fledgling's status at its culmination." He glanced at Hafthor. "This Earthbounder hasn't yet completed her training?"

"Correct. Arien will remain at Invicta until her graduation and assessment period is over, or when the next council convenes, whichever comes first," the Magister said. I tightened my grip on my fingers. This meant, either way, I was stuck at Invicta again. For another year.

Life on the run suddenly sounded more appealing. But I couldn't and wouldn't put Kole and the P6-ers at odds with the Earthbounder community and the council. I was ready to accept my place among the Earthbounders—whatever that might be.

"The matter of the fledgling Arien Blair is now closed and will be revisited twelve months from now." The Oath Keeper ambled to his chair and settled in it as the council members echoed another "I concur," in unison.

Xavier nudged me. I followed him out of the chamber with Kole behind me. My mind was processing what had just happened. One thing was for sure, I wasn't a demon even if some of my DNA pointed that way. I might be fine. I might survive Invicta and the Soaz. I might...

FOURTEEN

The guards closed heavy chamber doors behind us.

"I must return to the proceedings. Mezzo will escort Arien to my quarters for tonight," Xavier said to Kole. Not once did his eyes swivel my way. I glanced down the grand staircase to find Mezzo by the water fountain. The chamber door grunted as the guards again pushed it closed after Xavier re-entered the room. I glanced at Kole. His forehead creased in thin lines.

"What do you think?" I whispered to him as we descended the steps.

"That was too easy," he whispered back.

I turned my head trying to get his attention, but he avoided my gaze. A somber atmosphere descended upon us.

"I agree," Mezzo said unexpectedly. "The Magister wants you here. You're now his leverage."

"Leverage?"

Mezzo paused and looked me directly in the eye, his usual unaffected expression plastered on his face. He tired when he had to explain things to me.

"I'm a new shiny toy. Something new..." I thought out loud, seeking confirmation.

"Hafthor doesn't like to play."

"Then what?" I asked.

"A weapon," Kole said, his brow furrowing. "You're a new weapon in his arsenal. We must be careful. You will report to me if you observe or hear anything suspicious?" he asked me.

I swallowed. "Aren't you going to be around? As my protector...?" I thought Kole would accompany me to all events, although I felt torn about the protector mark and having Kole tied to my side. He shook his head slightly.

"I am privy to all matters surrounding you. But there are ways to go around it. I've no doubt Hafthor will keep me away whenever he can."

"I will tell you everything when I see you next then," I assured him.

"Good." His lips curved. Then he opened the door for me, and I stepped inside Xavier's suite with resignation. We both lingered, staring at each other. Me inside Xavier's office and Kole by the threshold. Until Mezzo grabbed the door-knob and yanked the door closed. I blew air and pivoted for the suite. I wished Kole could've stayed closer, but if staying with Xavier kept me out of the underground cell, I'd trade the cell for an insufferable roommate in a heartbeat.

Nelia's emergence from behind the fridge door startled me.

"I brought some food. Angels know, these warriors never think about substance, or where the food comes from actually."

I smiled. "You don't have to attend the meetings?" I asked.

Nelia glanced at her smartwatch, looking up with guilt.

"I have some duties..."

"Go. I'll be fine. I'm perfectly capable of prepping a meal," I said.

Nelia's shoulders relaxed. "Anhelm will be outside if you need anything," she said, making her way toward the door. I scrunched my nose up. I didn't need protection up here. Only authorized personnel could access this floor. Unless Xavier feared I'd try to leave... I guess I had earned that one.

***

I woke up to hazy light streaming in through an opening between blackout curtains, announcing the sun breaking the horizon. I freshened up, washed my hair, and put on training gear, not knowing what today had in store for me. My elusive wings had retracted in my sleep. I tried sensing them and a tiny pinch and burn spread over my shoulder blades, but no wings erupted. I had no control over them.

Not a single sound reached my ears. I shuffled quietly across the space, checking sitting areas and scanning couches. Judging by an empty glass sitting on the bar top, someone had been in here. When I entered the kitchenette, I went for the fridge. Nelia had brought a loaf of soft fresh bread, butter, and a small selection of jelly last night.

I let out a squeal of delight when I spotted a small coffee maker deep in the corner of a lower cabinet. A couple of coffee filters sat in a drawer with loosely strewn silverware, and above the stove, I found an unopened bag of ground coffee next to a poor selection of spices.

I cut through the stiff bag with a knife and poured the aromatic grinds into the filter cup. A hint of staleness hit my nostrils, but I was willing to ignore it this once. I flicked the power button on and was rewarded with the sweet hum of the coffee maker heating the water. I made a quick piece of toast with butter, stuck it into my mouth, and poured a full cup. As I wheeled around, my heart skipped a beat at the sight of Xavier nonchalantly propping his arms on the bar, his gaze fixed on me. Some of the scalding liquid splashed my wrist. I quickly set the cup down and shoved my burned hand under the faucet's cold water. I glared at the warrior. He could've given me a warning.

Xavier rose and strolled to the coffee maker, serving himself the rest of my coffee into the largest mug. I grabbed a kitchen towel to dab at my hand.

"I'm surprised you know what a coffee maker looks like." I bit my lip. I couldn't help myself. One day, I'd pay a hefty price for my smart mouth.

"While you're here, make me toast, too."

My jaw dropped. Xavier sauntered past me with a smug look on his face. I bit back my retort, realizing he was joking. At least, I thought he was. I definitely wouldn't be making him toast. I grabbed my cup and joined him in the living room, deliberately choosing a seat furthest from his. As I faced him, it struck me for the first time this morning that the Pure was half-naked. His tattooed pecs glistened with beads of water as if he hadn't bothered to use a towel after showering. The gray sweatpants hung loosely on his hips exposing a deep cut V. I averted my gaze as soon as the cup left his mouth, and his eyes bored into mine questioningly. My face heated, and I immediately brought the cup to my own lips.

Sounds from the flat screen above the fireplace drew my attention. The reporter with velour green eyes and green streaks in her hair posed in front of a wooded open field I recognized. That couldn't be. I sat up straight. The take switched to a studio setting, then to a new reporter in front of Invicta's gates. As luxury cars with tinted windows entered Invicta's grounds, a group of reporters and cameramen tried to get a shot of the occupants. Cameras flashed and the group shouted at passing vehicles.

"I had no idea you had your own paparazzi or news channel," I said. Xavier muted the TV and threw the remote on the coffee table.

"They have their uses." Xavier stretched his long bulky arms. Noticing my bewildered expression, he asked, "You didn't know?"

I shook my head. I couldn't recall a single instance of watching TV while I stayed at Invicta. Partially because the secondborn rooms had no TVs.

"The Earthbounders have the same means of communication you experience in the human world, including social media. But we use our own apps."

"But some of your technologies are nothing I'd ever seen," I said.

Xavier looked at me like I was off my rocker. "Of course not, we have access to divine materials and knowledge that can't be shared with humans."

"Why not?"

"Simple. They wouldn't be able to handle it. Have you heard of cognitive dissonance?"

I opened my mouth to answer him when Mezzo, Anhelm, and Kole waltzed in. I couldn't contain the coy smile threatening to spill all over my face and making me feel so childish. Kole's eyes found mine immediately and softened around the edges but hardened again when he surveyed Xavier's attire or rather the lack of it. Kole stuffed his hands into his pockets, positioning himself behind my couch and my back. Something about his move screamed of him staking a claim. I just didn't know if it was the protector claim or something more. Delicious heat radiated from him. It soothed my nerves.

Xavier tilted his cup and emptied it. The other two warriors settled leisurely on the third couch, facing me.

"Nelia's on her way," Xavier said before picking the remote up again and turning the volume up. The next several minutes passed without a single word among us. Another woman would've dreamed of getting stuck in a suite with four hot warriors, but at least three of these men either repulsed me or were a complete iceberg to me. The TV held no more interest for me either.

I hopped to my feet and crossed the living area to the corner library. Although pristinely clean, this section exuded a cozy ambience with a sizable wingback chair tucked in the corner. There was an indentation in the chair like someone sat there often. That someone would've been Xavier. I never suspected him to be a book connoisseur. Built-in dark mahogany shelves brimmed with a variety of books. One shelf drew my attention in particular with its brown leather-bound book covers. I hesitated, unsure how Xavier would react to me touching the older, fragile books. But curiosity won over. I gently slid a couple books out. The first one was titled *Kinder- und Hausmärchen* by Jacob and Wilhelm Grimm. The book next to it was *The Fairy Tales of the Brothers Grimm,* seemingly the first English edition. Xavier had a twisted fascination with fairy tales. He'd referenced Sleeping Beauty and alluded to Hansel and Gretel fairy tales at different times when he and I butted heads.

Biting my lip, I slid the book out completely and flipped the cover. In an elegant hand, an inscription took over the bottom half of the title page: *For my beautiful and strong boy — Cerah.* Guilt overcame me, and I replaced the book in its rightful place. Xavier's mother had died when he was a little boy. I'd seen no pictures of her in his place or Hafthor's office. But his holding onto this book meant more than an old dusty picture. I glanced over my shoulder. Xavier reclined with his hands behind his head, his back to me. Only Kole was facing me from his position behind the couch I'd abandoned. A line above his brows wrinkled in question. I offered a small reassuring smile in response.

I turned away from the books when the door creaked open and heels tapped on the wood floor. Nelia came in, wearing a navy suit with a pencil skirt. She had elegantly styled her blond locks in a high updo. She held a folder and a notepad in one hand and a pen in the other. I approached the warriors along with her.

"The bearer of bad news," Xavier said instead of a welcome. Nelia perched on the arm of his couch.

"It's not bad if you don't count extracurriculars, additional training, meeting with the Magister, fancy and pretentious dinner parties, and figuring out how her wings work, or her powers." Nelia smiled up at Xavier, then at me.

"I see sarcasm runs in the family," I said. "Please tell me not all of it is on today's agenda."

"Today and every day until..." Nelia trailed off with a shrug. "But, on the bright side, it won't go on forever." I hiked my eyebrows. Nelia was horrible at reassurance.

"Let's take one day at a time," Kole said. I focused on my protector who'd lived the longest life among the warriors present and nodded in agreement. Although anxiety had made a permanent residence in my stomach, I wouldn't back down. Being back at Invicta as a "recruit" created a déjà vu effect. Except this time I was a Pure. That fact alone should increase my chances of succeeding. It simply didn't feel that way though. Because I was now high profile, a new Pure, an enigma. The question was to what lengths would the Magister or the Soaz go to crack the mystery surrounding my ancestry? To crack me?

FIFTEEN

Walking the familiar hall with marble busts of prominent figures throughout history should have felt refreshing, but knowing my destination made me abhor them. Today they resembled gargoyles more than works of art, watching me as I entered the mouth of evil.

The Magister, Hafthor, reclined in his overstuffed leather chair, drumming fingers on the exquisitely carved mahogany-stained wooden arm. He studied me with a stoic expression, the usual arrogance, judgment, and distaste absent.

I strolled in with my head held high, mimicking his own demeanor. I wouldn't be the first to crack, and it was only a matter of time before Hafthor hinted at his true intentions. I sat in the visitor chair Exiousai Seth had occupied once, avoiding any glance at the other visitor chair—the one I sat in when I was first called into this office. Hafthor had made me feel unwanted and little then. And I was a new person, a new Earthbounder coming into her power.

The corner of his mouth lifted. I couldn't tell whether he approved of my choice or simply mocked me. Did he think any more of me than he did the last time we met? I suspected the only person he held on the pedestal was himself. Everyone else was a toy in his arsenal.

"How are your accommodations?" he asked.

The question took me aback, and I examined it from every angle.

"Lovely," I intoned. I wasn't sure yet what he was getting at. He leaned in, settling his elbows on the massive desk.

"Neither of us is good at small talk, so let's cut it. We haven't started off well, and I don't blame you for harboring resentment. Let's put that aside. You're now a Pure, and I am offering you more than adequate shelter, necessities, and training until you graduate from our elite program. You're also granted Invicta's protection."

I nodded.

Hafthor slid a sheet of paper over the top of his expansive desk. I picked it up. The Magister had troubled himself to outline my daily schedule—how nice. I had a packed schedule; even the evenings had "Attend evening functions as required" blocked off. I guess I'd become Hafthor's beck-and-call girl. I fumed inside. Hafthor inspected his nails.

"As you see, you will be required to attend some functions. Especially while the council is still here." He bored his hardened eyes into mine.

"I expect you to be on your best behavior. Your performance in training and during social events will determine your good standing with Invicta. Don't disappoint me."

I inclined my head. No further explanation was necessary. The Magister still pulled the strings, regardless of the council's wishes. He cocked his head.

"Why so silent? That's not like you," he said.

"And it's just like you to hold everyone in your tight fist," I said with a bite.

Hafthor grinned, and the act reminded me of Xavier.

How did they have so much in common when they acted in such contrasting ways? One craved power at all costs; the other put his duty above all.

"Ah, there you are. We are clear then. You do as I ask and your stay at Invicta will be a pleasant one."

The door lock clicked open.

"You called me?" Donovan asked from behind me, sending an unsettling tremor over my body. I'd seen him in the council chamber, but I hadn't expected facing him so soon.

Hafthor reclined again.

"Arien needs to catch up with her cohort in order to graduate on time. I've included extra sessions with seasoned warriors in her curriculum. That includes you most mornings."

"Yes, Magister," Donovan said.

"Perfect. You can begin today." Hafthor peered down at me showing dismissal. I rose to my feet and turned, poised and ready to confront one pissed warrior.

Donovan led the way to the Pure's gym. As with everything else, the Pures and secondborns had separate training places and, mostly, didn't mingle.

The Seraph used to pursue me as his *Amorei*, a lover, but then apparently had made snide remarks about my warrior potential behind my back to the Magister. I planned to remain vigilant around him.

Donovan wore designer jeans and a white polo shirt. His hair still glistened from a fresh shower. He hadn't expected to have to train me or anyone today. I studied his gait for a sign of the injury he'd sustained during the battle with Bezekah, but I saw no signs of it. He'd probably gotten the healing serum the P6-ers so desperately needed for their ranks.

"This way," he said, steering me around sparring arenas to a vast open space with mats covering the floor. He left me in the middle and stripped his shoes and shirt, throwing them on a bench. He returned with nothing but his jeans on. I cocked an eyebrow.

"If you want to go grab some workout clothes, I can wait," I said.

"This is no workout for me."

Oh... So that was how we were rolling today. I wouldn't let him intimidate me. He gave commands to strike, and I followed them. He'd tap my flabby arms and kick my legs from underneath me when my stances were not up to his standard, which happened every single time.

"This is not helpful. You criticize but you don't tell me what I need to do to improve," I said.

"Perhaps it's because I don't care." He regarded me down his nose and crossed his arms over his chest.

"I recall you not so long ago offering to train me. To give me your one-on-one attention," I goaded him.

In a swift move I hadn't seen coming, Donovan swept his leg and knocked me down. I lay flat as a pancake on my back, admiring the ceiling. *Shit.* How was I ever going to match his level? Or that of Kole and Xavier, or even Vex? I wasn't even five percent there.

Donovan bent at his waist, hands on hips. Veins popped on his forehead, and the little exercise he'd done wasn't the cause for it.

"If you'd become my *Amorei*, none of this would've happened." Donovan sounded irate, which put me on the defensive.

"Then I wouldn't have stopped Bezekah," I replied with

the same heat. Wait a minute. "What side are you on?" I asked.

Donovan's dark laugh made me wince. He straightened, glaring ahead and then back down at me.

"The best one there is—my own."

I inhaled sharply. Donovan gathered his clothes. I rolled to the side, intent on continuing this convo, but found him already dressed and leaving while perplexed warriors bounced glances between us. *Argh!* I flopped to my back. I had no clue where I was or how to get back from here. I'd need to talk one of the Pures here into showing me a map on their fancy watch. I still hadn't gotten one. Apparently becoming a rare Pure didn't equal smartwatch-worthy.

SIXTEEN

"Is this really necessary?" I asked, staring at my reflection in the mirror. The silk plum material highlighted my curves without clinging. I could actually breathe in this corset-like top with an A-flare bottom. Nelia, as usual, had outdone herself on the outfits for us. She wore an emerald beauty, cut like mine but with a single shoulder strap. Nelia styled her hair in an intricate fish braid, interweaving emerald silk between her blond strands. I asked the hairstylist who'd accompanied her to style my hair the same way, but she'd said she had strict instructions from an undisclosed individual to leave my waves loose.

I scowled at the revelation but decided against picking this battle. I had promised Hafthor to appease. At least he hadn't chosen my dress.

My makeup was striking. The deep, matte eye shadow extended beyond the crease in a dramatic and daring effect. The line upturned on the outside corners with a precision that could cut glass. A gunmetal eye shadow colored along the lower lash line and silver glitter in the inner corners reflected light. Mauve blush sculpted my cheeks, and a vampy burgundy lipstick balanced the intensity of the eyes. The fair tone of my skin stood in stark contrast to the fierce makeup. I bit my lip and turned to face satisfied Nelia.

"This is perfect," I said. She scooted beside me and inspected our images side by side. In her classy dress and elegant evening makeup, she embodied her inner angel. My edgy makeup portrayed me more as a badass.

"I wouldn't send you over there without a little confidence boost. You look fearless, even if you don't feel like it sometimes."

A ball of emotion lodged in my throat.

"Thanks," I whispered.

The Magister had extended an invitation to me today, although it seemed more like a requirement, for a cocktail hour and dinner hosted for the council and all families of importance currently stationed at Invicta. He invited Kole as my protector, and I couldn't shake off the giddiness of seeing him in a tux tonight.

He stood by the fireplace with one arm propped on the mantel. When he lifted his head, his eyes widened. My core heated at his reaction, and a strange tingle ran across my shoulder blades. I glided over to his side, never dropping his eyes as he held onto mine. There, I finally let myself inspect his graphite jacket and matching pants. The white cuffs of his shirt peeked out slightly from underneath his sleeves, but he didn't appear to care.

"You're missing a bow tie," I said.

He leaned in. "Funny thing, the delivery boy lost it." His eyes softened around the edges and a dimple erupted on one side.

"I hope you gave him hell for his carelessness." I smirked.

The sound of ice cubes clinking drew my attention to Xavier. He stood on the other side of the bar holding a crystal glass filled with golden liquid. He raised the glass my way and emptied its contents. His black tuxedo was complete with the bow tie.

Kole lifted my hand and entwined it with his arm. I bit my inner cheek to stop myself from grinning. Why did I feel so giddy when I was about to enter a room filled with intimidating Seraphs? I summoned calm and composure to overrule the other emotions. Kole was with me now, but I had to be able to stand on my own. They wouldn't tolerate a Pure hiding behind her protector's back. Kole had my back as much as I had his.

The ballroom was in the south wing. Before the grand entrance, a receiving line of liveried footmen welcomed guests with flutes of champagne. They wore pristine white gloves and tuxedos. I swiped a flute to occupy my trembling hands. Kole still held my other arm on his, but I suspected we wouldn't remain that way for the entire evening.

Golden lines filled the contours of the grand white double doors. Beyond the threshold, high sprawling ceilings drew my immediate attention. Elaborate paintings adorned the dome-like segments of the ceiling, providing a stark contrast to the dark paneling of the walls. Delicate crystal glasses, fine bone china, and silver flatware created an elegant display on the massive rectangular table. And strategically placed candelabras cast a warm ambiance.

Xavier guided Nelia to an open chair at the end of the table. He kissed her hand before she got seated. His own seat was at the Magister's left hand. Kole strode confidently toward open seats by Nelia when a servant stopped in front of us, bowed deeply, and gestured with his hand to show the other end of the table. Kole stilled.

"Only the lady," the servant said, staring down at the

white marble floor. I glanced at the seats leading up to Hafthor. They were filling up fast, and soon only one open seat remained—by the Soaz. I clenched my fist.

"I'll go," I said to Kole, who was glaring in that direction. He flinched when I slid my hand out of the crook of his elbow. For a moment, I feared he'd make a scene. Nelia placed her soft hands on his other arm and whispered into his ear. He relaxed enough to let me walk away. The servant ambled by my side in case I disobeyed. I couldn't blame him, though, and if I took offense with him, I'd be misdirecting my animosity. No, the target of my ire sat at the head of the table.

Xavier appeared disinterested as I slid into the chair by the Soaz. The bloodthirsty monster sat directly on Hafthor's right side. I counted all the sharp utensils on the spread in front of me and memorized their locations. But, most importantly, I avoided giving the Soaz any of my attention even when he partially turned to face me. I scanned the faces of the guests. The council members sat near the head of the table with their spouses. Next were some of their offspring, I assumed, all elite Seraphs and their dates, including Donovan and Paulyna. She swiveled her head my way as if I'd spoken her name. Even across the expanse that separated us, I sensed her hostility. Other less prestigious guests occupied the other end of the table. There, I found the faces of the warriors I adored most— Nelia and Kole.

Kole sipped on a drink as if he had no care in the world. But I knew better. He hated this event and the elitists attending it as much as I did.

The first dish was served—a creamy white soup that melted in my mouth. It had a rich savory flavor of herbs and some root vegetable that I couldn't quite place.

"*Planning to ignore me all night?*" the masculine voice of the

Soaz echoed in my head. The spoon I was holding clanked against the fine white bowl and bounced to the side.

"Oh, I'm sorry," I said to the council member seated to my right. Elyon? Was that his name? He sat next to the Oath Keeper. The Magister of the Northeast region caught my hand mid-air. Before I could react, a servant picked up my fly-away spoon and laid a new, shiny piece of silverware by my bowl.

"Thank you," I said. The councilman released me and chuckled.

"We don't thank the servants," he said.

I inclined my head. First impressions were never my strong suit.

"Arien has much to learn about Earthbounder ways, particularly those of a Pure," Hafthor said.

"She hasn't been around the Pures. Perhaps we should all rotate Arien through our institutes. She can learn more and faster from all of us. My children, Zephyr and Seraphina, would provide exemplary guidance." Elyon glanced down the table at a handsome male warrior with blond hair smoothed into a ponytail. I peered at the faces of other council members, who nodded in agreement.

Hafthor sipped his wine before he replied. Tension lines formed at the outer corners of his eyes. "That is a valid notion we can explore later, my dear friend," he said.

I lost my appetite. My plans didn't involve swapping institutes.

"*Cheer up. Hafthor will never let you leave.*" Ominous laughter followed the Soaz's words in my head. I hated he could do that. Still, I refused to glance at him. Instead, I stole glances at Kole and Xavier to anchor my sanity in this asylum.

Throughout the meal, the Soaz kept intruding into my head and, I suspected, took pleasure in startling me.

"It isn't polite to hold a private conversation while in

company," Xavier said with nonchalance. He swirled his favorite drink around while scowling at the Soaz.

"Hmm, I concur," another councilman said. "We're all vying for our beautiful fresh addition's attention. I call for Damian to refrain from further sharing his thoughts with Arien." I let out a breath. And for the first time, I peered up at the offender.

His name was Damian? His true name. I'd never heard it spoken before. I averted my gaze before our eyes connected and grasped my glass of wine. Knowing his name felt... empowering? He was no longer the frightening Soaz. Although he was still scary as hell, the name would remind me he wasn't as omnipotent as he claimed to be. A smirk tugged at my lips, and I brought the drink to my mouth to hide it.

"My son will honor your request," Hafthor said.

I choked on the wine, coughing up the small amount I ingested. *His son?* The Soaz grabbed my arm and clapped my back with a force that rattled my spine. I snatched my steak knife and brought it to his rib cage.

"Don't touch me!"

Silence filled the room. I realized then I had done something unthinkable. To the Earthbounders present, the Soaz was merely helping me, and I threatened to stab him in return. My hand trembled. The Magister's eyes narrowed to dangerous pinpricks. I laid the knife down and waited for him to decide my fate.

"She's a fighter," the councilman who sat between Xavier and the only female Magister said. He was from the Southwest region; his name was Adon. He stroked his chin thoughtfully. "The Southwest would like to host Arien at our annual games next month."

Oh.

Xavier straightened and turned to his father. He didn't

miss a beat when it came to the Soaz's—I mean his brother's
—actions, yet he shot an accusatory glance my way next. I
held air in my cheeks, afraid I'd say something I could only
get away with in private with him. Because he so graciously
allowed it.

"The South is throwing an open invitation as well," a man
with grayish hair but a youthful face said. If I recalled
correctly, his name was Gavriel.

Elyon clapped his hands. "Yes. You see, Hafthor, we need
to revisit Arien's schedule prior to her graduation. She should
experience all regions to become a well-rounded Earthbounder."

The Magister snapped his fingers at the service. "Next
course," he said in a dark tone that made my skin crawl.

*"I must say I've never enjoyed Invicta's formal dinners, not until
today."*

SEVENTEEN

Hafthor announced the conclusion of the main course and rose from his seat. I couldn't wait to get away from the company of my neighbors. I pushed the chair backward only to find three men hovering over me with extended hands—the Soaz, Xavier, and the councilman, Elyon. I blinked, hoping my eyes were deceiving me. I knew which hand I wanted to take, but I thought back to Hafthor's actions today and made a move that was a sure trigger for him.

I plastered on a smile and slid my hand into Elyon's. He beamed down at me, inclining his head. Without another glance at the other man, I let Elyon parade me across the ballroom. First, he introduced me to his son and daughter, who were in attendance. He explained his eldest son had stayed at the institute as his second in command. A few other council members joined us for a conversation. They all sang praises over their institutes and explained how I would benefit from visiting. It reminded me of a sales pitch. The initial sense of alarm I had about being wanted by these institutes quickly developed into a dangerous idea. Could one of these places offer a safer place for me and Kole?

"*Careful,*" the Soaz intruded into my head again. *Argh,* there had to be a way to block him. I glanced across the room to the open bar, where he stood by his father's side. Hafthor appeared poised and relaxed, but he wasn't in control and that seemed to gnaw at his insides. The Soaz smirked, staring directly at me. He wasn't in control either at the moment, but his confidence made me suspect he was three steps ahead of me. Maybe even ahead of Hafthor.

I raised an eyebrow in challenge. The councilman asked me a question, and I answered succinctly and followed my response by asking questions of my own. I inquired about everything that came to mind—the count of their Pures, new recruits, recent demonic activities—and they appeared genuinely happy to answer my innocent questions. I didn't have to see Hafthor to know my interactions were making his blood boil.

A string quartet soon joined the somber piano, setting a perfect tone for refined dancing. They played passionately, transitioning from lively waltzes to slow ballads with ease.

"Excuse me, I must steal Arien for a dance." Xavier smiled sweetly at the small crowd before he ushered me away. The conversation with the council members had shifted into politics half an hour ago, and I was dying to get away. A few other couples drifted in perfect rhythm around the floor. Xavier kept the tempo slow and the steps easy for my benefit. If he even tried a waltz, I was going to step on his toes every chance I got. I was a poor dancer.

I scanned the room for Kole.

"He's watching you, even when you don't think he is," Xavier whispered into my ear.

"Where is he?" I asked.

Xavier sighed. "With Mezzo and Anhelm, that way." He

jutted his chin in the balcony's direction. Sure enough, my protector leaned against the marble balustrade, his eyes on us. The weight of the day slowly flaked away.

"You failed to mention you have a brother," I said.

"You never brought it up," he countered.

"I don't know if you realize this, but it's a big deal. Like... colossal."

Xavier snorted. "It's only an issue if you make it one. Everyone knows we're related, but we've grown apart ever since my...*our* mother died. He became the Soaz. I became the greatest demon hunter of our time. End of story."

I pinched my brows together "Maybe."

"We have no brotherly love between us."

I scanned his striking face. They shared the same eyes, but Damian's irises had no traces of blue. They were ink-black.

"You're both Pures. How is that possible?" Only the first-born Earthbounder child inherited the complete angelic gene and could transcend into the winged form.

"We're twins. Multi-births are rare among our kind, but when they happen all babies become either Pures or second-borns. Our mother had foreseen us coming, and her mother prophesied about Pure twin babies who'd set the world ablaze."

My eyes widened.

"Grandmother's prophecies didn't always come to pass," Xavier said. His lips curved lightly. I followed his gaze to a young man with a purposeful stride, heading directly for the Soaz. The Soaz's eyes darkened in an intimidation effort, but the Earthbounder didn't seem to notice. He halted a mere foot away with a sly grin, posing a question to Soaz and gesturing towards the dance floor.

"No..." I gasped, shocked. The size of balls it would take for anyone to approach the Soaz. My eyes involuntarily fell to the guy's crotch—nothing out of the ordinary there that I could tell. The Soaz's jaw clenched. Without a single word, he strode away, tossing his empty glass at a servant. The poor guy nearly fell as the glass bounced off him while he balanced a tray with cocktails.

The Earthbounder who'd approached the Soaz shook his head and twisted around in confusion.

"What on earth?" I wondered aloud.

"Compulsion," Xavier said.

My head swiveled to the balcony because the gift of compulsion was unique, and I knew one ballsy warrior with such a gift. As Mezzo and Anhelm grinned and clapped Kole on his shoulder, my heart stuttered. Kole's smoldering eyes stared directly at me, declaring the lengths he'd go to avenge me. And publicly embarrassing the Soaz both warmed my heart and made the mutant less scary. I suspected the distance he'd go to was limitless. A lazy smirk appeared on his face before he broke the eye contact and chatted away with an enraptured Anhelm. I wished he was dancing with me instead of Xavier, but the protector mark took that possibility away.

Nelia had warned me that anything more than a body-guard and protectee relationship would strip Kole of his mark, and people did not look upon it lightly. Kole's reputation was at stake. Not to mention, Hafthor would be more than happy to take Kole away from me. The fewer allies I had, the more influence he'd have over me. At least, he'd try. What Hafthor or the Soaz didn't understand was that having my friends close kept me in check. Without them, I'd be volatile like a freely released neutron bouncing in a particle accelerator.

"Your team despises the Soaz," I said.

Xavier's chin dipped as he studied my face. "Keen observation."

I rolled my eyes at his sarcastic tone. "I get a sense it's not only your men. I thought his position as the Soaz is revered?"

"The position, yes."

I held myself back from pressing Xavier any further. We were in the company of Pures with superior hearing after all.

I absorbed what little information Xavier had divulged. If the Soaz had enemies among the Pures, especially among the council members, then I'd try my damnedest to make them my friends. After all, the enemy of my enemy was my friend...

EIGHTEEN

I jerked awake from the pounding on my door.

"Get ready." Xavier's voice was authoritative. I buried my face in my hands, wanting to scream. I hated being startled, and I hated being woken up violently. I peeked outside the curtain. The dawn had crept its way into the day which meant it was around five-ish, maybe? I looked forward to days when I wouldn't require much sleep. But never one to keep Xavier waiting, I rubbed the remnants of sleep out of my eyes and got ready.

Kole, Xavier, and two of the Magister's guards stood in the living room, staring and avoiding each other all the same. A low tension infused the air.

"The council requires your presence," one guard said.

I nodded and ambled toward the door. I was relieved when Xavier and Kole followed us. We marched into the white marble hall below Xavier's floor. This time the guards opened the door opposite Hafthor's office to a grand room with an oblong conference table suitable for fifty or more.

The council members and their advisers congregated

around Hafthor at one end. Between them, a holographic 3D image of a forested area was displayed.

Hafthor sat at the head of the table with a stern expression on his face. Guards instructed us to take seats at the middle section of the table with Xavier and Kole on either side.

"The druids finally agreed to meet," Hafthor said.

"Not until after some persuasion—" The councilman Adon was silenced when Hafthor cocked his head toward him.

"They set conditions. They want to meet our newest Pure—"

"Father—"

Hafthor growled. "She will go along with her protector. That should assure you of her safety. Besides, we need our own men to go as well, and they specifically asked for you." Hafthor's eyes hardened with suspicion. "You will turn on your recording so we can see and listen. You will demand they turn in Kwanezerus to us. His crimes are egregious, and he must respond to Invicta. The council also suspects the disgraced druid has information on Arien's origin. We demand that they turn him in to us."

I squeezed my thighs under the table to remain still. I sought answers myself and I was angry with Paulie, yet I'd never wish him to be captured by Hafthor.

"We're ready to leave," Xavier said.

"The coordinates are already on your smartwatch. We expect to receive an update in an hour."

Chairs scraped the floor as everyone heard the dismissal in Hafthor's tone.

"When was the last time Invicta met with the druids on an official business?" Kole asked.

"A century? Not for the lack of trying. They operate on

their own terms and only meet when they want something..."
Xavier pursed his lips and stared at me. Kole mimicked him.

"What? What am I missing?" I asked.

"You can't kill a druid in their nature form, but you can
incapacitate them temporarily." Kole gave me an impromptu
lesson on druids while Xavier drove us to the destination.
Xavier retrieved a small dagger with an emerald nestled in the
handle from the weapons room prior to our departure. The
men took turns explaining the dagger was rare and special
and the stone held a spell. One touch of it would send a druid
into shock. I'd begun thinking of it as a taser.

Two black SUVs with the Magister's guards and some of
the best warriors followed us.

"Why would they want to attack us?" I asked.

"You never know what you're getting yourself into with
them. The druids have their own agendas and they're often
not clear until it's too late." I mulled this over. At one time,
I'd thought Xavier and Paulie had some history together.

"Do you really think they'll give Paulie up?"

"No." A straightforward answer that settled my nerves.

"Then why are we doing this?"

"Because while they wouldn't sell one of their own even
when they stripped his powers and sent him on a path of
destitution, they might offer some clues to your ancestry.
They are curious enough about you to entertain Invicta's
meeting request after a century of rejections."

NINETEEN

We parked the SUV on the side of a road at the base of a wooded hill.

I used my hand as a visor to block out the sun and gazed up. Thick forest covered the hill like a blanket with no clear path for us to travel.

"How are we...?"

Xavier released his wings with a stealthy *woosh* and took off into the sky. Oh, joy. My heart did a pitter-patter thing when I glanced at Kole. I couldn't fly yet, so there was only one way for me to get up that hill.

Kole's eyes darkened as he stepped forward, picked up my floppy arms, and wrapped them around his neck. Then he pulled me against his hard body. I wasn't prepared for that— the flight or the contact between us. I stared up at him, lacking the ability to react in any other way. His majestic charcoal wings unfolded with leisure and stretched to the fullest. My shoulder blades fired up in response like somehow they could communicate with Kole's wings. I wished I spoke *angel-wing-ish*.

Kole winked, taking my breath away with this one small

facial expression. A sudden gust swept my loose hair into my face as Kole flew us with rapid speed over snow-covered tree-tops until a small clearing appeared at the summit. Xavier's red wings contrasted with the white and green surrounding him. The descent was my least favorite part of the flight. I scrunched my eyes shut until my feet touched the ground.

Our boots crunched on the undisturbed snow. The winds whistled and the trees swayed in gentle rhythm. We stopped in the middle.

"Where are they?" I asked.

"They're already here," Xavier said.

The snow by the tree line rose and spun, revealing a human figure with blueish skin and aquamarine hair spewing down his back with fluid properties. Behind them, the surfaces of the tree trunks deformed until men with tanned skin and different shades of blond hair stepped out of them. The wind whirred around us and settled in between the druids, revealing four men with raven hair and pale skin. They all wore trousers reaching their calves but no longer and nothing else. Their bare chiseled chests gleamed in shifting sun rays. They measured my height for the tallest of them, but they weren't midgets either.

Their eyes had a vibrancy of the otherworld and wisdom beyond my comprehension. The ethereal sky blue, dense orange with brown speckles, and deep dark blue of stormy waters stared at us with scrutinizing expressions.

They shuffled to either side to reveal a new druid behind them. He wore a fur coat that opened over his naked torso. His pale skin shimmered like someone had rubbed glitter into it, and his brown hair hung low to his waist. He took measured strides toward us, cocking his head from side to side while his eyes traveled up and down my body. The sensation of his perusal left me uncertain and weirded out. *Remember, you have the dagger.*

The druid flared his nostrils and blew air, flapping his chops in a way that reminded me of a horse.

"Great druid, Invicta formally requests that you relinquish Kwanezerus into our custody," Xavier announced.

The druid blinked. "Kwanezerus has not been with us since his banishment four decades ago. As you're aware…"

"We're also aware he was at the black line fissure, assisting you."

"Bezekah posed a significant threat to us all, did he not?"

"Yes—"

"As the great druid, I lifted the ban temporarily. Kwanezerus possesses the ability to wield power with a precision that few of us possess, even when borrowing that power. And we stopped the plasma from oozing, did we not?"

"Yes—"

"Then Invicta approves of our actions." The druid kept examining me from ear to ear and head to toe, even looking behind me. I had a strong urge to peer behind my back, but I was too afraid to move. I bumped my hand against Xavier to get him to speak again. Silence prevailed, and he bumped my hand back. I glanced at him. He was speaking, but no sounds left his mouth.

"What did you do to him?" I asked.

"He started getting annoying with all this Invicta questioning. The other one knows to stay quiet."

Kole smirked, and a tiny dimple cut into his cheek. I flinched when icy fingers picked up my hand and turned it over. With his other hand, the druid traced one finger down the lines etched into my palm. I drew my brows together when his brows cinched and hiked them up when his brows rose. The druid chuckled, and it lightened my mood too.

"I can feel our life forces enjoying each other's company. They like to play off each other." He dropped my hand and a sort of sadness settled in my gut.

"I don't have answers for you. Except that I understand why Kwanezerus hid you from everyone else, including his own kind. If he had brought you to me, I'd have provided you with protection. No demon would've ever touched you. But your lines reveal you're on the right path. I can't hold you back when the Heavens have spoken."

"A path to what?"

"Greatness," he said with awe. "Your journey has only begun. And your lovers will support you on the way."

I stared at the druid like a deer caught in the headlights. Lovers?

"They're not... We're not..." My tongue tripped over the words.

The druid laughed. "I guess I misspoke. When a druid is seen with a woman it's because they're lovers. But then, perhaps I only spoke what your palm lines revealed." He grinned. "We must go now, little one. May our paths cross again."

The druid transformed into a buck and tromped into the woods. Winds swirled before us mixed with the snow. When the air elements finally calmed down, all the druids had disappeared.

"You knew he was going to do that." Xavier directed his accusatory tone at Kole. My protector shrugged.

"Would that have stopped you from asking questions?"

"No," Xavier admitted. His jaw tensed with displeasure.

"Why are you smirking?" Xavier asked.

"Me?" I placed a hand on my chest, faking confusion.

"Yeah, you."

"No reason."

"So, what did we learn?" Kole asked.

"They lack knowledge of Kwanezerus' whereabouts and have no interest in them," Xavier said.

"They are palm readers," I said and quickly regretted it.

Crickets followed my comment, and I could sense both warriors rolling their eyes internally.

"Arien's aura is familiar to a druid's life force, which isn't surprising since chikakas are drawn to her, too," Kole said.

And they thought the two sexiest warriors alive standing in front of me were my lovers. I glanced from Kole to Xavier and back.

"But that's not all he read from her..."

No, he said you're my lovers.

"He will keep the information to himself though," Kole said. He turned to me with his wings testing the wind. Xavier flexed his wings to prepare for takeoff.

"Why did he say he wasn't surprised that Paulie kept me hidden?" I asked. Paulie had been protecting me from this world since we'd met. I never doubted his intentions, but something in the way the great druid said it made me uneasy.

"He's a druid stripped of his power and cast out of his home. I imagine he craves revenge, and you were about to step into your power as an Earthbounder, power he could steal and wield as his own."

"No. I know Paulie—"

"And I knew Kwanezerus, once. We fought epic battles together before they stripped him of his power and exiled him. He's not the druid I used to know."

I sucked in a breath. Was I so desperate for friendship that I only ever saw the good side of him? What about when he tried to create a protection salve against the Archon and the trackers? Was that to protect me or to keep me hidden too?

I shook my head, certain of one thing—I wasn't thinking clearly. Kole took that as an invitation and scooped me into his arms before launching us into the air.

TWENTY

leep evaded me. The events of the last two days replayed in my mind whenever I closed my eyes—the council's ruling, Hafthor's words, Donovan's cryptic warning, the Soaz's mental intrusion, the party... I reexamined my interactions with council members, gauging their interest in me and the power dynamics in relation to Invicta and Hafthor. Who could wield influence over Hafthor, maybe multiple someones?

Soft knocking interrupted my thoughts. I slid out of the bed and traipsed to the door, cracking it open by a sliver. *Gah,* I was hallucinating. Two handsome male faces side by side stared back at me. I bit into my lip, and shit, that hurt. My eyes widened in shock.

"Wait!" I slammed the door into Kole's and Xavier's faces and dove for the sofa where I had stashed some yoga pants and an oversized sweater. I had opened the door in my flipping sports bra and underwear. They hadn't noticed, right? With cheeks burning, I swung the door open, and Kole barely concealed the quiver in his lips. *Oh, angels smite me.*

Since they wouldn't budge, I squeezed past them toward the kitchenette. I mindlessly filled a cup with already-made coffee and took a sip, only for my stomach to churn and my eyes to water. Grimacing, I dumped the coffee into the sink. I checked the coffee filter. Someone had filled it to the brim. The men made their way to the bar, observing me with curiosity. I must have looked unhinged.

"Coffee's too strong," I said. I washed the bitterness down with tap water. It probably didn't make me look any saner when I ducked my head under the faucet. Wiping my chin with the back of my hand, I faced them.

"What's the wake-up call for?" I asked.

On cue, Anhelm stuck his head through the door.

"We're ready," he said. I raised my eyebrows at the two mysterious warriors in front of me.

"Let's get you better coffee," Kole said.

We loaded into Xavier's SUV with Mezzo at the wheel.

"I planned this meeting with Talen before we left the cabin. I suspected Invicta would monitor my communications. I need a debrief on P6 and the Exiousai," Kole said.

"Oh, only Talen will be there?" I asked, hoping to see all of my P6 friends. Kole's lips curved downward.

"Yes, we agreed it would be the safest."

I gestured around the car. "When did the holy trio become part of the plan?" I asked.

Xavier turned in his front seat. "He wasn't planning on taking you, either." That felt like a slap in the face. I swung my accusatory eyes at Kole. We had promised not to keep secrets.

"I came by this morning to tell you I was leaving," he said.

For some reason, this answer didn't satisfy me either. Granted, we'd only promised not to keep secrets from each other and not that we'd tag along everywhere. The thing with Kole being my protector and always nearby had grown on me. I shouldn't have gotten attached, again.

"And Xavier felt like getting some fresh air." The warrior in question stared out the windshield. There was more to this story. But Xavier had mastered obscuring his own motivations. At least I got to tag along. Thanks to Xavier.

We arrived at the Great Lake an hour north of Invicta. Anhelm secured a permit and paid rental fees, while Kole convinced a group of teenagers that they were boarding the wrong speedboat, which had already been rented to us.

We took off at a high speed. I hid my face from the obtrusive wind. I peered up when Mezzo finally shifted the gears down. A vast island surrounded by the lake and boat docks greeted us. Luscious vegetation stripped of leaves by winter grew up the hill. We took a boardwalk upward. It soon merged with other docks' access points into a well-traveled road. We passed a handful of nautical-style houses and entered a small marketplace shaped into a square. Kole led us to a café.

Warm air saturated with the aroma of coffee and freshly baked goods blasted my face. As I stopped to admire the chalk-written menu above the barista, slender arms pulled me into a crashing hug. Rae giggled.

"How?" I asked, staring at Rae's and Zaira's beaming faces.

Rae waved a hand. "Do you think these men can keep us away?"

"We have ways." Zaira winked at a brawny fisherman seated by the window. I glanced at my entourage, who were now standing by a booth with Talen. They didn't look thrilled, but Anhelm was outright pissed. He glared at Zaira, who scoffed and flipped her red curls in response. The move told me Zaira was interested. She wouldn't have deigned to react otherwise. Well, that would be interesting to watch.

The bell at the front door chimed, and Vex strode in. Barefoot. And wet from his thighs down. He came directly for Rae and scooped her in a rough hug.

"I do like a good chase, babe. But you know water is not my friend." Rae snickered.

"Who ran a jet ski up my ramp?" an angry voice called out from the entrance.

"That's my cue," Vex whispered to Rae and scurried toward our not-so-small group of five—now six in total—male warriors. We scooted up the line to place our orders. Rae updated me on the supernatural developments outside Invicta. The fissure was now entirely inactive. However, it had failed to seal. A fence and signs warning people away surrounded the six-foot-wide zigzag opening. The scientists from Invicta and other regions were studying the phenomena. So far, they hadn't even reached the bottom of the mini canyon. They'd lost connection with the drones at certain depths. The images received prior to disconnect revealed no end.

The barista took our orders, and Rae directed us to the counter directly in front of the milk frother. I didn't care for the noise, but for their company, I'd suffer it.

"Psst." Rae drew my attention to a piece of folded paper she slid into the small side pocket of my yoga pants. I raised a quizzical eyebrow. The barista engaged the steamer. Zaira crowded my other side.

"Roan contacted me yesterday. He had a message from his contact at the Fringe, the one who helped him get you out," Rae said. "Don't mention it, or they will overhear."

I acted casual, although my adrenaline had kicked up a notch. Who could that be? And what did they want? I smiled at the barista. With drinks in our hands, we joined our group. Kole and Talen sat quietly in a booth by themselves, watching videos and reports on tablets. Xavier chimed in about underground cells Invicta had located recently, and Kole reluctantly extended the tablet to him, inviting him to take a seat. Mezzo stood by their booth, looking over Xavier's shoulder.

Vex happily accepted a cappuccino from Rae and drew her into his lap at a nearby table. That left an awkward triangle between me, Anhelm, and Zaira. I sipped the hot gold in my hands—this place had instantly become my favorite coffee spot—bouncing glances from arms-crossed and blank-faced Anhelm to glowering Zaira. She sipped her drink, her eyes never leaving his. I probably should've walked away, but being their third wheel was oh-so-entertaining.

"Ha, you blinked," I said with glee, pointing a finger at Anhelm.

"I did not," he said in his deep voice.

I high-fived Zaira, and she grinned.

"I wasn't aware this was a competition." Anhelm glowered.

"Anyway, I haven't yet properly thanked our transport over here. Arien, you must meet Zack." Zaira grabbed my arm before any words could leave my mouth. Zack's glum demeanor brightened when we approached.

"Zack is a merman," Zaira said. Confused, I checked the man for scales.

"What?"

"Sorry, my friend is new to shifters. This is Shifter Island, a safe place for all supernaturals," Zaira added for my benefit.

"Yet, the Seraphs never step foot on this land. Should we be concerned?" the burly man in a fisherman hat asked. He had remarkable eyes, large emerald green with golden flakes that twirled around.

Zaira rolled her eyes. "The Seraphs are buried too deep in their own asses. Ignore this little gathering; they will disperse soon."

The merman grinned at her word choice.

I tilted my head, studying him. I couldn't get over meeting a mermaid...er, merman...for the first time. He indulged me by answering my questions and sharing tales of his folk.

"Are merpeople related to the water nymphs?" I asked. Zack blanched.

"Oh, uh, I think it's time for us to go." Zaira stood and shoved me out of the booth. "Thank you again for giving us a lift." The man smiled up at her but wouldn't even glance my way.

Bewildered, I pivoted toward the badass warrior. "What did I say?" I whispered.

"The nymphs collect their scales." She widened her eyes for emphasis.

"Ah, as in..." I didn't finish.

"Yeah. It's excruciating."

Rae met us halfway, hiding her smirk behind the rim of her coffee cup.

"Listen to this," she said, eye-rolling to her left. Vex stood by disinterested Anhelm, preaching away. My enhanced hearing was still developing, but I got a boost now and then.

"...it's not about how deep you're fishing. It's about how you wiggle your worm," Vex said.

The three of us cracked up. Anhelm stiffened, swaying his blazing eyes in our direction. His neck flushed red. Holding Zaira in his sight across the shop, he said, "That might work for a Power. Seraphs have bigger worms. There isn't any wiggle room."

He abandoned Vex, who raised a finger in protest. Rae sauntered over to him and corralled him our way. I glanced at Kole's table. Talen stuffed tablets into a backpack, and the warriors rose to their feet. When Kole's eyes met my expectant ones, I experienced an emotional sucker punch. Sorrow filled his chocolate depths.

TWENTY-ONE

The air was brisk, but the blaring sun made the outdoor weather tolerable, or perhaps my body had done its Pure thing, protecting me from the elements. Sometimes, I couldn't tell where the human in me ended and where the angelic genes kicked in. Kole picked the top of a hill overlooking a beach on Shifter Island. The buildings of the marketplace were visible, but the distance afforded privacy from Earthbounder ears.

Thump, thump... My heart slammed in my chest. I couldn't form a single question. Instead, I waited for Kole to deliver the news.

"I will have to leave Invicta."

There it was. Right to the point. I expected nothing less from Kole. Yet nothing could have prepared me for this. I'd only had him for two, three days?

"But...you're my protector," I said. Grooves of irritation formed on his normally smooth forehead. This wasn't easy on him.

"What's going on?" I asked.

His lips thinned. "It's the Exiousai. We think the rebels captured him."

"Oh," I breathed, my heart rhythm softening to a pitter-patter. I still hated for Kole to leave, but this was important. P6 needed its leader back, and regardless of how things had ended between Seth and me, if he was in trouble, I'd help in whatever way I could. I put my imaginary "big girl panties" on and gazed Kole straight in the eyes.

"Then you have to go. I'll be fine. Actually, more than fine —I think I'm making progress with the council. They've been surprisingly...inviting."

Kole's hand covered mine resting on the pillowy sand.

"About that, stay vigilant. I've known Hafthor far too long to believe he'd ever agree to any terms about his most valuable assets without it benefiting him first."

"The Soaz said as much," I said, trailing off. Kole's hand tightened around mine.

"When?"

"At the dinner last night. He spoke directly into my head. Is his gift telepathy?" The first time he'd spoken to me that way was during the council meeting, but the next day I convinced myself it was my own imagination playing tricks on me.

"Yes, it's one-directional. He cannot hear thoughts, only project his own on others. What else did he say to you?"

I pinched my nose.

"Nothing significant besides that. He's been trying to get my attention, that's all."

Kole's stare intensified. "I don't like that."

"Ditto." We stared at the gently undulating waters and the sun's rays rippling across the surface. A flash of a silver dolphin-like tail broke the serene facade of the water in the distance. It arced and disappeared beneath the surface.

"How long will you be gone?" I asked in a small voice. I

didn't care if I sounded desperate. With Kole, all gloves were off. He abandoned my hand, and I felt the separation in the pit of my gut. Why was this so hard? I'd been alone most of my life, and I had sworn not to need anyone. Ever. Even losing my best friend, Brie, to her new life and the Fringe didn't feel like someone was sloughing the remnants of my fractured heart.

"I don't know. Talen is working with Anhelm to secure a safe comms channel between Xavier and me. I will report to him daily. He's as vested in this as we are. The underground resistance is one of Invicta's top priorities."

I read between the lines. He'd check in on me every day, and I'd get a daily reassurance of his safety. Xavier would be my lifeline to him, and surprisingly, I trusted both warriors.

I reached into my small side pocket and retrieved the piece of paper Rae had stashed in it. Kole watched me with curiosity. I recounted to him what Rae had said in the coffee shop and unfolded the scrap of paper.

"We need to talk. It's important. Ashton." I read the note out loud. On the bottom, my best friend's fiancé had written a phone number. I swallowed, confused as hell. Ashton directed the Fringe crew that had delivered me to the Fringe and tossed me in a cell. He wasn't to be trusted. But...what if the message was about Brie? What if she was in trouble?

"It's a trap," Kole said. "Rae shouldn't have given this message to you." His nostrils flared.

"No. Don't be angry with her. I couldn't count her as one of my friends if she hid this from me. You're not being fair, and you need to stop trying to protect me from everything. Protector mark or not."

Kole nodded, although the stubborn set of his jaw revealed he didn't like it.

"Promise me you won't contact this guy," Kole said. I

gazed nostalgically at the note in my hand and closed my fingers over it.

"I promise," I said.

Kole hiked an eyebrow, peeled my fingers off one by one, and removed the note.

"Kole," I warned him. A corner of his mouth wavered. He ripped the paper into tiny pieces not even a shredder could replicate.

"Kole!" I punched his bulging bicep, only half-upset. He knew me all too well at times. Although I hadn't planned to phone Ashton, the number and questions about Brie would've eventually bored a hole in my pocket. Plus, I had a tendency to draw danger like a moth drawn to the light.

Kole sprang to his feet and flung the sand off his pants. He pulled me up after him. A breeze plucked red and brown leaves from the branches, nudging one into my hair. Kole stepped closer as he reached over my head to free it. The warmth of his body was tempting. As if he read my thoughts, he gazed down at me, smirking. Heat flared up in his eyes and then swiftly extinguished. Kole could rein in his emotions like a cowboy corralling a herd, with undeniable confidence.

His mere glimpse fed my soul with promises that could never come. Maybe I was delusional for holding onto the idea of us.

Someone cleared their throat.

"Hate to ruin the moment and eclipse your wildest dreams forever, but the almighty Seraphs are being impatient," Vex said cajolingly. My shoulders slumped.

"I didn't know you were a poet?" I said, smiling at Vex. His interruption wasn't welcome, but it beat Xavier storming down the beach, which I suspected Vex prevented. The three of us headed for the dock.

"When will you leave?" I asked Kole, afraid to hear the answer but wanting to know all the same.

"Hafthor is hosting another fancy dinner tonight. I figure that's the only time I'll get to speak to him, and I have to inform him of my temporary absence personally."

"Why?"

"It's customary. At least, it used to be observed two hundred years ago when the last protector mark happened. In my temporary absence, the Magister, as your host, must step in and assure me of your protection."

I tasted something sour. Hafthor wouldn't protect me unless it benefited him in some way. Right now, I was a novelty, a pet he paraded about. That was as good of an assurance as I could get.

"So, you will leave after, then?"

"In the morning."

I chewed on the inside of my cheek. I worried about Kole. His safety was in danger, not mine. Although he'd laugh at me if I said it out loud. I paused at the top of the boardwalk leading down to our boat and faced him.

"Be safe out there," I said. His lips trembled with the beginning of a smile he seemed to save for my eyes only. I would have loved to witness it at any other time.

I grabbed his arm. "No, I mean it." Tense seconds passed with us staring into each other's eyes. When I thought we were clear—crystal clear—I stepped in front of him and bounded two steps at a time. I didn't want him to see my face at this moment. It was torture to see him leave so soon. But worse than that, I worried he'd get hurt or worse... Kole remained silent. He offered a gentlemanly hand to assist me in stepping into the boat. I grasped it and didn't want to let go, but in the end, I did.

TWENTY-TWO

The crowd had doubled from the previous night. I did not recognize the fresh faces. But I smiled politely at everyone looking my way—which was most of them.

"Who are these people?" I asked Xavier. I hung on his arm tonight. Kole had received a last-minute uninvite. The Magister himself expressed his disappointment in Kole for applying his gift in such a disrespectful manner toward the Soaz at the last event, blah, blah, blah... Who knew the mutant Earthbounder was so sensitive? *Geesh*.

"They are all here for you," Xavier whispered. I narrowed my eyes at him, convinced he had to be joking. But no, he remained stone-faced.

"Don't let it go to your head," he said. I rolled my eyes. Returning my attention to the crowd, I widened my inviting smile for the council members and their families whom I'd met yesterday. My mood soured upon seeing Magister Mariola in Hafthor's circle. That woman gave off strange vibes. Xavier tugged on my arm, and I shot him an irritated glare.

"Grabbed you some food while you were gawking at her."
He held a small plate with hors d'oeuvres in his other hand.
He guided me to a tall cocktail table designed for standing
around. Today was a cocktail night and not another formal
dinner—thank the angels. I was even able to pick my own
outfit and hairdo—a simple A-line dress and a quick updo. I
hadn't seen Nelia today at all, but she'd sent the stylist
anyway.

A server weaved by with a full tray, and I snagged two
champagne glasses. I chugged one right away and returned an
empty glass to his tray. The secondborn avoided my eyes,
which grated on my nerves. What was I doing posing as one
of them? As a Pure? I thanked the man and watched him jerk
in surprise.

Xavier pilfered the second glass from my hands.

"Hey—"

"Are you trying to get him punished?" Xavier's cold eyes
bored into mine.

"No, I only thanked him. Something you should do more
often." My blood turned ice cold. Xavier pinched his lips
together, then emptied my second drink. *My* drink.

"I could explain why you're wrong, but I know you
wouldn't listen."

I sighed. "Can I go back? I showed my face as I'm
required to do. I don't think I'm good company tonight."

"Kole won't leave without seeing you first." Disgust
stained his tone.

"That's not—"

"Xavier," Hafthor's deep voice traveled across the room. A
vein on Xavier's temple bulged. Without hesitation and
without looking at me, the Seraph strode off. Good riddance.
He was getting on my nerves. I pretended to busy myself with
the tiny food portions on my plate, avoiding eye contact with
eager Earthbounders in the room.

Long, familiar masculine fingers glided over the edge of the small table, coming into my view. Black ink swirled on the back of the hand in a pattern I now knew too well. I schooled my features before I dragged my eyes upward to the scarred face of the Soaz.

"Fancy to see you around here again. Ran out of innocents to torture?" My mouth blabbered out the inane words. No reaction. He rested both elbows on the table, bending at the waist, which brought his face to my level. The blackness surrounding his pupils was unnatural. Knowing he wasn't simply an Earthbounder but something else altogether explained the phenomenon. Did that make him scarier? Very.

He scrutinized my face, which should have scared me shitless from this proximity. Instead, I stuffed another tiny pastry into my mouth and chewed it up, smiling.

"I prefer your hair loose," he said.

"Oh." I arched an eyebrow. "Your hair could use some conditioner, but then, who cares? Split ends may be back in style." The truth was his dark luscious curls shone with vibrancy even I envied. He had damn good genetics. I doubted a single split end thrived on his head.

A corner of his eye twitched. He stole a snack from my plate and popped it into his mouth.

"Help yourself," I murmured, pushing the plate away. I wouldn't be eating from it anymore. My eyes wandered around the room, welcoming company this time around. I had to shake the Soaz off. Nothing good ever came from us talking. Well, not for me, anyway. The Soaz sighed.

"No one will come to your rescue. Unless they wish to upset me."

"You think an awful lot of yourself," I said. He was right though; everywhere I looked, the Earthbounders averted their gazes. What a bunch of cowards. The councilmen ranked higher than the Soaz, but they'd followed Hafthor and

Xavier to an adjacent chamber. I had to deal with the maniac in front of me on my own.

He ignored me. Then, after a pause, he said, "In my foot soldier days, I stopped massacres from occurring—"

"Because of your self-control?" I blurted out.

He snickered. I froze, confused as hell because I'd never thought him capable of laughter. His brows drew lower as he contemplated his odd behavior.

"Why are you talking to me?" I asked.

"There is something I need." His eyes skimmed over my exposed neck. I swallowed.

"No."

He flashed a full set of teeth at me. His grin was grotesque, and he meant it that way. The drumming of fingers against the table came next.

"You have questions. About me. *The Fringe. Perhaps you'd even like to know how your friend is doing over there?*"

It took me a second to realize his mouth was no longer moving. The Soaz switched to mind-talk in the middle of his speech. And he knew about Brie. I couldn't tell how, but I had no doubt he meant my childhood friend.

"Leave her out of it," I gritted. Now he had my heart pounding, and I was losing control in this power play. He jeered.

"She's of no interest to me—at least not right now." I gripped the edge of the table so I wouldn't launch myself at him. "*And you haven't even told anyone about what you witnessed.*"

Shit, he was right. I was still grappling with the shock of his transformation. I hadn't even told Kole. I inhaled deeply and lowered my eyelids.

"What do you propose?" I asked.

"Easy. I call it a *nick-n-pick*. One drop for some answers. I will allow one question."

"What if you lie?"

"What if I don't?"

I bit my lip. "What if I want to ask more questions?"

"Be ready to pay the price." He ran his tongue over a slightly protruding incisor. I grimaced. That wasn't an option.

"So, a drop of my blood in exchange for information?" I asked, searching for any deception.

"One question."

"What are you going to do with my blood?"

He arched a brow. "Is this *the* question?"

Damn him. I shook my head. If I was going to take this deal, I'd better make it count.

"Answer first," I said.

He nodded without hesitation. Too easy.

"If I sense a lie, we have no deal."

"*I will not lie to you. But be prepared that you may not like what you hear,*" he spoke inside my head. He upturned his hand, palm side up, inviting me to lay my hand atop it. My internal alarm wailed in warning as if I was making a deal with the devil himself. I ignored it and dabbed my hand to his.

"Are you working with the Fringe against Invicta?" I whispered.

His lips stretched, pulling at the scar.

"*That's two questions.*"

I huffed and began pulling my hand away.

"*Wait.*" His tone darkened. "*Yes.*"

I gawked at him in shock.

"*I told you to prepare. And before you think about running your bruise-worthy lips to your protector, remember it's your word against mine. Kole will lose his credibility and standing if he challenges me. Rumor's spreading that his obsession with you runs deeper than his protector duties. Maybe you even charmed him with your demonic blood.*"

I listened to his words in a trance, falling deeper into despair. I might have thought I had a semblance of a family with the P6 crew, but I'd only end up bringing them down with me. The curse of my lineage would always hang over my head.

I hissed when a sharp object pierced my thumb. Before I realized what happened, the Soaz pocketed the sample. I wrenched my hand free.

"Why?" I asked.

"Shhh... In due time, I will be able to talk more freely about it. Now is not the time. I revealed more than I expected to already."

"You said a one-syllable word. I don't see how that's a lot of information," I deadpanned.

"It's not the response I gave, but the question which I didn't expect. You're more observant than most Pures. I give you credit for that."

I narrowed my eyes. The compliment sounded genuine, but I wouldn't let it steer me off course. His confirmation could mean the overturning of governments or general antagonistic relations between the Fringe and Invicta that posed no threat. Surely, the Magister would know. Maybe even Xavier. I pinched my lips to one side. I was naive at times, but this was a nothing-burger. I regretted losing blood over it.

The Soaz cocked his head, mild confusion overriding his mask of indifference.

"*Do you think I'm bluffing?*" he asked.

"Your statement is general. Anyone in this room could say that, and it wouldn't make a tiny difference in my universe. Not unless they had a plan, timeline, and powerful forces backing them up. You've not proven any of it. It's like reading horoscopes—full of probable possibilities."

The Soaz snarled loudly enough for some heads to turn our way. I wished they were eavesdropping, but even if they were, the Soaz spoke in my head alone. My word against his wasn't enough to incriminate him.

"I don't dabble in fortune-telling; I give spoilers. Cram that into your little head," his voice boomed inside my skull. He stomped out of the room, leaving me rattled. That didn't sound like an uncertainty. His words were a promise of things to come. But what exactly were his twisted plans?

TWENTY-THREE

I sat cross-legged on the floor by one of the elegant armchairs, watching the color-changing patterns in Xavier's electric fireplace. The chairs on either side of me groaned under the weight. I glanced to my right to confirm what instinct had already told me. Kole's eyes took hold of me. A small smile graced my lips.

I picked up the book lying in my lap. Ever since we'd returned to Xavier's suite following the party, my mind was scrambling. As soon as we were alone or had some semblance of privacy, I planned to tell Kole about my bizarre conversation with the Soaz. Xavier was too unpredictable to be trusted with this information right now.

Ice cubes rattled in Xavier's glass as he set it down on the table behind me. The two warriors had closed themselves off in Xavier's office shortly after we returned. I'd had time to shower and browse Xavier's small library for way longer than necessary. I stole glances at the door separating us and tried to listen in. My improved hearing refused to cooperate. Finally, I settled on a book about the mysterious properties of the Everlake.

Since hearing Kole's story about being gifted his protector mark there, I'd been curious. The problem was that with my hectic daily schedule and extracurricular activities, there was no time to ask around or research. I wondered if the Magister purposely kept me out of these quarters and away from the warriors whose company provided me with solace. I'd had more conversations with the freaking Soaz than I had with Kole. And now, with Kole leaving, the shell he'd cracked little by little before my jump on the day of the black line implosion wanted to clamp shut again.

I gave up on trying to read and rested my head against the side of Kole's chair. At some point, my head slid lazily forward until it rested against a firm and warm cushion. My consciousness tugged at my sleeping self with an important message, but I couldn't bring myself to care. I was tired and deserved to rest a little. I rose in the air and floated, surrounded by warmth. Steady motion and a band of pressure under my knees and back strung my consciousness through the haze to reality.

My eyelids fluttered open to the view of Kole's corded neck as he carried me across the doorway to my bed. I felt like a Peeping Tom, staring at him in secret. He laid me down gently. I didn't protest or move. I was tired after all, wasn't I? He grabbed the sheet I'd kicked down the bed last night and pulled it up my body, his forehead crinkling the higher he went. Cold, warm, warmer...hot! His eyes snapped to mine, which were tracing his graceful movements and studying the power that had emanated from his body for the last several minutes. There was nothing done without utmost precision and calculation.

I could get lost in the dark chocolate of his eyes, or was it milk? If it was, that was the richest milk chocolate I'd ever seen. The tension didn't leave his face. *What internal monsters are you fighting?* He kissed my forehead, eliciting a hiccup of want and frustration from me. If I didn't have "I want more" written all over my face, I'd have to be dead because only the dead could hold a straight face forever in a moment like this.

He blinked and some of the light in his eyes fled. Without much thought, I grabbed the back of his head with one hand and rose on an elbow, claiming his lips, fearing he'd withdraw if I didn't act fast enough. He'd expressed strong emotions for me before coming to Invicta, but I'd never pushed the boundary.

Kole made a guttural sound, taking over the kiss, then hastily pulled away. His eyes shone with desire. I imagined mine glistened like those of a crazy woman. I shouldn't have done it. If Kole lost his protector mark, Hafthor wouldn't stop at removing him from Invicta. He'd make sure I never saw him again. Exhaling, Kole lowered his forehead to mine.

"I don't get surprised often," he said.

"Stick around and I promise to surprise you more," I whispered. My lips still tingled from the kiss, and adrenaline coursed through me.

Sadness flickered through Kole's eyes. Then he rose to his feet, gazing down upon me. His features closed off. He was the lethal Pure once more.

"Tell me about the Everlake. I've been curious ever since you revealed your protector mark, but the only picture I could find was small and in black and white." In the picture, the white-capped mountains surrounded three sides of the lake, and even in a black and white photograph, they gave off a surreal and tranquil vibe. I'd definitely visit the place if I could.

Wonder entered his eyes again.

"I wish you could see it. The vibrancy of colors is out of this world. The peace is palpable, and the water itself is so clear you can see a reflection of yourself in it."

"Like a mirror?"

He cocked his head to the side, considering it. He huffed a laugh. "I never thought much about it in terms of comparison, but the quality of it reminds me of glass. Like a liquid window into a different world."

Huh. Glass water.

"Get some sleep." His voice vibrated around me, eliciting a yawn out of me.

"Will I see you in the morning?" I asked sleepily. My eyelids drooped. *Wait, stay awake. You must tell Kole about the Soaz,* the small part of my brain that was still alert screamed at me.

I forced my gaze to find him.

Kole was already opening the door. He looked at me, but shadow obscured his face. Then he slipped out, the door clicking shut behind him. I plopped on my back, exhaustion taking over. My last thoughts were of the clear waters of the Everlake.

I traipsed on a pebbled beach toward the Everlake. The mountains towered over the water like old, stoic sentries. Their snow-capped tips glistened under the early morning sun rays with tenfold intensity. I could only steal a glance. A colorful songbird danced on a small promontory above the deeper water and trilled a tune before taking off. I smiled at it and changed direction for the rock, thinking it would be a perfect spot to gaze into the clear water.

After a rock-climbing adventure with Rae and Zaira, this climb was a breeze. I knelt by the edge and gazed down. My mouth fell open. The marine life in there was...impossible. The lake was home to a vibrant array of multicolored fish and plants swimming lazily around each other. There were fish with stripes, polka dots, neon colors, and hues I'd never seen before. An exotic fish tank wouldn't do it justice. And above them, if I focused, was my own reflection. Clear as day, my blond waves framed a fragile-looking face.

I realized then that the surface of the lake was perfectly still. No air bubbles or fishtails disturbed it. As I scanned the vastness of the lake's body to the right, I only saw the pristine still surface, resembling an iced-over sheet.

I sucked in my lower lip. This was a dream—a still active small part of my consciousness recognized that truth. And I could do whatever I wanted in my dreams. I lay on my stomach and reached with one hand. My finger created a single ring of disturbance on the surface. My reflection distorted and then worked its way into a proper image again, except the hair, now pale blond and shoulder-length, didn't match my own. Thick brows and ageless eyes with the irises of shimmery sky blue stared at me. A masculine straight nose and firm-set lips completed the image of Sylvan. I gasped and scrambled away from the water. Getting to my feet, I teetered and fell backward...

My eyelids flew open. I ran my hands over the cover Kole had pulled up to my chin. The ceiling, painted black and adorned with an intricate design, the assortment of furniture, and the imposing standing mirror against one wall all struck a chord of familiarity. It had only been a dream. The clock showed a few minutes past midnight. I strained my ears and chatter came in from the living room. The doors opened and closed, announcing comings and goings.

I wished I didn't require as much sleep. I'd read that Pures who'd lived a few centuries barely ever slept. They mostly required sleep to recover from tapping into their higher power for prolonged periods of time.

Whatever they were planning on the other side of that wall, they didn't want me to be part of it. *Where are you?* I asked for the hundredth time. The mystery specter who had saved my life and prevented an apocalyptic event when she blew Bezekah into nothingness and...the warrior who'd vowed to find me? Sylvan. That was the first time I'd seen him in my dreams in weeks.

Sylvan was the Pure Earthbounder who existed on the same plane as the stone—*Sky Ice*. He looked like he belonged in a Greco-Roman era, surrounded by white marble columns and imposing facades in his domain.

Maybe the Everlake held a key to my dreams? And now it was calling me.

TWENTY-FOUR

I crept out to the living room, wrapped in a sheet.

"Psst, Kole," I whispered. The dawn was breaking, and I hoped he'd spent the night here or waited for me. However, only silence and emptiness greeted me.

Emptiness filled my stomach and foreboding embraced me. I knew it. I freaking knew he'd leave without saying goodbye. After he used his gift of persuasion to will me to sleep. Part of me understood he'd used his gift to help me as I'd been a sleep-deprived mess these past few days. But the other part roiled in anger.

I slumped into the chair he'd occupied merely a few hours before. The fireplace was now a dark tinted glass that reflected my naked legs peeking from between the swaths of the sheet.

An edge of some white paper stuck out from between the cushion and armchair. I pinched it and pulled out a note. From Kole. It said he wouldn't be back for several days and that the operation required more consideration and planning. I crumpled the paper. He should've explained it to my face. We'd promised not to keep secrets between us, or was it only

I who had promised it? A dry laugh escaped me. Of course, in my naivete, I *assumed* when I promised not to withhold information between us he was making the same promise in return. But Kole would remain the controlling Pure who always knew better and didn't have to explain himself to anyone.

"Do you love him?" Xavier stepped into my line of vision unexpectedly. How long had he been watching me? I massaged my forehead. That was such an odd question to ask. I had no understanding of what love truly meant. The feeling had been foreign to me my whole life. Although I'd made room for Brie in my heart, and now, apparently, a small sliver belonged to Kole.

"I care about him, and there aren't many people I care about," I said, shrugging.

I let a few tears of frustration roll down. I didn't feel the need to hide them from him.

"Do Earthbounders feel with the same intensity humans do? I mean, except for the fury you unleash on demons and the condescension you seem to possess for all other living creatures, what drives you?"

Xavier's reply was a "Hmm." What was I expecting, really? I freed my bent legs, set on retreating to my room.

"I mourned my mother—" Xavier inhaled. "—after her death." He slumped forward on his elbows, eyes set on the floor. He hid his face from me. What emotions did it betray? I played with the fronds on a decorative pillowcase. The moment stretched.

"What was she like?" I asked softly.

"Beautiful, loyal, charismatic. Loving. She loved my father more than he ever deserved to be loved. And she loved her children fiercely."

Children? Until a few days ago, I'd thought Nelia was Xavier's only sibling, his half-sister from a different mother.

"What happened between you and your twin brother?"

"He's the reason our mother is dead." There was animosity and hurt in the way he said it.

I shifted uncomfortably, chewing on the inside of my cheek. The curiosity was eating me up, but the hurt his loss reignited hollowed out what remained of me.

"It seems like it's ancient history now. Centuries have passed..."

"But it hurts like it happened yesterday..." I said. The ache in my gut cut my words short. This wasn't about me. But I could relate on so many levels. At least they didn't blame Xavier for his mother's death. At least he had that.

"He swore on the sword of Gadriel that he witnessed my mother having relations with one of the council members. Anton was a flirt, but I always doubted he'd risk his Magister of the South seat for a folly. Even if she was interested, and she wasn't. She was loyal to my father to the core."

"She was his *Ashanti Rosa*?"

Xavier nodded. "More proof why she couldn't have engaged in adultery. But my father took the word of a seven-year-old over his own wife's." He hit his tightened fist on the table.

"What was the punishment?"

"The council assembled, and they sentenced her to beheading."

I gasped.

"They said her unparalleled and mystic powers of prophecy could make her immune to the *Ashanti Rosa* bond."

"What about Anton?"

Xavier scoffed. "My father supposedly killed him upon hearing about my mother's betrayal in an act of temporary insanity. Hafthor swore Anton confessed the crime before he died."

"There were no other witnesses?"

"No."

I mulled this over. "Do you ever think your father—?" I wondered out loud.

"Yes. All the time." His danger-filled eyes locked on mine.

The sound of a lock twisting had me glancing at the front door. Mezzo and Anhelm marched in. *Oh shit!* I so didn't need more witnesses to my pity party. I dropped to the floor, throwing the sheet over my head. I prayed they hadn't spotted me. Xavier fell silent, and only the scraping of approaching boots filled the air. That bastard could've walked over to them and let me hide in peace. But of course, he'd revel in my misery.

"Arien?" Mezzo asked.

I stuck out a hand from underneath one corner and waved it.

"Um...hi. I was just practicing...something." I shuffled on all fours, under the cover of the sheet, in the direction of my room. The men fell into an awkward silence, especially when I nearly bumped into a wall. It would've been nice if they had said something! I turned a corner and slithered down the wall and out of their sight.

"What's wrong with her?" Mezzo asked, not even bothering to be discreet about it. *I can hear you*, I wanted to say but he wouldn't get it either.

In the safety of my room, I kicked the door closed. I threw the sheet away, and within a few minutes, I stepped out dressed in my trainee uniform. I kept my face straight as if the Pures hadn't witnessed anything ridiculous and cringeworthy only moments ago.

"Where are you off to, little one?" Xavier asked.

I fumbled a coffee cup and caught it after it bumped into the counter. The warrior hadn't called me that since before my transformation to a Pure.

"You have my schedule. Donovan is my first punisher of the day."

Someone brewed coffee again. This time, I poured in only a quarter of a cup. I slurped a tiny amount and savored it like a professional wine connoisseur. I was pleasantly surprised when it didn't cause an acidic burn down my throat, and the flavor was absent the burnt quality of his last attempt. I topped off my cup and turned around.

"I'm shocked to say this, but you can actually improve in some things." I drummed my fingers on my cup.

"Sorry to disappoint, but Kole set the coffee maker before he left. He's quite a homebody. Who would've thought?" Xavier said with his usual sarcasm.

The taste in my mouth instantly soured. I dumped the remnants into the sink and hurried for the door. Donovan was waiting for me, and he'd whip me if I was late. At least that's what I told myself.

TWENTY-FIVE

I'd practiced with a dummy for the past half an hour, drawing glances from the Pures working out in the arenas and weapon centers. A few even came up to correct my positioning and technique. It'd become clear with every minute that Donovan was a no-show. He was also MIA from most of the social events unless he'd hidden in the shadows. And when he showed up, Paulyna draped from his arm or stuck to his side like a leech, annulling all my attempts at having a civil conversation between us. Only the two of us. Ever since I'd entered the gates of Invicta, the competition between Donovan and Xavier was clear. I thought jealousy fueled their animosity. But considering his latest comments, Donovan's antagonism stemmed from something more than a dispute over social standing. And I planned on getting to the bottom of it.

Just like you were planning to get to the bottom of the Soaz's involvement with the Fringe? A dry laugh escaped me. I had no leads. Unless the Soaz, Damian, straight fessed up. I sensed his intense desire to divulge his plans simmering beneath the surface. But, as compulsive as he was, he was also disciplined and patient where it counted. It made my skin break out in goosebumps every time I thought about it. Because there was a larger plan at play here.

Bezekah was no longer a concern. He was one and gone, and the return of his soleil to the Emporium was confirmed. There were no further developments with King Cygnus either, and with the help of a mage, Rae had patched all alluras on the northern continent. Another group had the task of developing alert spells. Since I was never alone outside Invicta, the chances of contact were scarce. And, so far, the four fae I'd brought into the Earth realm had not popped up on any Earthbounder radars.

But wait? A thought registered that required my immediate attention, and the punching bag I'd been hitting swung back at me with vengeance. I sprawled on the mat, immediately sitting up and drawing numbers with a finger on the mat. All but the last number were clear, and there were only ten possible combinations... A dangerous plan hatched in my head.

The heavy presence of muscular bodies drew my eyes upward. Four, no five, hands shot out in offering. I picked one at random, and the four other men strode away grumbling to themselves. A Pure I recognized from the *chikaka* challenge pulled me to standing, smiling.

"Are you all right?" he asked.

"Yea...no." I cradled my left elbow. "I think I need to get that checked at the infirmary. But I have no way of contacting Donovan."

The warrior flashed a smile. "I saw him packing weapons and leaving this morning. If he's on a stakeout, you won't see him for days."

"Oh." I bet the Magister didn't know. And it was best to leave it that way. "So...I can go?"

"I'll walk you there," he said.

I plastered on a smile. I didn't want witnesses, but I held onto a small hope he wouldn't stick around once we got there.

I missed the P6 elevators. The walk to the infirmary took at least fifteen minutes, filled with stories showcasing prowess, creatures he'd fought, and the next assignments he was looking forward to. I had to admit I encouraged him with expressions of awe and well-timed remarks.

"I'm aware that you're staying in Xavier's suite, but should you want a change in scenery, come by room five-oh-five. I can show you some of my battle spoils—I have the hooves of a rhinoquiem." His eyes rounded from excitement I tried to mimic.

"Sounds amazing," I whispered before stepping into the infirmary. The Pure assumed a self-satisfied smirk like he'd just hooked a fish but didn't even attempt to cross the doorway. In case he was still watching me, I crossed over to the nearest med bed and sat down like a good patient.

Zed, my favorite secondborn medic at Invicta, frowned as he approached me.

"And you're here because...?"

A quick glance at the door confirmed the Pure had left. I hopped off the table, glad to see Zed was alone.

"I've come to see you, of course." I beamed at him. Zed crossed his arms and gave me that patronizing look a teacher wears when a child is totally bullshitting their way through an explanation.

"Fine. I need to use a phone."

He sighed, pointing at the smart tablet on his desk. "You can dial Xavier from my device."

"Mmm... What if I need to call someone outside Invicta?"

"Then you're asking for trouble." He scampered toward a cabinet and busied himself with its contents. I followed.

"All connections are traceable and monitored. You call,

Hafthor gets alerted, and I get in deep shit not even a horde of dung beetles could dig me out of."

"Ew...Brother, the visual of that is horrifying." Dez stepped out of the adjacent supply room.

"Dez!" I approached the secondborn.

He swallowed in jest. "I'm scared."

"Ha." I swatted his arm. "I suspect you have exactly what I'm looking for." I whispered the item into his ear just in case.

Dez rubbed his chin, his glance flitting to his twin, who shook his head trying to dissuade him. So, I stepped into his line of vision.

"And?"

"Come with me." He pulled me into the supply room. Several rows of shelves later, we stopped at an IT graveyard with haphazardly stacked boxes of outdated electronics. He removed the top four of them and dove into the fifth one, coming up with an ancient flip phone.

"What the...?" I took the phone out of his hands and flipped it open. The worn-out buttons looked familiar. "You kept it?"

Holding my trusty phone in my hand, a remnant of my old life, made me want to weep.

"Not really. We simply haven't had the time to dump this pile."

My old cell phone powered on with half the battery life and one bar of signal. I checked the balance and four minutes of call time remained on my prepaid plan. Connecting with an incorrect number would easily eat up the balance.

"I'll leave you to it." Dez strolled out, leaving me alone with my phone.

I leaned against the wall with my eyes closed. What was that last number? It was either a six or an eight. Or a three. I dialed in the first combination, and a woman picked up. I hung up, immediately convinced he would answer himself if he was waiting for me to contact him. The second dial rang and rang, no voicemail. I canceled the call. My hand trembled. I punched in the last number combination, ready to hit the call button when my cell phone buzzed with an incoming call. The second number I dialed was calling me back. I hit accept and brought the phone to my ear.

"Arien?" a gruff male voice asked.

TWENTY-SIX

The clock on the wall struck half past the hour Donovan was supposed to meet me in the training arena. I picked up my bag and descended the bleachers. The sparring matches taking place between the Pures garnered quite an audience. I tried for inconspicuous, but everywhere I peeked a warrior stared right back at me with curious and inviting eyes.

Fingers glided through my hair, and I glanced up. Mattias, with his signature red mohawk, hung over the ropes, smiling down at me. The Pure had been in charge of the *chikaka* challenge a few weeks ago, which I'd failed miserably.

"Leaving already? Thought you were enjoying the show," he said. My brows drew together, and my mouth opened. I stepped to the side, finding the warriors from other rings also paused their sparring and stared my way.

"Um...I can tell you work out a lot," I said, slapping myself mentally. *Stupid!* I readjusted the strap on my shoulder and pointed my thumb at the door. "I have another session I have to get to. So...bye." Mattias vaulted over the ropes and blocked me.

"Usually you're here with Donovan for another hour. You can get your workout in with me in his absence." As he inhaled, his shoulders inflated.

"Oh, no, I really need to go—" I glanced around for a plausible excuse. "—because..." Anhelm stepped into the gym. "Anhelm!" His pretentious eyes landed on me in an instant.

"You have a training session with Anhelm?" Mattias's gaze flickered between Anhelm and me. Maybe Anhelm never trained new recruits? But there was always time for firsts, especially when it had to do with me.

"Yes. See you around," I said. Anhelm had already stepped out of the gym. What a jackass. I chased after him down the corridor, then another.

"Wait!" No response. I lost track of turns. I stepped into a cavernous room with a double ceiling and pallets loaded with weapons all the way up. A security check was the only access point. Two guards stepped out of their stations, heading for me.

"Anhelm!" I hissed. I suspected this little stint was going to cost me a detention. I shouldn't have been there, and the guards knew it. Their bored expressions soon gave way to animosity.

"What are you doing here?" a voice whispered into my ear. I flinched and spun around. Xavier's bemused smirk boiled up the anger within me. But I squashed it. I kinda needed him right now.

"Donovan didn't show up. When I tried to leave I got ambushed by Mattias, and Anhelm showed up. I sort of lied that he was training me and left, but then he wouldn't stop and—"

"Shush," Xavier said, rolling his eyes. I wheezed air in and out.

"She's with me." He waved the guards off.

"Really?" I sounded so hopeful, like a teenager who was just asked to a dance. Xavier snorted.

"Hell, no. You will take your sweet ass back to my room." He engaged his comms while I stared at him with mouth agape. He'd never spoken to me that way. Should I be offended? Probably, but I couldn't bring myself to be. I placed my hand over his watch.

"Take me with you." I stared into his eyes with sincerity and pleading. "I hate to sit and wait. That's not my style." He lowered his arm, and I withdrew my hand.

"It's not my style to babysit."

"You've done decent job so far. Minus the lack of food and a few other essentials, but who's counting," I said with an overexaggerated nonchalance.

Xavier raised an elegant eyebrow.

"I mean what are you going to do now?"

"We're going on a patrol downtown." My eyes rounded. My city, my streets were calling my name. Xavier crossed his arms over his chest. "You won't stop begging, will you?"

I clamped my mouth shut. Mezzo and Anhelm checked out the weapons and brought a duffel bag out to Xavier.

"Goddamn, I was certain I lost her," Anhelm said. I stuck a tongue out at him when he wasn't looking. Mezzo snorted.

"Hmm, perhaps her tracking abilities have kicked in?" Xavier studied me, and I stood up taller. "Fine." Those four letters kick-started my heart.

"You don't seriously—" Anhelm began.

"Since Donovan stood her up, *again*, it's my responsibility to arrange for the next best training session. Nothing can beat field experience. With us. You can accompany us, but there will be rules. Should you break them, this will be your last time outside Invicta's allura until you graduate." The stern tone was unmistakable. It drove the message home.

"Cross my heart and hope to die," I said, bouncing on the

balls of my feet. Two warriors stared at me with puzzled expressions.

"What does that even mean?" Mezzo mumbled. I smirked at Xavier. He knew.

I bounced my leg restlessly. I sat in the back of Xavier's black SUV, glued to the window. We were in the city! I tapped into my mental map and dropped unfamiliar sights and streets. I had a general idea of where we were thanks to the ring-like layers of New Seattle stretching in all directions. We were heading towards the busiest district, where hundreds of thousands of people waded through the crowds every day, either heading for the subway or the city bus and tram lines.

Xavier pulled into a parking garage a few blocks away and parked in an empty corner on the fifth level. The warriors jumped out of the car and armed themselves with the few items they had stashed in the trunk. Xavier shut the trunk door with a thud and scowled at me.

"We're going incognito," he said. At the same time, Anhelm and Mezzo released their wings. Well, damn. They hadn't told me that was the deal. Xavier quirked a brow as his magnificent red wings unfurled to their full width.

I clasped my hands together in front of me, biting my lip.

Xavier ticked his head at me while gazing at Anhelm.

"What?" My mouth felt dry.

Xavier and Mezzo ambled away toward the staircase. But when I followed, Anhelm blocked my way. A satisfying gleam entered his eyes as he stalked me. My feet shuffled backward until my butt hit the metal barrier of the car exit ramp.

"What are you doing?" I asked.

Anhelm stretched his neck to a side until it popped and

he sighed with satisfaction. "You need your wings," he said dryly.

I held up a finger. "Yes, but—"

I shrieked when Anhelm seized my legs and flung me over the barrier. I saw death awaiting me. The levels flew by in smeared colors. My heart was in my throat and a burning sensation spread over my shoulder blades. My wings!

They stirred and a spark of hope ignited. I concentrated and by the third floor, the extra appendages had unfurled. I slammed into the half wall. Firm hands grabbed my waist and pulled me into a hard chest. Xavier lowered us down to the street level. "Thanks" rolled off my tongue, but then I remembered he'd ordered Anhelm to drop me from the fifth floor.

I leaned against a column and bent over, resting my hands on my knees. That wasn't necessary! I looked up to tell Xavier that but he was already walking away toward the exit. I rushed after him.

"Where are the others?" I asked.

"Waiting," he grated. Was he upset with *me?* I didn't get to inspect his face as we merged with the tumultuous sea of people. Mezzo and Anhelm stood in the middle of the sidewalk while people stepped around them.

"I thought they're not supposed to be able to see us?" I asked.

"They don't," Mezzo said. "They're automatically guided to avoid us. Sometimes, they will see a human in our place or a tree, a bench, anything that keeps them away and allows us to work unobstructed."

I scanned the passersby and waved in their faces. No reaction. A grumpy guy was next, and I stuck my hand out again. This one snarled at me, and I plowed into Anhelm's back as I turned around.

Mezzo sighed. "This one's possessed."

I gawked at him.

"What do you mean?" I'd heard of possession before but that was before I heard of the Earthbounders, druids, shifters, fae... I wasn't sure what was accurate anymore.

"The possessions or attachments happen all the time. Although humans may not be consciously aware, they generally consent to have them. We can't interfere with voluntary attachments," Xavier said. He and Anhelm led our little group while Mezzo marched beside me.

"Because of free will, right?" I asked. Xavier nodded.

Anhelm launched from the ground to the top of a street lantern. Mezzo landed on the rooftops. I glanced at Xavier standing beside me. I was the weakest link in the group, with not being able to fly and all. I was slowing down their operation.

I stepped up to Xavier, committed to assist.

"What are we looking for?" I asked.

"You're here to observe. Leave the hunt to us." I bit my lip since I'd promised to behave. Mouthing off wasn't a good idea. Xavier's smirk dug deeper into his cheek.

"But, since you're here... Did you notice anything different about the man who warned you off?"

"The possessed guy?" I didn't wait for his response, asking rhetorically. I mulled it over. I hadn't paid attention at the time, but there was something different about him.

"His eyes. They strayed in my direction for a moment. He noticed me."

"Good. Anything else?"

"No." What else could I have missed?

"It takes some practice, but when we're in our true form, we can see the aura of each human. The ones with an attachment will have an unsettling, frazzled aura about them."

I concentrated on the people around me. Faint multicolored glows emanated around them.

"Are they supposed to be different colors?" I asked, hesitantly.

"The coloring varies, and you can't rely on the shades alone. It's the quality of their energetic field that gives the attachments away." I concentrated but noticed nothing out of the ordinary about the energies surrounding the humans. Even when Xavier pointed a few of them out, I remained blind to it. They usually frowned when we talked about them, and some scowled in our direction. That was the only sign that suggested we'd come across a demonic attachment.

We crossed the street, leaving the financial district behind. The warriors scoured both populated and deserted streets and buildings. A couple of minor demons edged onto the streets tonight, and Mezzo sent all of them back to their realm with precise arrow shots.

Crossing yet another street, I peeked into a back alley. A reddish cloud hung low to the ground a few yards away.

"What's that?"

Xavier paused at the entrance with me.

"*Hongaek*," he said, studying it. "It's energy, not a demonic presence, so it's out of our concern."

I cocked my head, not sold on the whole *not our concern* attitude. "What does it do?"

Xavier sighed. "In Korean it means 'red disaster.' It's a cloud of fear and confusion that often appears at a scene of murder. It dissolves on its own after a day or two. If a human walks through it, they could get bad luck that day." He shrugged. I asked him how to dispel it, but Xavier insisted that wasn't their job. He appeased me by promising to send a secondborn unit over to neutralize the cloud.

He spun around, and I shifted to follow when an older

lady stepped out of the restaurant's employee-only exit and turned in the cloud's direction. There was no time to think. I dashed into the cloud and started shooing it away with my arms and legs. The vapor rose to my nose and entered my nostrils. I swayed, and Xavier pulled me out. When I came to, Anhelm dispelled the *hongaek* in time for the woman to pass safely. I exhaled, resting my forehead on a cool brick wall.

"I should've anticipated you'd do something stupid like that." Xavier's voice dripped with scorn.

I waved my hand. "I saw her..." I coughed. A broad palm covered my mouth.

"Don't talk. You need a breathing treatment. We're going back."

TWENTY-SEVEN

Xavier called a medic to meet us in his suite. I didn't recognize the girl, but the medics were rarely at the infirmary since the Pures refused to use it. It was below their dignity to fraternize with secondborns or use any facilities their lesser brethren used.

She attached a small tube underneath my nose and adjusted the setting on her tablet. Immediately, the fog residue from the red cloud began lifting. I was able to actually hold a thought for longer than five seconds. Mezzo explained hongaek would eventually paralyze my brain cells without a treatment.

I relaxed against the couch, staring into space. How did regular people carry on every day without knowing the dangers surrounding them? How had I ever survived on the streets at night? And the only answer I could come up with was that someone protected them on some level. Whether it was by God or guardian angels, or maybe spirits of the ancestors... And the Earthbounders who were less ethereal in nature but necessary, nonetheless.

Deft fingers disconnected the tube. The medic packed

her bag and departed without a single word. I frowned. I was too inside my head to even thank her. And the *originals* in the room wouldn't even think about it. The *OGs*. I snickered under my breath.

"Did she get too much oxygen?" Anhelm asked.

"I'm afraid that's her normal self," Xavier said. The corner of his mouth quivered.

Something banged into the door, and Mezzo pulled one side open to reveal a large rolling garment rack filled with dresses and boxes. Nelia's slender frame came into view as she pushed the cart to the side. She dusted her hands clean while the men collected their weapons and left. Xavier whispered into her ear as he passed her, and she laughed.

"Don't worry, Brother," she said.

"Why are they leaving again?" I asked Nelia when the exterior door shut.

"Strategy meetings. Now that the council is here, my father runs a tighter ship than ever."

One book after another landed on the cushion by my side. I narrowed my eyes at Nelia.

"Just because you can't go to your library session doesn't mean the library can't come to you."

She was right. I couldn't afford to miss my study time. I picked up the books and read the spines.

"Nelia?"

"Hmm?"

"What do you know about the Fringe?"

Her eyes snapped to mine. "That's a topic we don't bring up with the recruits." She carefully chose her words.

"Come on, Nelia. They held me captive there. I am aware that they are shifters, mostly. And the Soaz was there, of all people. How do you explain that?"

"I don't think the council understands the danger. The Fringe has been operating for decades, and my father kept a strict finger on it. He still portrays an image of him being in absolute control..."

"But..."

"I don't know. No one talks to me about it, not directly anyway, but I have access to Invicta's expense sheets. Over the past year, Invicta's financial contributions to the Fringe have quadrupled. So, I've been asking myself why are we paying them money if we're in control over the happenings there?"

"Unless Invicta is no longer in control."

"Exactly. I can't ask my father though, and I can't go to the council."

The Soaz interrogated traitors. But I doubted Nelia worried about her own safety as much as she worried about Xavier's reaction to their father's action. What if he beheaded her like he had his own wife?

Nelia grabbed a small box from the cart of a thousand things and tossed it to me again.

"Open," she said.

I flipped the box over. "But it's addressed to you?" I frowned at her.

She smiled. "You have clever friends. We don't celebrate Christmas or any religious holidays. And I don't eat *that*." She twirled her finger, pointing at the ripped side from when she took a peek inside earlier.

I shook it gingerly and small compartmentalized items rattled inside. I slid a box of chocolates out with a note attached. *Merry Christmas, you filthy animal*. The latter part was written in a different hand, and my lips trembled imagining Vex scribbling on Rae's pretty note behind her back. The chocolate couldn't have come from anyone other than Rae.

"They're safe. I scanned the box for any toxic substances. It came back with sugar only."

I rolled my eyes. "You know how to take the fun away from eating a simple treat." I thrust the open box at her. She sighed and took one chocolate.

"I don't see what's so special about this."

"Bite..." I said.

Tired of me, she bit half of it and chewed. I waited. She popped the other half in her mouth and closed her eyes. Her throat bobbed as she swallowed the last bite. When her eyes opened, there was a light there that was missing earlier. I slid the box on the coffee table between us and popped an entire piece into my own mouth. I was going to suggest to the medic to add chocolate to her oxygen regimen for the red fog intoxication. The combination of the two worked wonders.

I peered at Nelia who snagged another piece.

"So, what are all these boxes and fancy dresses for?" I asked.

"The Magister announced a Christmas ball celebration to take place tomorrow, on Christmas Day. He even invited the secondborn recruits."

"I thought you said Earthbounders don't celebrate religious holidays?"

"We don't. That's why it's a ball. Don't expect Christmas trees or caroling."

I twirled another chocolate in my mouth with my tongue, enjoying the transient sweetness. "I don't know. I'd rather enjoy hearing Hafthor sing."

Nelia laughed somberly. "My mother was from the Northeast region. They observed many customs. My father refused to allow decorations at Invicta, but she'd hum the melodies when Hafthor wasn't around." That sounded like a miserable relationship.

"What happened to your mother?"

"A demon happened." She snickered nervously. "Isn't that

what usually ends our lives?" I sensed her discomfort. She pushed the chocolates my way as if they'd turned repulsive.

I tapped my fingers on a hardcover in my lap. I turned the cover and the front pages and began reading. At some point, Nelia left, and the suite was again a stark and lonely space. The black glass front of the fireplace reflected the living area in darker tones, creating a reflection of my experiences at Invicta. Things always turned out worse than what was visible on the surface. I could not afford to become comfortable or go with the flow when I wasn't the one in charge of the current.

TWENTY-EIGHT

I gathered my dress and ascended the broad steps leading to the mansion. I'd never seen it properly in the daylight or from the front before. Luck had me always entering this particular building from the lakeside garden. The structure appeared to have been carved out of a single marble piece. Everything seen from the outside was white marble with a gray mosaic pattern, except for the roof, which was covered in a black layer of shiny composite and a set of dark wooden doors with an archway design.

The doorway stood ajar, inviting guests into a circular foyer with high ceilings and a grand staircase to the first floor. The addition of marble columns throughout created an ambiance of sophistication and antiquity. I wouldn't have been surprised to encounter Sophocles or any other famous ancient world philosopher here.

I was running late. There was a minor sort of misunderstanding about my ride over here. At the last minute, a guard informed me that there was a car available for me parked in front of Invicta. The problem was I'd never driven a car before. Getting a driver's license had never been a priority for me since public transportation was available and I couldn't have afforded a car even if I scraped for it. Everyone had left by the time I realized my unfortunate situation. So, I'd barged into the secondborn wing and banged on some doors before a brave soul opened for me. The rest was a mix of me begging and demanding the poor recruit drive me over here.

All the other cars were already valet parked and not a soul was in sight. I hurried along a wide hallway toward where the sound was emanating from. A string quartet played a classic melody of melancholy and revival. The entrance to the grand room was open, and I sneaked a peek at the guests congregating in small groups throughout the vast space. I hesitated by the threshold. Coming in alone and covered in the layers of chiffon Nelia insisted on, I'd immediately draw attention to myself and the fact that I was late.

A familiar figure with a blond ponytail was ambling over to the snack table nearby.

"Psst." I made the sound and hid from view.

Zephyr moonwalked out of the ballroom, sporting a cheesy grin. "Ah, everyone's been wondering where you were. Stage fright?" Elyon's son asked.

"No, I just got here." I bit my lip. "Can you escort me inside?" I doubted I could deceive Hafthor with this trick, but I hoped some council members wouldn't notice.

Zephyr offered me his elbow, which I gratefully accepted.

"Thanks." I breathed a sigh of relief.

"Don't thank me yet. I see an agitated Pure on my seven," he whispered as we stepped into the room. Heads swiveled in our direction, prompting me to offer small smiles and nods. Some scowled, but nothing could compare to the narrow slits of Xavier's deadly expression. I flicked my brow over my shoulder.

Zephyr directed us toward a group of the council members' spawn. I glanced at Xavier reluctantly out of the corner of my eye. A slender hand ran up his arm, and a beautiful female with long chestnut-colored hair stepped out from behind him. She was the Magister of Southwest's—Adon's—daughter and a perfect match for him in beauty and social standing.

I forced myself not to stare and instead devoted my attention to Zephyr and his circle.

"I do like your dress." Seraphina ran a finger down the side of my bodice. That felt too intimate. The sparkle in her eyes was unmistakable.

"Uh...thanks. I wouldn't have picked it for myself. The compliment belongs to Nelia."

"Hafthor's daughter." Seraphina's eyes swept the room in search of her. Nelia nursed a drink by Mezzo's side. Neither of them spoke, and I suspected that was how they both liked it, to enjoy each other's company in companionable silence. She wore a stunning deep green gown with an off-the-shoulder neckline and a flowing skirt that cascaded to the ground like a waterfall.

Seraphina cut through our circle in a direct line for Nelia.

"Are we heading out after these festivities?" a male warrior I hadn't placed yet asked, sweeping his long bangs to the side.

"Last night, Caelum and I ventured out downtown. We wrestled four vampires and spent a few hours with lovely pixies at that other place... What was it called?"

"The Moonshine," I said.

The men gazed at me with curiosity.

"Are you familiar with that place?"

"I used to serve drinks there." Except I never knew the petite women with rainbows in their hair and colorful outfits who always hung there weren't actually human. I guess that made sense now. But the vampires?

"Eww, you actually worked...for the humans." Seraphina,

unsuccessful in getting Nelia's attention, screwed her face with distaste.

"Yeah, I did. I just don't get why the Earthbounders are so repulsed by humans when you protect them. Perhaps you *serve* humanity more than anyone else."

A genuine grin spread across Zephyr's face as he clapped. "Bravo," he said. "I've been wondering the same thing for decades."

A glass chimed from the far end of the room, drawing heads toward Hafthor standing by the musicians. At some point, the string quartet had gained a pianist and two more violinists.

"I'd like to formally welcome you to Invicta's ball. One good thing stemming from recent events is that we can enjoy this rare celebration with the Magisters from most prominent institutes present—"

"You're welcome, you scumbag," I whispered to myself. Caelum choked on his champagne, and Zephyr snickered. I bit into the inside of my cheek. I kept forgetting whose company I was in.

"And now, let us begin with the enchanting waltz a la monte," Hafthor said. A server ran up to take the glass from Hafthor's hand as he approached the Magister Mariola, inviting her to dance. Her eyes brightened as she slid her dainty hand into Hafthor's sizable grasp. The music commenced, and other couples soon joined on the floor.

"You realize it's mandatory for prominent Pures to engage in dancing, right?" Zephyr said.

"Oh, sure, I'll find some other corner to blend into," I said. And a drink or two.

Zephyr laughed. "I'm pretty sure that now includes you."

I stared at him with widened eyes. "I-I can't dance." I winced as the words left my mouth. Sure, I could move in a club, but not *dance*-dance, especially not a formal dance like the waltz.

"Certainly, I am an excellent teacher." He slid his palm down my arm and clasped my hand. I resisted stepping onto the floor, but his grip was firm, and my reluctance soon began drawing attention. Shit on a stick. I was going to make an ass of myself at this ball.

Zephyr squared with me and adjusted my arms.

"If I fall—"

"Shh. We'll go slow." He nudged my toe with his, and I stepped my left foot back, then the right. We glided with fluidity, so I assumed I was doing something right. When he shifted backward, I followed. I released a long exhale. Maybe this wasn't so bad after all. We picked up our pace.

"Mmm," I whimpered when Zephyr's shoe jammed into my toe.

"Let's slow down," he said.

"Good idea," I said through gritted teeth.

I felt an overwhelming sense of relief when the song finally stopped. I shot Zephyr a glare before he could even suggest another dance and stomped off toward a table laden with food that was calling my name.

I stacked food in four layers onto a petite plate and claimed the nearest high-top table. Who gave a ball without proper plate-ware? The answer, apparently, was the Earthbounders.

"You mind if I join?" the Soaz asked, setting his tiny plate with only two items opposite mine. I curled my fingers into fists. It was fight or flight with the Soaz. I preferred neither, but it never hurt to be ready.

"Yes, I do. Yet I have a feeling you don't care either way."

"Enjoyed the relic dance?"

"No."

He huffed a laugh. "Humanity has a built-in Luddite

mentality. They resist change. It's a shame to see our race fall into the same trap."

My eyes shifted to the couples dancing on the floor. "It's only a dance," I said.

The Soaz breathed with exasperation.

I tried a different angle. "So, it goes deeper than the dance... The Institute? No, the council then?" I worked off the cues he was giving me. I had to think larger. His disapproving stare relaxed.

"The council lost sight of what's best for our race. We stopped *evolving*." His coal-dark eyes bore into mine. Was he referring to my unknown heritage or his shape-shifting ability? His ability wasn't common among the Pures. As with everything concerning the Soaz, there was more beneath the surface. He was *more*.

The Soaz stomped away, abandoning his plate of untouched hors d'oeuvres. I gaped at the blood orange slice and pomegranate seeds. Symbols of hidden dangers and betrayal, life and death... I doubted he planned to eat that. He meant it as a message or a warning. My heart pitter-pattered. I scanned the crowd in search of him but he was long gone.

TWENTY-NINE

It was only a matter of time before they would notice I was missing. I hiked my stupid dress up and sprinted across the underbrush of Invicta's forest. I'd abandoned my heels by the fountain. The trees thinned out, and the barrier came into view. Tonight, vibrant turquoise auroras weaved through the surface of the allura, pulsating. Was it expecting me?

I approached it with caution. Its magnetism made the hairs on my arms stand at attention. Without overthinking, I dipped my fingers in first to test it, then boldly stepped into it, focusing on a clear destination.

The other side came into view, and I stepped toward it, landing on both feet this time. Below me sprawled the familiar vista of the Fringe. Ashton had explained that the gate at the end of the tunnel marked "F," which I'd traversed all those weeks now to visit Brie, was in fact a portal. It explained the chains and padlocks covering it. Clearly, the gate was not intended for mundane use.

Rustling branches caught my attention. I was weaponless,

having placed my trust in a man I would never otherwise
trust. But he said Brie was in danger. Now, doubt crept in.
Was this another of the Soaz's schemes? Cautiously, I edged
closer to the gate, ready to leap back to Invicta at the first
sign of deceit.

Ashton emerged from behind his cover with Brie
clutching his arm.

"Brie!" I rushed to her, only to halt abruptly. Her belly
protruded strangely. I stared, mouth agape.

"You're... You're pregnant?" I blurted out.

That was the wrong thing to say, apparently, as Brie buried
her face into Ash's sleeve and began weeping. Ohmagod.
Ohmagod! I raked my hands through my hair.

"I thought you said she was in danger, not that she was
pregnant," I said, my voice tinged with disbelief. Ashton's
scowl deepened. It was clear from his protective yet gentle
hold on Brie that he cared for her deeply. Perhaps even
loved her.

"Will you help her or not? I'm already risking a lot by
being out here with her." His tone was gruff and demanding,
bristling my skin. But this wasn't about him. I watched my
brittle friend cling to him. How had I not realized she was
pregnant? She had mentioned being engaged to this man, the
same one who had thrown me into a cell with the Soaz. I
doubted Brie knew the full extent of his actions. A sudden
urge to pull her away from him surged within me. What other
misdeeds had he committed and lied to her about?

I extended my hands. "Give her to me."

He hesitated, perhaps hoping for my refusal, then
tenderly kissed the top of Brie's head and whispered to her.
After a moment, he kissed her belly while she still hiccuped
with sobs. Gently, he guided her to me, and she leaned her
head on my shoulder, breathing deeply.

"What do I do?" I asked, feeling the weight of the situation.

"She will need medical attention soon. Our baby, against all odds, is a shifter like me. Shifter offspring mature faster than humans do. Brie has all the paperwork to claim refugee status with Invicta. They're obligated to provide her with shelter and necessities until she can manage on her own."

What about you? hung heavy on my tongue. It didn't sound like he was in the picture going forward. But I stopped myself from asking in front of Brie.

"Why can't the Fringe provide for her?"

He averted his gaze.

"Tell me."

He studied Brie's face. She seemed to have checked out completely. "If I tell you, you can't speak of it to anyone," he said gravely.

I nodded.

"The Fringe is a hub for genetic experiments on creatures of all types, even the Earthbounders. They call it a Super program, but I think there is more to that than simply enhancing us. Our baby being a shifter means he's likely to be enrolled in the program as an infant and taken from us. The younger the subject, the better the results, or so they believe. This isn't common knowledge, even among regulars at the Fringe."

His haunted eyes conveyed the horrors he'd witnessed.

"Some experiments get terminated." His Adam's apple bobbed. I suspected terminated was a euphemism for killed. "I'll do whatever it takes to protect my family. I know you don't owe me anything, but will you promise to look after them?"

"I will protect them with my life." The words left my mouth as soon as they formed because that was the truth. I guided Brie toward the gate, remembering how I transported four fae with me a few days ago. The difference was they knew how to navigate through the portals. I tightened my hold on my friend, inhaled, and stepped into the portal.

I imagined the same allura location I'd departed from. We were about to disembark from the portal train when the iridescent green darkened, clouding my vision. I sensed the barrier was rejecting a human with a shifter baby. It tried to strip me away, but I clung to Brie, determined. When the fog cleared, a dozen angry warriors stared back at us, their swords raised. We stood in a spacious room with high ceilings, encased in a cylindrical, semi-transparent energetic field within Invicta's alluron.

I nervous smile broke on my face. "I can explain..." The warriors' faces hardened. Mattias stepped forward, and I sighed internally. He'd recognize me.

"You're either who I think you are, or you're a demon shifter in her form," he said.

"No, it's me." I inched forward, and the weapons engaged with clicks and charging sounds penetrating the air. Brie moaned and burrowed her face into my shoulder.

"I'm Arien Blair, and this is my friend Brie. She needs immediate medical attention." My voice was clear and carried in this space.

Mattias signaled for the warriors to lower their weapons.

"Prove it."

I shuffled to the barrier, Brie's weight slowing me down. *Don't let me down now*, I thought at the alluron. If it didn't let me pass... I couldn't afford to think that way. Innocent lives were at stake.

I pressed my foot through first and relief flowed through me when it went through the alluron as if no barrier existed. I nudged Brie forward with me, clutching her closer and making a sort of shield out of my body. A force like amped-up gravity but in reverse pushed against me, and I had to strain to push us both through. I teetered on my feet when we emerged on the other side. One small victory in this precarious situation.

Mattias called the infirmary through his comms device and described Brie's medical needs with efficiency. The next call he made was to the Magister's office. I stared at my bare feet, noticing minor cuts that now stung, but that was the least of my worries. I had breached my agreement with Hafthor and broken trust with Xavier. There'd be hell to pay.

The medics rushed in, and I helped them administer a sedative. Brie wouldn't be easy without me, but she couldn't come with me. I retrieved the paperwork Ashton pointed out and handed it to Mattias. He'd know what to do with it. I hoped.

I chewed on the inside of my cheek as the medics and Brie left the room.

"You escaped Invicta only to return less than an hour later?" Mattias shook his head as he shackled my wrists. Pointless but orders were orders.

"Where to?" I asked.

The warriors nearby laughed and Mattias smirked.

"I can't decide whether it's the bravery or the naivety driving your actions."

"Oh? You'll let me know when you decide?"

A wide grin lit up his face. "I will. Right now, I have bad news for you."

"What's new?" I whispered.

Mattias chuckled. "You're in a pile of trouble, but along the way, you've garnered quite a fandom."

My eyebrows shot up to what seemed like my hairline.

"Come on," he said, circling his long fingers around my bicep rather gently. "I must escort you to Xavier's quarters."

I winced at the mention of his name. If I had truly gained any fans, Xavier wouldn't be among them...

THIRTY

"Ariiien!"

The front door slammed, and the door to Xavier's suite didn't fare any better. I pushed deeper into the couch, shackled hands between my legs, eyes on the looming threat in the room. Xavier's face was flushed. The angry features were reminiscent of his father. He tossed his weapons on the floor with brute force as if he needed to get his frustrations out. I considered it a good sign because at least he wouldn't be bringing those wicked sharp weapons near me. His suit jacket and tie were gone.

Catching his breath with hands on his hips, he stared at Mattias propping up the wall behind me. Mattias had remained silent throughout Xavier's unusual outburst.

"You're relieved," Xavier said with his common poise.

The red-haired warrior marched out of the suite without a glance back. Immediately after his departure, Xavier leaped over the back of the neighboring couch and settled in, sitting with his legs spread and his hands cradling his head. Well, shit. I had no idea how to deal with him like this. I bit into my lip, waiting. Seconds ticked by. I made myself sit still and wait.

"Damn it all to hell. Do you have any sense of self-preservation?" His dark eyes pinned me down. I gulped. Growing up, all I'd thought about was myself and how to get by until I met Brie and later Paulie. Then a handful of kind Earthbounders crossed my path, and caring for myself alone was no longer an option. So, no, I didn't think self-preservation was a priority these days, but I didn't say that out loud. I was fairly certain his question was rhetorical.

He let out a scoff and leaned back against the couch, his hands running through his curls as he stretched his legs out broadly. The door opened and Nelia stuck her head in. She breathed raggedly. Her eyes swiveled between the two of us.

"Just checking that everyone is still alive... I'll go now."

But before she could retreat, two bodyguards forced her inside the suite. Mezzo and Anhelm, also heavily armored, ambled over slowly.

"Invicta is secure. We detected no demonic presence. The disturbance was all *her* doing." Anhelm aimed his words to deliver a punch, but I didn't care. "The emergency shutdown was called off, and council members are meeting shortly."

That piqued my attention. I glanced up.

"I'll assist Arien in changing. They'll want to see her. Mezzo, can you free her?" Nelia said.

"No!" Xavier growled. He examined my shackles, bare feet, and the frayed bottom edges of my dress. "She looks perfect. What a renegade should look like. Perhaps my father will insist on me returning you to a cozy cell in the underground after all. I will deliver you there myself."

I couldn't resent him for thinking that.

"What? No response? Not a single one-liner?" He laughed with that bored quality to it. The light on his smartwatch came on, and he slapped his knees before rising to his feet.

"It's time."

Outside the right wing was an escalator. I'd never taken it before. It was select personnel only, and so far, I had gained zero access privileges to any secured areas. Xavier rolled his dress sleeves up while I stared at his back. We faced a transparent inner door. Mezzo and Anhelm positioned themselves in the back of the escalator, behind me. Nelia squeezed into the side. Her face had lost all color.

The enclosed shaft opened up to a space ten times as wide with an emergency stairwell hugging the walls and rectangular openings at regular intervals. We plunged into momentary darkness when the walls closed in on us again and came to a stop.

I followed Xavier out. Crowds amassed wherever we were at the moment and parted to let us through. Tiny goosebumps erupted on my arms, and I peered into the doorway ahead. The energy coming off the green-speckled dynamic barrier of alluron drummed on my skin. *Why were we here again?*

We stepped through, and the audience thinned out. The Magister stood at the helm, his back to the alluron. Council members, their families, and a security detail faced him. I breathed a sigh of relief, grateful for the floor-length dress that shielded my wobbly legs from prying eyes. Forcing my chin up, I gaze forward. I had broken a promise, and there'd be a price to pay. But I wouldn't cower. It was for a good cause!

Hafthor pointed a finger at the floor by his side, beckoning me to him as if I were a dog. He had to assert his dominant position with the onlookers. I joined him and faced the council with an expression void of emotion.

"All of you are aware of the situation. Pure Arien Blair has defied our wishes and my explicit orders to remain within the borders of Invicta until her graduation and the next council meeting. With sadness, I must report that Invicta has observed this type of behavior since the day we offered Arien a prestigious place among us." I gritted my teeth at the way Hafthor represented the situation as if I'd begged to be taken in by the Earthbounders when in reality I'd had no choice. "We do not tolerate disobedience."

I took a deep breath, anticipating his next words.

"But considering the unusual circumstances and your sage advice of giving it more time—" I glanced around at the faces in front of me. Someone, or a few someones, had stuck by me. "—I agree to your wishes. Arien will remain in the Invicta trainee program and will be treated equally...with one minor change."

Hafthor flicked his fingers at a small secondborn in a lab coat. He approached with a tray. A polished metal band lay in the center. While I studied it, a guard with the Magister's office insignia removed the shackles. My eyes snagged on Xavier, who studied the object with interest. He must not have known about it. The Magister didn't appear to share much with his son—unless that son was the Soaz. It was only a suspicion at this point, but that gut feeling told me there was something to that.

Hafthor clasped the band on my right wrist, then lifted it toward the crowd.

"Thanks to Invicta's ingenuity, we're equipped to deal with transgressions swiftly. This band inactivates Arien's ability to portal travel and only I can disable it."

My features morphed in shock. *Was it possible? Could this little thing do what Hafthor proclaimed?*

He faced me.

"Go on, touch it." He meant the alluron.

I scanned the crowd again, their faces intrigued by this recent development. I stilled my nerves and shuffled over to the barrier. Swallowing, I raised the hand. The electric charge I associated with allura's energy was absent. The tip of my index finger tapped at the alluron, and a lava of energy erupted. A sonic boom lifted me off my feet and threw me yards away, over and past the crowd into the hands of one of the guards. Under the force of the impact, he took a few steps backward to avoid a fall.

He set me down on my unsteady feet. I brushed the hair out of my eyes and directed unpleasant thoughts at Hafthor. A dark smirk stretched his lips.

Elyon stepped forward and faced the council.

"The Northeast region is fully satisfied with the resolution of this matter. We commend the Magister of Invicta for taking such foresighted steps. It illustrates your readiness and adaptability," he said, nodding at Hafthor who assumed a proud stance. "And we eagerly anticipate Invicta sharing this technology with all of us."

Hafthor's expression fell flat. He stepped forward to reclaim the room's attention.

"Yes. Well, let's not let this one unfortunate incident stop us from enjoying our evening. The talented Orphelia will sing for us in the auditorium. Let's head over there now."

The announcement aroused some excitement among the council members' families. They drifted toward the door, guards following. I expected someone would escort me back to Xavier's suite, maybe one of his men, but it became apparent I was on my own. The threat of me leaving Invicta was removed, Xavier hated my guts right now, Kole was still MIA, and even Nelia, my supposed orientation leader, had departed without me. But Brie and her baby were safe. Relatively speaking. And that was worth all the misery it inflicted upon me.

THIRTY-ONE

Barc, scraped feet, a torn dress, and a jail bracelet made by the devil himself. He wanted to shame me. Yet, I strolled the halls of Invicta with my head held high and a glower worthy of an award for the best "fuck off." Most secondborns had shunned me before I'd turned into a super freak Pure. Now, I thought I made some tremble. The Pures I passed had mixed reactions. Some smirked, others made smooching sounds, and a handful just glared back. The point of this was to leave me alone on my walk of shame.

"Hey." Zephyr stepped to my side as I entered the staircase to the first floor. I guessed my intimidating persona didn't work against him. Against probably most Pures if I was being honest with myself.

"You're gonna miss Orphelia's tantalizing performance," I said dryly.

He flashed a grin. "My siblings and I always sneak out from these events. Besides, Caelum is planning a ghoul hunt later tonight." He rubbed his hands together.

"A ghoul hunt?" I peered at him with a skeptical expression. He bumped into my shoulder.

"You almost look the part. Maybe you can act as our bait if nothing shows up?" He twitched his eyebrows.

I blew out a breath. "I suspect they plastered pictures of me on all Invicta gates."

He bellowed with laughter. "You always say the funniest shit. But, no, he did you one better. Face recognition cameras alert him of your whereabouts every half hour." I stopped with one foot on the next step.

"How do you know?"

"As Elyon's son, I have to sit in on all council meetings." I resumed walking, stealing glances at him. This statement made me see him in a different light.

"I now understand why ghoul hunting is an appealing diversion."

"As is your company."

We paused at the security door on the fourth floor. Also known as Xavier's floor. Zephyr lifted my hand to his mouth for a kiss. His eyes sparkled with mischief.

"I applaud your chivalry. Isn't that too mundane for a warrior race?"

He showed off perfectly white teeth. "You've been hanging out with Invicta brutes. A true warrior knows how to win a lady's favor." Wait, what? Zephyr spun on his heel, leaving me completely speechless.

Buzzing behind me alerted me to a lock disengaging. I stepped into the hallway.

"Hello?" I asked. I expected to find Mezzo or Anhelm there. Someone had unlocked the door for me. Absolute silence greeted me. Zephyr's words returned to me—security cameras now traced my every move. Someone, perhaps even Xavier, had let me in. I pushed on the door handle to his suite. It didn't move. I waited for the lock to disengage, and nothing happened. I tried Mezzo's and Anhelm's quarters. All locked up including my only exit point—the hallway security door. Whoever let me in had played a joke on me. Fine. I slid down Xavier's door to the ground and propped my head against it. Eventually, he would have to return to his suite. And then...I didn't know what.

There was too much on my mind. The Fringe with its monstrous labs underground, Brie and her baby, and now this stupid band on my wrist. This whole time, I had been too blind to see that the odds were stacked against me graduating and leaving Invicta on my own terms. What a stupid angel I'd been, indeed...

A slight nudge to my foot startled me awake.

"Do you mind?" Xavier towered over me. His brows pinched together in agitation. I tucked my feet under and sprang up as gracefully as possible. I stepped to the side while he pushed the handle down and strolled inside. Huh? I frowned at the handle that had failed to yield to me. Xavier was somewhere inside his suite already. At least he didn't shut the door behind him. So, I was still welcome here.

When I emerged from the shower, Nelia waited outside my door. She wore a new outfit since I'd seen her last—another pencil skirt with a delicate loose top.

"I'm so glad you're here," I said. "You're my only anchor to sanity right now." I pressed myself to the window. My former class of secondborns was out for their early conditioning. I could no longer socialize with them. Even my time with Master Pietras was limited to once a week. I glanced over my shoulder. Nelia was unusually quiet.

"What's wrong? Is it Brie?" My heart did a little double-tap.

"She's fine. She's at the infirmary surrounded by an expert group of medics."

I blew out a breath. "When can I see her?"

"I'm still working that out..." She considered something, then ambled over to me. She unclasped her smartwatch and entered settings, scanned my eye, and pressed my thumb to the surface.

"Why are we doing this?" I asked.

Nelia didn't answer. In one swift motion, she had the thing on my own wrist. The band molded to my skin but felt weightless all the same. I gaped at her.

"Here is how you operate it—"

I grabbed her shoulders and shook gently. "Take it off."

Her fists came down on my elbows, and I hissed, letting her go. That hurt worse than when I'd been kicked in the shin.

"Listen. There are things happening I'm not supposed to know about and even more I don't understand. Stop wasting time and learn how to use this thing. I reprogrammed it to respond to you. The watch is traceable, but you've already got that tracker band, so I guess it doesn't really matter now, does it?"

"Does *he* know about this?"

"You forget I'm the Magister's secretary. I put in an order on his behalf to fit you with one of these. To any guard checking, this will appear legitimate—"

"Shit, Nelia. Why? What if he sees this on me?"

She shot me a death glare. "You will wear it in incognito mode. And because my father is a proud snob who would never suspect me of doing this, he won't ever suspect a thing."

I went along with her whims. We spent the next hour going over commands and programs. Unfortunately, I couldn't use it to unlock security doors because that would draw everyone's attention to me. I would pretend I had limited privileges on the device. The feeling of dread kept burrowing deeper inside me.

"What about you?"

She shrugged a shoulder, avoiding my eyes. I found myself speechless. Saliva kept flowing in my mouth and I struggled to find words. What was it Nelia kept from me?

Nelia squeezed my shaking hand. "I'll meet you at the library in the afternoon," she said in a hoarse voice. Then she grabbed her purse and left abruptly.

THIRTY-TWO

I skipped the training with Donovan and headed straight for the weapons warehouse. Lately, I was in the habit of noting Xavier and his men's movements—not in a stalker-ish kind of way—and if I was correct, they had a scheduled patrol today. I leaned against the wall across from the sliding door. I knew better than to try entering. I'd learned that the hard way the last time I'd followed Anhelm inside.

Mezzo and Anhelm didn't spare a glance my way. *Fine, let them be that way.*

A few minutes later, Xavier's footsteps beat the stone floor. I recognized the rhythm of his stride and soon his silhouette gained clarity. Including a very pissed-off face.

"No," he growled.

"But—" The sliding door opened and closed, and I was standing alone again.

Fine. I kicked at imaginary dirt. Plan B it was then. He couldn't complain that I didn't come to him first.

I reactivated Nelia's smartwatch and hit Contacts.

Zephyr's name displayed on the screen with chat and call options. I debated this move. It could mean more to him than I intended. But then didn't "taking advantage of someone" require a degree of deceit and promises that couldn't be fulfilled? I intended to smash my index finger down on the call button when someone captured and wrenched it backward.

"Ow, ow..."

"I said *no*." Xavier glared down at me with my finger still bent at a painful angle.

"You say that a lot lately," I said with tears in my eyes. He released my hostage finger, and I shook the poor hand. Ever since I'd rescued Brie, he'd been avoiding me or communicating in single words.

"That boy isn't stupid enough to take you outside Invicta."

"So there is nothing to worry about then." I spun on my heel and trotted away from him.

"Get. Back."

I paused, smiling to myself. I masked my winning expression with a blank stare when I turned around.

"Why?"

"Little angel..." There was a shudder-inducing warning in his tone. I approached him precisely in time for Mezzo and Anhelm to emerge from the warehouse laden with knives, swords, chakrams, and other gadgets.

"I implore you, sir—" Anhelm said at the sight of me.

"She's coming." Xavier's harsh tone ended the argument.

We loaded into Xavier's black Humvee. Guards at the gate shot curious glances my way but didn't dare to question their leader's son.

I stared out the window the entire time, scouring the landscape for any sign of Kole or the P6-ers. Blinking had become a nuisance. At one point, I held my eyelashes up by framing my face against the window. That almost resulted in eyelash loss when I sneezed.

The outskirts of the city sprawled against the backdrop of trees at first. Buildings slowly condensed the in-between spaces, winning the battle for space with nature. Soon, crowds populated sidewalks, and recognizing Kole became impossible. I should've been able to spot a green fedora, but I doubted Paulie wore it these days. He was lying low some-where—hopefully not in a graveyard.

With a frustrated sigh, I fell back into the seat.

We crawled in the lunchtime traffic by the Chinatown gates, its colorful mythical beasts laughing at me with those bulging oversized eyes. Four men surrounded and pressed someone against the gate's red pillar. With their backs to us, I couldn't tell for sure, but their height, fight-ready stances, and a weird feeling seeing them gave my stomach a twist. I yanked the door handle, but the door didn't open.

"Let me out!"

Anhelm, who sat in front of me, was on the sidewalk in a flash. Mezzo was by his side only a millisecond later, but my door still wouldn't cooperate. I flattened my face against the window, but at that angle it was now impossible to see anything other than Mezzo and Anhelm disappearing into Chinatown. Xavier entered the next parking deck and pulled into a street-level spot.

"Did you spell my door or something?"

"I believe humans call it a *child lock*. Interestingly, I never had a use for it until today." I had a strong urge to smack him.

"Could you let me out now, *dad*?"

The air inside the vehicle was suffocating. I tugged at the collar of my thermal. When the lock released with an audible *click,* I tumbled out of the car to my damn knees. My chest hurt. Why was it so hard to breathe?

Strong hands cinched my waist and put me upright.

"Breathe." His voice was gentle.

"Those men out there... I think they were the fae from King Cygnus's court. The ones who returned to Earth with me."

"Hmm, they definitely were supernaturals. Anhelm and Mezzo will investigate Chinatown. But if they were Andromeda fae, they're long gone."

"You sound...confident."

"If you think the likes of me or my father are ancient, then the Andromeda fae are prehistoric. They live long lives and fight even longer battles. There's a reason the Earthbounders cast them out. Or at least that was the belief."

"What happened?" The large Bible-like book Nelia had first handed to me when I arrived at Invicta told a story of the powerful fae who broke an edict. "Did they break a law?"

Xavier scoffed. "Supposedly."

"You have your own theory?"

"Let's suppose you belonged to an elite group who protected an entire world and held all its affairs in balance. One day, a mightier being shows up at your doorstep and asks for temporary shelter in exchange for the fae's services. With time you see that being has garnered a following because he's swift and just in exacting justice; maybe even the people start gravitating toward the fae. But they are not the saviors and don't deserve the worship. If you ask them to leave, you will lose reputation with the people—"

"But not if they are accused of committing a crime against humanity..." I finished for him. "It's all about control with you guys, isn't it?"

We entered one elevator, and Xavier punched in a few too many digits.

"You say it like that's not the ambition of all rulers? Even the smallest man given a taste of power is bound to abuse it."

"What an optimistic worldview you have."

He squared his shoulders, any hint of playfulness waning away from his expression. "You forget I have a few lifetimes on you."

True.

The elevator slowed down and rocked to a stop. Bright light poured in when the two metal sides retracted. I followed Xavier onto the roof. We were in the middle of the business and entertainment center and on the top of one of its highest buildings. Xavier strode to the very edge. Standing with his legs apart and head bowed, he resembled a superhero surveying his city.

The thought of looking down from this height made my stomach upturn. I stared at the horizon instead. A strange warmth ignited underneath my shoulder blades.

"You like that, don't you?" I whispered.

"Hmm?" Xavier squinted in my direction. My cheeks heated.

"Just having a little chat with my wings." I shrugged.

Xavier touched two fingers to his lips in contemplation.

"Is this the part where you tell me we're going to be jumping off the edge in an unforeseen twist of events?" I didn't think any repetitions of "Geronimo" would've saved me from falling to death.

"I could always catch you..."

"Don't. Even. Think. About. it. Besides, you're not training me today. I am tagging along on your job, remember?"

His forehead creased. "How often do you train with them?"

"I don't. They only come out if something scares me shit-less, and that's not even guaranteed. But, hey, if you know a wing whisperer, send them my way, would you?"

Xavier hopped off the ledge and stalked toward me.

"You're saying no one is teaching you how to use your wings."

"Uh... no... I mean, yes?"

His nostrils flared enough to alert me to him about to go pissy on me.

"You know what I mean." I tried to placate him.

"Yeah, I do. My poor excuse of a father doesn't care about your abilities, only your bloodline. And Donovan is a selfish bastard."

I stood still, surprised that he didn't direct his anger towards me. "Donovan has a chip on his shoulder. I'm unsure what that is though..." I lingered, waiting to see if Xavier would pick up that thought. He didn't.

"Anyway," I continued, "I haven't seen him since my first day. I don't think we're good training partners." I shrugged.

Xavier spat to the side. "I've been...occupied with the events my father puts up to impress the council. I needed this day out. What do you say we skip tonight's fancy dinner and after-party?" Mischief gleamed in his eyes.

I grinned. "Hafthor will have my head."

"Not when he hears about the fae. It only makes sense we continue our search."

I snorted. "In your dreams. He will have both our heads."

"And?"

I sucked my lower lip in. "I'm all in."

THIRTY-THREE

We marched for what seemed like several miles, across streets, food markets, and subway stations. The sky darkened, and we were currently in a city park, strolling by a pond with a sprawling fountain when Xavier's watch lit up again. He'd been receiving updates from his men all afternoon. His brows drew together.

"One of our contacts thinks he saw our fae in the club district."

I was thankful when Xavier called us a cab. As much as I enjoyed strolling through the city, my legs were getting tired. No wonder the warriors' thighs were bulging. Even when they weren't working out, they did cross-training while on a job.

Not much had changed in the city's party zone. Yellow outdoor lights hung in a zigzag pattern from one side of the bars and clubs to the other, over a paved pedestrian-only street. Patrons filled half of the space, enjoying each other's company, meeting up with friends, and groups of made-up teenage girls who definitely shouldn't have been there.

Some bars had elevated stages and outdoor seating with live music. Others leaned to the darker side with blood-red decor and black walls, smoke coming from who knew where, and deafening heavy music that had the potential to scramble your head. It was all a facade, though. I used to pick up all sorts of odd jobs at these clubs not so long ago. I was the dishwasher, bartender helper, or invisible cleaner on the floor who made refills appear magically while their patrons engaged in activities on the dance floor.

Xavier's face screwed in disgust. Many women shot him hopeful glances and a few men too. I chuckled mildly.

"What?" he barked.

"Oh, nothing."

"No, that was something."

"Fine, take all my fun away. You seem very much out of place, and I've never seen you outside of your element. It gives me a tiny bit of joy." I grinned at him.

His eyes narrowed. "I may not be accustomed to this... atmosphere, but I'm always in full and absolute control. As long as we agree on that."

"Agreed to agree."

He cocked his head to the side, studying my face. "You have a tendency to speak in flattering ways with double meaning."

"Oh?" I quirked a brow.

"It's clever." He ducked his head under the sign hanging lopsided over the entrance while I stood frozen in place with my mouth partially open. Had he just complimented me?

"You coming?" Xavier stepped one foot out, pushing the sign to the side. He pushed my chin up to close my mouth with his free hand. "Careful, you may catch flies. Or ash from the cigs they all smoke here, or even worse, someone's spittle." He punctuated his words with a fake tremble.

I rolled my eyes and sidestepped him. "Says a guy who bathes in demon gore."

The narrow entrance opened up into a wider corridor with five steps down. This was Kill Bills, the only club on this strip with pool tables and a full bar in the front room. Across the front room, double doors opened into the dance floor with lounge areas tucked away. DJ Muffin was mixing techno-pop records on a black platform in a corner. Xavier took the lead toward a booth behind the VIP rope. Anhelm wore a bored expression on his face. He leaned back in his seat with arms spread across the back of the couch, looking like he belonged there.

Xavier made me slide in between him and Anhelm. *Oh, joy, I guess there'll be no dancing for me tonight.* Mezzo slinked into a cushion in the corner. Where had he been all this time? I hadn't seen him approach us at all.

"I inspected the perimeter. No sign of them," Mezzo said.

Xavier rubbed his jaw. "Maybe we're too late."

A server approached with a tray laden with beer bottles. He wore a vest over his naked chest showing off his muscled arms and a pair of ripped jeans. His expression brightened when our eyes connected.

"I thought I spotted you here," the man said.

"Hi." I returned the smile. The server worked at Kill Bills when he wasn't touring with Chippendales. He made solid tips and often teased me about exposing more skin to increase mine. The problem was I didn't tolerate patrons touching me. He was a performer who craved physical contact.

The warriors stared at the server while he set bottles on the table.

"We worried about you, but I see you've been busy." He winked at me, and my cheeks heated. "Enjoy these on the house."

"Thanks. We'll catch up later," I said. Although I doubted I'd be visiting that district any time soon, it sounded like the right thing to say. The server grinned and hopped over to the next booth.

"You know him?" Mezzo stared at me with disbelief.

"I worked at most of the bars on this strip."

"You worked here?" Anhelm frowned.

"Well, yeah, if I wanted to eat..."

I attributed the silence to the warriors' brains dealing with the idea of a Pure having to work to earn a living.

"Describe what the four fae look like again," Xavier said. I recounted what I remembered—tall, dark, and fae. There wasn't anything extraordinary about them other than slightly pointed ears and their handsome otherworldly looks. Then Xavier insisted I retell the entire encounter with King Cygnus, how many fae warriors there were, how many rooms were in his castle, and so on. I was parched by the end. I downed half a bottle.

"Have you been watching the dance floor?" I asked.

"Hmm?"

"For the fae. If they came here, it'd be to have some fun. They live isolated from the world and their own people, assuming there were other survivors." I recalled how their eyes gleamed with excitement when the king announced their departure with me.

"The women," I whispered.

"What about the women?"

We all observed the dance floor now.

"They have none. I wasn't able to see the entire complex, but I saw the longing in their eyes when they gawked at me. I don't think there are any women there."

"So, you're saying King Cygnus's secret mission was for his men to get laid?" Anhelm deadpanned.

I rolled my eyes skyward.

"Hook-up after a job?" Mezzo asked.

I stood up.

"Where are you going?" Xavier asked.

"Someone's got to get in that crowd, and I don't see any of you volunteering to dance. Among the humans," I added with mock horror.

"No." Xavier's response was immediate.

"That's a good plan actually," Mezzo countered. "And we can track her thanks to the Magister's generosity." I glanced at my new smartwatch.

Xavier gritted his teeth.

"She can blend in," Anhelm said.

"One wrong move and—"

"I know, I know." I removed the thermal and tugged my tank top lower. Xavier glided out of the couch, letting me out. I weaved my way into the crowd and soon got sucked into it. The wave of bodies carried me deeper. Blaring techno assaulted my ears and strobe lights blinked rapidly like an old picture frame. One second, it was dark and I couldn't see shit, and the next it was like lightning had brightened everything around me.

I yelped when Zephyr's face popped in front of me.

He steadied me and lowered his head to yell into my ear. "What are you doing here?"

I tiptoed and yelled back. "I could ask you the same question?"

He grinned. "Me and few others decided we had enough of the posturing at Invicta." Others? I glanced over his shoulder. Caelum was grinding against a pretty woman in a red mini dress. A head of blond waves that had to belong to Seraphina laughed while dancing with Thalassa. Zephyr started dancing in front of me with impressive fluid moves. He could dance more than the foxtrot his upbringing required. He surprised me yet again when he snagged my waist and pulled me against him. I had no choice but to dance with him, feeling the hard planes of his broad chest pressed to mine. I bit my lower lip. *How was I going to get out of this conundrum?*

"I'm here on a mission," I yelled again. Zephyr quirked a brow. "I need to investigate the back." I pointed at the back wall and spun out of his embrace. I shuffled my way around his friends and into the sea of people when a body pressed into my back.

"Mind if I go with? I can help you blend in." Zephyr was a freaking talented dancer. He matched my steps and took the lead often, but I didn't mind it. We were at the end of the throng of dancers now, facing a black wall, and the fae were nowhere to be seen. Patrons filled the booths on both sides, and none of them were the four fae. Someone emerged from behind a curtain I hadn't spotted earlier.

I grabbed Zephyr's hand, not wasting time to explain, and slinked us behind the curtain into a corridor lit with black light and a red exit sign at the far end. Dark shapes lingered against the walls. I draped Zephyr's arm over my shoulders to blend in as I inconspicuously inspected males engrossed with female bodies they'd pinned against the walls. But the next one, he had his back against the wall, arms behind his head, and a girl on her knees in front of him. I froze.

"Wasn't aware voyeurism was your thing," Zephyr whispered into my ear.

"Shut up." I dropped his arm and touched my smartwatch before claws wrapped around my neck. The fae tossed me into Zephyr, and we crashed to the floor. The girl wept next to us. City lights lit up the corridor as the exit door swung open. I slid, coming up on a substance I didn't want to know the origin of, and had righted myself against the wall when Zephyr shot past me for the exit.

"Wait!" He didn't know what we were dealing with. I ran after him and tapped Xavier's name on the watch.

"I see you," Xavier said. The rest sounded mumbled as I pumped my arms to keep up with Zephyr's shape in the back alley. Two winged shapes rushed above my head in the runner's direction. I was losing sight of them and after rounding another corner, I was alone and...lost.

THIRTY-FOUR

riiien." The whisper came from my right, and I turned, staring into a narrow gap between two buildings.

"Oh, Ariiieen." This one came from behind me, and I whirled around. I was in the middle of a narrow one-lane street lined with small shops and living spaces above them. The shops were closed, and the street was quiet.

"Ariiien!" A man chuckled. The fae. Two of the Andromeda fae stepped out from the shadows on either side of me.

"What do you want?" I asked.

"You found us out, sly vixen." The fae to my left doubled over, laughing hysterically. "Get it—vixen?"

My brows drew together. I wasn't getting it for sure. I scrutinized the other man's flushed expression and lopsided grin.

"What's wrong with you?" I watched both men for any threat. The fae to my right shrugged.

"What's it to ya?"

"Oh, nothing." I shrugged my own shoulders. "Just curious, you know. Since you disappeared on me, I've been wondering what my least favorite fae have been up to..."

"Well, we didn't think about ya one bit." The fae chuckled.

"Or about King Cygnus, apparently."

The fae sobered up.

"Does he know you've been frolicking around? How long has it been now...?" I tapped my chin. The fae came in closer and a tremble ran down my spine. Their silly expressions morphed into scowls.

"She worries too much about the king," one said to his companion.

"Perhaps we should bring her back with us?"

"He rather liked her wings." The other fae nodded. I widened my stance on instinct.

The air whooshed behind me, and a winged figure appeared by my side. I halted just in time from serving Xavier with a round kick.

"Invicta and the council wish to know your interests on Earth," Xavier said.

"Invicta, ya say?"

"Invicta has no jurisdiction over us," the second fae warrior said.

"Kindly answer my question, then."

"Civilized this one, yeh?"

The fae were stalling.

"Ahh, ya fine. You mustn't worry your head about it. We were retrieving an object for the king, that's all."

"What—" I began to ask.

Earthbounder figures landed on the roofs of the surrounding buildings.

"Stand back," Xavier ordered.

The fae exchanged a glance.

"It appears our brother got away."

"Wait," Xavier demanded with a growl. As if he sensed the conversation was over then. The fae touched their sternum with two fingers connected and flashed out of there. I covered my eyes.

"That light," I mumbled.

Xavier scowled at the men when they joined us. Mezzo, Anhelm, and Zephyr.

"Sorry, Commander. We couldn't tell what was going on down here," Anhelm said.

"Get the car," Xavier commanded. His men darted into the sky.

Zephyr inclined his head to me and took off.

"Did they say anything of value before I arrived?"

"No."

Xavier faced me. "You wouldn't lie to me, would you?"

"For god's sake, no. They tried to spook me at first, and afterward they appeared drunk."

"Hmm. They're susceptible to human wine, but the effects don't last long."

We began walking, and I stuffed my hands into my pockets.

"What's in your pockets?"

"What?" I sounded appalled even to my own ears. I removed the hands and waved them in front of his face. "Happy now. I'm not hiding anything from you."

"You sure forgot to mention your plan to rescue your friend," he gritted. He directed his stormy glare at the street. So that was what all this was about.

"And you know why…"

He marched on, his brows dipping lower. I didn't owe Xavier that much. I didn't owe him my trust. I wasn't sure even Kole deserved my trust since going MIA. I grabbed his elbow.

"Listen…" My mouth quit cooperating. The cerulean in

Xavier's eyes spilled over the white. He appeared eerily other-worldly, with his blue orbs and tiny black pupils fixed in a distant stare. My breath quickened.

"X?" I whispered. His eyes focused on me, and I stepped back. When he blinked, the whites of his eyes returned to normal. "Sounds like I'm not the only one with secrets."

Xavier huffed. "It's no secret. My mother was a seer. I simply inherited a bit of her gift."

I mulled that over. Xavier was known for his gift of heightened olfactory senses. That meant he had two gifts.

"I'd never heard of an Earthbounder with more than one gift."

"It is rare." He said it with a blasé attitude.

"I guess..." We resumed walking, but I couldn't help myself. Since he wasn't forthcoming with the information, he could only blame himself for this. I spun around toward him, almost tripping over his giant foot.

"Can you not?" he murmured.

"What did you see just then?"

He hesitated. "I'm not sure. There was a lot of action. Usually when that happens, I need a good night's sleep to allow my brain to make sense of the vision."

I nodded. I'd take that explanation for now. "It happened to you in the car after the kelpie attack?"

"Yes."

I sighed. "What did you see then?"

He stopped. "You. I saw us in front of an altar." He shook his head. "You wore a wedding dress, and I stood opposite you."

My heart hammered in my chest. Well, that was... unexpected.

"Earthbounders wear wedding dresses?" I asked.

Xavier simpered. "They are different from what humans wear, but yes, the women do."

I narrowed my eyes and pointed a finger at his chest. "That's why you tried to claim me?"

"I did claim you."

I scoffed. "Semantics. You thought we had to *marry* because of a vision?"

"Yes, that's what I thought. Obviously, that wasn't written in the stars, or the stars played a trick on me. The last time I had a vision prior to the kelpie attack was over a decade ago. They come sporadically, but they have never misled me. Not until that day."

"Oh? But what changed?"

Xavier ran a hand through his waves. "Honestly, the only difference is the people in it. Perhaps when it comes to you, my gift can't predict your trajectory. You're too dynamic, or your fate isn't set. These are merely my suspicions. Your bloodline is still quite a mystery."

We ambled the rest of the way to the club district in silence. Although that clarified some of Xavier's bizarro behavior in the past, one thing gnawed at me. He said he couldn't be certain of the visions with me in them. And since he didn't want to discuss his latest vision, I bet I starred in it too.

THIRTY-FIVE

The SUV veered into the roundabout in front of the strip. Xavier and I both reached for the door at the same time, our hands touching, and I dropped mine as if someone had burned me. In a rare act, he held the door open for me. I chalked it up to his vision rattling him.

We peeled off from the curb. Mezzo and Anhelm occupied the front this time, scanning the streets and sidewalks as if we were on a hunt. Taking the appearance of the fae into consideration, that was precisely the mood they inspired.

Thud. I jolted, startled, as a heavy object hit the roof of the SUV, leaving a dent. Mezzo hit the brakes and tire screeching filled my ears. Two bulky figures stood on the road in front of us. Drunken pedestrians cleared the sidewalks, anticipating a commotion. I squinted into the alley my side window faced, from which another hulking figure strolled out and then stared squarely at the SUV.

"There is another one," I said calmly. Xavier nodded.

"I counted six, maybe seven," he said. What? How and when had he assessed this situation so fast?

"You will stay in the car, or I swear on the angels, Arien..." The threat hung heavy.

"All right, all right," I breathed. I actually didn't feel like arguing on this one. The three warriors hopped out of the car and Mezzo tossed the key fob into my lap.

"Wait..." The doors slammed on all three sides. Did he expect me to drive? He'd left the car running. I scrambled over the center console into the driver's seat and shrieked when the door locked automatically. I guess that was why he left the key with me, duh...

The shadows advanced closer. Two in the front, the one to the left of the car, and now, one on the right side came into the street light. I glanced at the rearview mirror and wasn't surprised to see another one approach from there. They outnumbered us three to five because—let's be honest—I was of no use to them. The strangers matched Pures in build and stealth. Shit, that wasn't good.

I squinted ahead when the headlights illuminated the enemy's faces. They were not the fae. These guys were something different but definitely supernatural.

I gasped. The blue bands on their arms meant these were rebellion warriors—Earthbounders who had revolted against the regime. Their faces twisted into ugly snarls as they charged Mezzo and Anhelm. The SUV rocked when Xavier and his attacker collided with it. A face at the passenger window nearly gave me a heart attack. The man gestured with his index finger to the door lock. I shook my head slowly. He insisted, yelling how they were here to save me.

For a second, I considered whether Kole was part of this. But if Kole were involved, he would've come for me himself. This rescue attempt made no sense.

"No," I said. The man headbutted the window, and it cracked into dozens of spider webs. He jammed his elbow into it. The reinforced glass would soon give way. I peered at the Seraphs who continued to fight the others.

I tried to shift the gears, but the stick shift was stuck. Glass pieces fell inside. I remembered to push on the brake, and I successfully shifted. I released the brake and floored the gas. My chest pressed into the steering wheel and a *thud* sounded at the rear of the car. I'd put the car in freaking reverse. I took my foot off the pedals. My heart pounded. The SUV's rear sat higher, and I feared what was stuck under it. With trembling hands, I shifted into drive and eased off the bump. My attacker knelt by the body. *Ohmagod, I killed someone.* The man pulled the body away into the shadows. I must have hit one of them, but that didn't feel any better. I'd never killed anyone before. I pressed the brake and used both hands to shift into park.

Screaming echoed when a body landed on the hood and the windshield. Xavier's face rose above the man he pinned down. A snake rope tattoo adorned the man's neck like a choker. He retaliated with a bone-crunching punch to Xavier's jaw that made him stumble. The man leaped to his feet on top of the hood. He ran across the roof of the car and disappeared into the shadows.

Mezzo and Anhelm ambled over, scanning the area for any new danger. Xavier's piercing eyes stared back at me as he massaged his jaw. Wait, no, he popped it back into place. My stomach squirmed.

Thump. I flinched and turned to find Mezzo looking in through the driver's window and gesturing towards the unlock button. I complied and stumbled on shaky legs to the backseat.

"Calling all units near the club district. Five rebels spotted..." Anhelm debriefed the intelligence center with the location and details while Mezzo put the car slowly into motion.

"Don't look at me like that. I don't know them, and I have no idea why they came for me," I said to Xavier, who'd been staring at me ever since he slid into his seat. His mouth formed a hard line. I rubbed my forehead. *Did I kill that man?*

"Good reaction there," Mezzo said. "Where did you learn to drive like that?"

"Oh, I've never driven before," I said. And I ran over someone on my first try.

"You're joking?" Mezzo said.

"Ugh. I'm gonna be sick." I cupped a hand over my mouth, fighting with the door handle. My skin heated, and yeah, if they didn't let me out, I was gonna beautify Xavier's SUV. Cool hands pulled me out of the car and dragged me to neatly trimmed bushes. I bent over and emptied my stomach. One steel arm held my waist from tipping over, and the other knotted my hair up. What a bestie would do. But, let's face it, Xavier wasn't my bestie and I hadn't imbued unholy amounts of alcohol. I had freaking killed someone today, and even if they'd meant to harm me, I couldn't justify it.

Xavier guided me back into the SUV and punched in my buckle. I leaned against the cool glass of my window, closing my eyes.

"They weren't rebels I remember," Anhelm's deep voice rumbled from the front seat.

"Mine was a shifter. But I couldn't detect which race. He had a mixed scent I'd never experienced before," Xavier said.

I twisted my neck to gaze at him.

"I will have the intelligence unit check the registry for any new shifter race. Every now and then they interbreed and mutations form."

"Rebels aren't tracked, but it won't hurt to check. We may want to activate another asset," Xavier said.

"Which will require the Magister's approval. Should I dial the emergency line?" Mezzo asked.

"No, we don't want to alert the council members. I will debrief him in person when he's alone."

Mezzo gave a curt nod.

"I thought rebels were a group of Earthbounders?" I asked.

"We've seen disgruntled shifters join the cause before. It's uncommon but not impossible," Xavier said. His forehead did that tensing thing when he didn't quite buy an idea. The men wore rebellion bands. They belonged to the group.

"You seem unsure," I said.

Surprised eyes connected with mine. Was it shocking I recognized some of his body cues? Xavier cleared his throat.

"Anhelm, contact Nelia. Tell her to add driving lessons to Arien's schedule."

Really?

THIRTY-SIX

I flinched awake as the smartwatch on my wrist vibrated with a new message. I had fallen asleep sitting on a stool, with my head pillowed by my arms on top of Dez's desk. The message read: *Soaz alert*. It came from an anonymous source. I jolted upward, my eyes zeroing in immediately on a sleeping Brie, with tiny Ash Junior moaning slightly in the bassinet by her side.

Xavier had received a top-level message about Brie going into labor on our way back to Invicta and allowed me to go to the infirmary right away. It was only my second time seeing her since I'd brought her to Invicta. The Magister's guards kept visitors away, but today, they were called off. I got to hold my best friend's hand when she needed someone. Ashton should've been the one, but he was a screwup I didn't want near Brie. I was aware she would've disagreed. I could see it in her eyes. Even after he'd put her and their baby in danger, she'd have forgiven him already.

My head swiveled to the mahogany door opening. The Soaz and two of his men stepped inside the infirmary with determination. They pushed medical contraptions out of their way and headed directly for Brie. I sprinted across and intercepted him only a few feet away from my friend. Seeing him get closer to her set me on edge.

"Wha-what are you doing here?" I tried for nonchalant, but we both knew he was here for Brie and her baby. I was only stalling the inevitable. But, no! I couldn't let him even point a finger at her. He'd have to go through me first.

The Soaz scowled. He glanced over my shoulder, then reached a hand to my side and shoved me away.

"Stop! She just had a baby. She can't talk." I wedged myself back between him and Brie. This time, my butt almost scraped the edge of the bed. If he were a dragon, I imagined smoke would lift from his nostrils about now. He stepped closer, towering over me. Menace radiated from him.

"She's human. She knows nothing." My hands trembled by my sides. "She knows nothing!" I repeated. But the Soaz didn't care about that. All he wanted was to satisfy his cravings for exacting suffering and cruelty on others. If they were innocent, well, I feared that was how he liked his victims most.

The men emerged from behind him in a clear sign of removing me, and I had no chance against the two mature warriors. I glanced around the room that now stood at a standstill as if someone had pressed pause. Horror and disbelief painted the faces around me. I couldn't count on any of them for help. I had to change my tactic, stat.

"Please, I'll do anything," I whispered into the Soaz's neck. He gave a cue to his men I must have missed because they stopped in their attempt to remove me. I set my eyes on his, unwavering, communicating I'd go to any lengths to protect my friend. Any.

He knew as well as I did he wouldn't get any information out of her. It occurred to me then that maybe he was acting on behalf of the Fringe. They wouldn't want any information about their experiments coming out, and Brie's life would always be in danger for that reason. I had to get her away from the Fringe and the Soaz. If I could hold him off long enough.

"Let's go," the Soaz said as he swiveled on his heel. I didn't miss a beat. I was by his side the next second, matching his stride with two of mine. At the doorway, I glanced back. Brie continued to rest, and a female medic attended to now awake little Ash. Love and sorrow intermingled in my heart. What would the future hold for the two of them?

The Soaz dismissed his men. He guided us straight down the corridor, past the staircases I was familiar with. The hairs on my arms stood on end, and the precarious situation I was in had slowly begun sinking in. He stayed quiet, not bothering to even glance at me. Like a wolf leading a sheep to slaughter.

I pulled up my mental map of Invicta, dropping this new placeholder into it. The Soaz kicked in a door to our right and shoved me inside. The space had an exposed brick for the walls and a rugged-looking, unpolished ceiling. This could have been a cellar at one time, holding spirits and non-perishables for the nobles living above.

I stopped in the middle under a miserly source of yellow light the Soaz flipped on as he nudged the door closed behind him. He stalked but didn't pounce. And it occurred to me that while he thrived on the chase, that was all he ever did. Warily, I padded toward him. His pupils dilated to the edges of his dark irises, and his incisors lowered. My heart thudded and it took everything in me to remain still. I didn't scream or hesitate. His elongated hard nails dug into my shoulders, immobilizing me in place. Unnecessarily, but perhaps that was a habit his inner creature or mutation had adopted.

"You will leave Brie and her baby alone," I said, scrutinizing his hungry expression. The monster scoffed.

"When will you learn you can't tell me what to do, nightshade?"

I hated the pet name he gave me. I grimaced. "I don't pretend I can control anyone. But I think you're capable of honoring a deal. You do live by some principles, don't you?"

He growled. "If I'm to grant you any leeway here, you'd better make this rendezvous worth my time." His tone was sharp enough to cut steel.

"Is my surrender to you not enough?" I asked. Had I miscalculated his reaction?

"It's a good start." There was a slight purr to his voice. His claws retracted, but he didn't loosen his hold.

I gathered my hair to one side and exposed my neck to him. His tongue shot out and he wetted his lips. It elongated and appeared unnatural. He brought his face to my neck, and I inhaled sharply, anticipating the pain. I closed my eyes. Instead of a bite, warm air brushed my neck. Damian laughed cruelly and tsked.

"Oh, nightshade, you're forgetting one thing."

I flinched. He wanted to play games with me. He wiggled a finger in front of my face.

"You can't heal from my bites yet. A mark here would be... risky."

Shit. I hadn't thought about that. "Where then?" I asked without thinking.

He ran the same finger from my ear down to the collarbone, pausing there and then drawing a line lower to the flesh of my right breast. Dread filled me. I shook my head.

"My dresses..." I whispered. Annoyance flashed on his face, and his pupils dimmed. Afraid he'd change his mind about Brie, I dragged the shirt over my head and tossed it away. "Fine, do it there. I'll hide—"

I yelped when his claws clicked into place again. He pressed one of them into my collarbone and pushed a bra strap down my arm. In a flash, his head was at my stomach and the most excruciating pain ricocheted across my body. I'd never been bitten there before, and my internal organs screamed from deprivation of their own life support. I wondered if he'd hit a major vein. Every pull hurt worse than the last. I gritted my teeth at first, but soon let out a bellow I couldn't hold any longer. I pounded and scratched his back, collapsing onto it. The edges of my vision blurred, and I sensed I was on the brink of losing consciousness. Maybe even my life? The Soaz would've blamed my death on an attack by a shifter. With his secret unknown to the Earth-bounders, he would never be implicated.

I crumpled to the floor. An invisible force plowed into me, jolting my body. I convulsed. *Not dead yet*, my soul sang. Through blurry vision, I recognized Damian's face hovering above me. Blood—my blood—stained his lips and dripped down from his mouth. He lapped it up with his elongated tongue.

"What the hell was that?" he asked, intrigued.

"I. Don't. Know."

I pushed up on one elbow and brought my crumpled shirt to the sopping wound. I shot a furious glare at him. If it weren't for my spirit, or whatever this thing was acting as my personal defense mechanism, he would have drained me.

"You seem to know more about me than anyone else. You tell me," I said.

My tormentor sneered. "Perhaps next time, nightshade." He sprang to his feet, the shifter features disappearing. He was the Soaz everyone knew once more. Satisfied with the inspection of his attire, he strode toward the door.

"Bullshit," I called after him. "You don't know."

His dark laughter resonated through the corridor and into the cellar. He turned halfway, sneering down at me.

"Your code is not the easiest to crack, but I always

succeed. Just like I sniffed out traitors at the Fringe. I was going to break the news to your friend myself, but under the circumstances, I guess you might as well tell her. As her *best* friend." There was glee underlying his words. Whatever he planned to say next he intended for the words to knife through me.

"Ashton took his punishment rather well. They raise them tough over there." Another pause. "But it could only end one way."

My mouth worked like a fish's. I wanted to ask the question, but in my heart, I already knew.

"He's dead," the Soaz said as an afterthought as he turned the corner. The echo carried the diminishing sound of his footsteps to me.

I collapsed, numbness overtaking my body and surrounding my erratically beating heart. Was that what mourning felt like? I'd never gotten to mourn my mother's death. As an infant, I knew no better. I didn't know Ashton well enough, so I mourned for Brie. No, my heart wouldn't go numb. I didn't deserve that luxury.

THIRTY-SEVEN

I stepped into the shower fully clothed and activated the cold jets. The water was supposed to bring me the hell back from the zombie state I was functioning in right now. Damian's parting words rang in my head: *He's dead. He's dead.*

I screamed into the wall of the shower, beating my fists against it. *You might as well tell her. As her best friend.*

Brie had just had a baby. I couldn't tell her about Ash. But she deserved to know, even if it broke her. I screamed even more at the injustices of this world.

The cold eventually forced me into action. I flung the wet clothes over the shower glass and scrubbed at dried blood and where the Soaz prodded me with his claws. Although my wound had already scabbed over, it pulsed angrily. I hoped my Earthbounder immunity was strong enough to fight off infection because dying from the Soaz's bite after everything I'd been through would be a crappy way to go.

I stepped out barefooted into the living room. As usual, it was pristinely clean and absent any presence.

"I heard you in there."

I blanched.

Xavier sat in his library with a book in his hands. I'd never seen him there or reading. I assumed his library was a display room no one truly used.

I swept wet strands behind my ear. "I...needed a moment." I swallowed.

"Join me?" He pointed at the other cushioned chair. I ambled over to the bookshelf. I'd been wanting to explore it more ever since I last ventured there. Xavier had some old volumes in his possession that deserved to be explored. From classics to writers I'd never heard of. He also had a collection of unique trinkets. A wooden box with an engraved feather on the top caught my attention. I ran a finger over it. Nostalgia and sadness swathed me. I snatched my hand back and masked a sniffle.

"I have something for you."

I wiped under my eyes before I turned around. Xavier held up my mother's bracelet. My stomach flipped.

"But I haven't graduated yet."

He gave a dry laugh. "Under the circumstances, holding onto it is pointless. Besides, Nelia would've wanted you to have it."

I took the bracelet from him, massaging it between my fingers. The familiar touch.

"I'm guessing she's the reason you have the smartwatch?"

I hesitated. Was Nelia's secret out? I thought I'd been careful with it.

"Don't worry. Hafthor doesn't suspect anything. I wouldn't have put the two together either if it weren't for the fact that she's gone."

My head snapped up. "What do you mean?"

He studied my horrified expression. "Glad to know I wasn't the only one blindsided by this." He flipped a page over. *What?* This wasn't a time to be reading. I wanted to rip the book out of his hands, but on a closer examination, I saw that the hard cover was bending under his grip.

"What...? When?" I struggled with words.

He flipped another page over. "My father informed me this morning that Nelia requested a transfer a few days ago, and he agreed. She left *two* days ago." The sound of the cover being ripped away filled the silence. Neither of us had known. I stared at my—*her*—smartwatch with disgust. I should've pushed her for more information. I should've suspected she was planning a move. But for what?

"Where did she transfer to?" My lip trembled. I was supposed to meet Nelia at the library yesterday, but I never made it.

"The fucking research institute in the Northern region. *As a reproduction volunteer*." He tore the cover in half and threw it across the room. The book was next.

I sank into the chair next to him, shocked. Nelia would've never done that. She was a sword master destined to fight battles, not a baby-popping machine. And she'd never leave without saying goodbye to her brother—the only family member who'd cared for and loved her for all these decades.

Xavier leaped to his feet and wandered to the bookcase and back.

"He's punishing me, isn't he?" I whispered. "I defied him too many times. And the stint in the city yesterday. I bet he just sent her off this morning..." I rattled off my thoughts out loud.

"Don't feel so special. He's putting me in my place."

I stood up, anger swirling in my chest. "Don't feel so special? Maybe you should take your own advice, Mr. Hothead."

His glower was all fire. He strode over, caging me against the bookcase.

"Finally, one thing we agree on—I'm hot. For you." He

crushed his warm full lips against mine. A shock wave rico-cheted to my toes and back up. I shoved him away and ducked under his arm. He remained there with his head hanging low.

"You're not being yourself. I'm going back to the infir-mary," I said, walking backward. Then I hightailed out of the suite, bumping into Mezzo outside the office door. He righted me.

"Is he still reading?" he asked. The question caught me off guard. My forehead furrowed as I shook my head from side to side. Mezzo sighed. "Reading calms him down." With those words, he pushed the door open.

I stared after him for several seconds, adjusted my shirt for no reason, and hightailed out of there. People did stupid things when they grieved. It was only natural for Xavier to kiss me since I was there and probably the only woman around him in the last several days. Right? *Right?*

THIRTY-EIGHT

"Hey, you," I said to a smiling Brie. Today, she sat in a rocking chair that the infirmary had procured for her. The clinic had never served as a maternity ward before. I was impressed with how quickly they adapted. And I was immensely grateful for the secondborns who had readily accepted a human with a shifter baby in their domain. Little Ash was contentedly suckling away.

"I'm gonna check in with Dez and be right back," I whispered. I didn't want to ruin their bonding time. Brie beamed at me. Clearly short on sleep and rest, the bags under her eyes attested to it.

Zed waited for me, leaning against his desk with his legs crossed.

"Any visitors?" I asked. I was specifically referring to one.

"No. Whatever you did last night worked." He folded his arms over his chest. "Did you know?"

"If you're asking about Nelia, no. I swear to you. Xavier told me before I got here."

Zed turned red. "He knew?"

"No. Hafthor told him today. She wouldn't have left like that of her own will. I'm worried for her."

"That makes two of us."

"Make that three." Dez popped out from behind the monitors.

"More like at least four," I added. "Xavier isn't handling this news well either. What do you know about the reproduction research?"

"Officially, they're trying to find a way to make Pures stronger, more pure. They're looking for a God gene in our DNA. But none of their protocols or research is in the public domain. It's all hush-hush," Zed said.

"Zero transparency," Dez added.

"So...what are you saying?" I swallowed nervously.

"That you're right to be worried about her," Zed said. He scowled into the distance.

"Our cousin volunteered in the program a few years ago. They offer significant benefits, and for those of us trapped in menial jobs, it's a definite way out. But we've never heard from her since. I hear that's more common than not, and the institute does not answer to secondborn families. There's no recourse."

"Why would they recruit female secondborns when they can't bear Pure Earthbounders?"

"They're surrogates for cultivated Pure eggs that are fertilized."

"Baby mama is looking your way," Dez said.

I glanced at Brie and waved. She gestured for me.

"Will she be okay?"

"As a matter of fact, Mandi is transferring her to the cottages in the mountains this evening. Her family runs a shelter there, and Invicta allocated a generous amount of funds to care for them. I don't think they'll ever lack a thing."

Only a husband and a father, I thought.

"Do you think...?"

"Yes. This has Nelia written all over it. The Magister is too busy with the council to check in on everything. By the time this detail comes out, it'll be too late. They have scheduled the press conference for tomorrow. Brie will be all over Earthbounder news, and Invicta's generosity will be on full display. Not even the Soaz will want to intervene. That'd be bad publicity for both."

Some weight dropped from my shoulders. Brie and the baby would receive excellent care. Thanks to Nelia.

I squeezed Zed's arm. "We will find her. I will jump through hundreds of alluras if I have to bring her back to us."

I strolled over to waiting Brie, who extended baby Ash out to me. I wrapped my arm around him and nestled his head into the crook of my elbow. His eyes were closed, and he yawned lazily.

"All stuffed, huh?"

Brie chuckled. "He eats nonstop, just like his father."

Tell her, tell her. "Higher metabolism?"

"Must be." Brie stretched and yawned herself. I picked up Ash's little hand and slid my thumb over his tiny fingers.

"How are you? Is everyone treating you well?"

Her bright smile warmed my heart. "They have all been wonderful." She deflated. "But I was told today I'm being relocated."

"Yes, to a cottage in the mountains. It sounds wonderful, doesn't it?"

"I guess. I just thought I'd be with you a little longer. I don't know anyone."

I placed the baby in her arms and knelt by her side. "I promise to visit as soon as and as often as I can. Since I'm not allowed to leave Invicta right now, it may be a while, but we can stay in touch through your caretakers there."

"Are you safe here? Ash didn't talk much about Invicta, but he despised Pures."

I stared into her concerned eyes. "I'm fine, as you can well see for yourself." I made a brave face.

"But you can't leave?" She pursed her lips.

Ah, that.

"I sort of broke a rule when I brought you in here without permission. It's temporary though. When I graduate, I'll be able to travel." I fibbed my ass off. Truthfully, I didn't trust Hafthor. Especially now when he sent off his only daughter to a life equal to slavery to punish Xavier and possibly me too.

Her smile wavered. She wasn't convinced.

I squeezed her arm. "You have to leave tonight. Trust me, this is not a place for you and Ash Junior. Besides, Ashton won't be able to enter Invicta. But he'll be able to reunite with you two outside the institute." And there it was—the lie that brightened her eyes, even though it ate at my soul.

THIRTY-NINE

As the hour to train with Donovan loomed over me, I said my goodbyes to Brie and the twins and headed out to the training facilities. Two of the Magister's guards stood by the entrance, their gazes set on me.

"Pure Blair, your attendance is required at the Pyre," one guard said.

My stomach twisted into a knot.

"Pyre?" There was only one reason the Earthbounders went to the Pyre—aerial training. I had not even gone through any basics of flying. Wasn't there a lesson in theory of flight I had to take first anyway? I sensed the blood draining from my face. I followed them on numb legs.

"This way." The guard gestured toward a small room that most definitely wasn't the Pyre. I stretched my neck to peer inside.

"Oh, here she is." A female secondborn in a flamboyant outfit with knee-high boots stepped over to greet me. She pulled me inside while the guards turned their backs on us. The woman had two assistants waiting by a portable vanity with an oval mirror, with makeup brushes and pencils in their hands. The stylist pushed me into the chair and ripped the elastic out of my hair. I winced.

"Sorry about that. They didn't give us much notice."

The stylist applied a styling substance to my hair while one girl tweezed my brows.

"So...what I'm getting ready for?" I asked.

The women chuckled, glancing at each other. The laugh died out.

"You really don't know?"

"I think my comms device ran an update or something." I shrugged.

"OMG, she doesn't know," one girl said.

"She doesn't know!" the other one squealed.

"Girls compose yourselves," the stylist said.

The assistants busied themselves with matching colors to my eyes and skin. The stylist handed me her tablet and brought up a TV app called *Earthbounder Style & Life*. It appeared to be a gossip site. An overdone young female presenter stood in front of Invicta gates and reported excitedly on a gauntlet tournament announced only last night and how the supernatural community needed that in these intense and uncertain times... The next shot showed her inside a rotund arena interviewing a few of the warriors training there. All Pures and elite, including the children of the councilmen. They kept the interviews light and fun. The reporter flirted with the men, and they charmed her with compelling smiles. What kind of nut house was this?

Mattias stood out from the crowd with his gruff demeanor and ignorance of the reporter's attempts to lighten up their short-lived chat. I smirked. She had picked the wrong Pure.

"What is she talking about?" I asked.

"The gauntlet. In your honor!" the girl couldn't contain the excitement any longer.

I stared at the video. "Is this live?"

"Yes, Irina always gets the inside scoop."

"Because she's the best," the other girl said. They continued back-and-forth compliments for the reporter, Invicta, and the warriors. They truly believed the Pures were this jolly and approachable. Hafthor had succeeded in creating an image of a benevolent leader. I bet the reporter wasn't "lucky" to be here. She was a controlled plant like anyone else the Magister allowed near him.

The stylist dressed me in a black skin-tight suit and leather boots. The heels on those things were five inches high and unsteady. The stylist put my shiny styled curls into a loose ponytail.

I twisted my lips in the reflection. I looked like a Barbie doll from space.

"What? You don't like?" The young women's postures slacked.

"Oh, no, you were phenomenal. It's just not my style." I wrinkled my nose.

"Blair. Time," the guard called.

I teetered over. If Hafthor hadn't killed me by the end of tonight, I was sure the heels would.

The Magister's personal elevator chimed to announce my arrival in his posh suite. The councilmen and their spouses had gathered by the hors d'oeuvre table and the bar. Three rows of red leather chairs faced the open wall into the interior of the Pyre. One guard nudged me along toward the first row where the Magister lounged front and center.

"You're late," he said without looking at me. He rose to his feet, and the hum from all viewing booths around the arena quieted. The councilmen assumed their seats. I was forced to stand by Hafthor's side. I risked a peek at the drop to the floor level far below where warriors gathered. From this distance, they appeared as miniatures of themselves. The Pyre stretched a similar distance upward to a glass-covered dome with steel arms pinnacled in the middle.

A holographic screen displayed halfway between our suite and the other side. It listed the names of the warriors—at least thirty of them—along with a large timer.

"Welcome everyone," boomed the Magister. "It's been a long time since Invicta held an inter-institute gauntlet, and I am honored to renew this tradition. The winner will receive a prestigious award and travel opportunities to institutes around the world to hone his mastery of combat. Begin."

Cheers erupted from all booths. The timer began ticking down from thirty seconds. As we sat, a clear barrier descended from the ceiling to the floor. The booths across from us turned into gray stone that blended in and created one smooth wall of the interior of the Pyre.

Five...four... The floor beneath us turned transparent and I squeezed the armchairs. The ceiling and half of the walls turned into translucent surfaces. Three... The warriors' weapons became semi-transparent. They stood still, exchanging casual yet calculating glances. Two...one... *Woosh.* Most warriors took to the air, where they clashed with their selected opponents. I glanced below my feet resting on the transparent floor. A few pairs of warriors sparred there. I flinched when the soles of warrior boots ran across the front view barrier and then pushed off into the air again. The scene reminded me of hummingbirds chasing after each other, although my newfound Earthbounder ability allowed me of track their fast movements this time versus only a few weeks ago. The warriors shot across the Pyre in all directions, hovered and sparred, assessed situations from some vantage point, and fought with the aim of delivering a killing blow.

Their weapons got disengaged somehow. Each hit counted and left a physical mark. Although no one showed their pain, the ones who got hit often slowed down, even if only for a second. The weapons affected them but didn't draw blood. The first warrior got eliminated, and a red flash appeared on the holographic screen. I didn't recognize that Pure, but the emblem by his name implied he was from Invicta. He held his side as he ambled toward an opening at the bottom of the Pyre.

A figure slid into the empty chair next to mine. He wore an all-black outfit including a black dress shirt. I immediately removed my arms from the armchair we shared and crossed them over my chest.

"*If you wanted to coordinate outfits with me, you could've just asked. For the record, I prefer none,*" the Soaz said in my head.

Get out! I thought back but, of course, he wouldn't hear it. So, I ignored him instead, focusing on the competition in front of me. The Soaz rested his elbow on the armrest between us, twiddling an item between his knuckles. His fist was practically in front of my face, so I had no choice but to notice the item in his possession. It was a large dark green button. No! Nelia owned an oversized knit sweater with buttons like those. Tension coiled through my body. I shifted my eyes to his smug face.

"*Are you enjoying the show?*"

Was he referring to the gauntlet or his little performance? I shook my head.

"*I guess you wouldn't when the winner is to take the place of your beloved protector.*"

My lips parted.

"*No one told you? Not even my little brother?*" His devilish chuckle rang in my head. "*It's ironic, isn't it? I'm the last person you'd ever trust, yet I'm also the only one who never lies to you.*"

FORTY

I stared forward for the remainder of the gauntlet, not seeing or watching. I tuned everyone out, including the Soaz who got rather agitated by my lack of reaction to him.

A bell announced only two warriors remained in the competition, and Hafthor called for a break before the final showdown. The spectators rushed for refreshments. Except for me and the Soaz. I glanced at him.

"If you always tell the truth, what's the Magister's plan when it comes to me?" I whispered, hoping to keep it below Earthbounder hearing levels.

"You're his way to sealing an alliance with the institute he deems worthy of the honor, most devoted to him, one that listens to him. Xavier refuses to marry and becomes more difficult to control year after year—honestly, that's the only trait I approve of in my brother—but it comes with consequences... But I digress. He's going to promise your hand in marriage. You've played into his hand quite nicely over the last few days by befriending the council. And many of their sons have become enamored with you, so it won't be difficult to convince them..."

Blood drained from my face. "You're lying."

"*Believe what you want.*" He got up.

"Last test, then. Where is Nelia?" I swallowed. I fought to ignore the fact that he had one of her buttons. I didn't want it to be true.

He jeered in that grotesque way of his. "*Unfortunately, not with me. I never had the opportunity to* enjoy *my half sister's company.*" He strolled over to the bar, his comment leaving a sour taste in my mouth. "Enjoy" his half sister? His enjoyments lay elsewhere. I believed him when he said Nelia wasn't accessible to him, though. Thinking back to all my conversations with the Soaz, I couldn't recall a single time he'd lied. He obscured, sure, but never outright lied.

The party returned to their seats, including the Magister. He rumbled off a few words of encouragement to the finalists. For the first time, I glanced down at them. Zephyr and Mattias were the last two warriors standing.

"*Choose wisely, little nightshade,*" Damian whispered into my mind from the back of the room. I scowled. *What did he mean by that?*

The audience around the Pyre erupted in cheers as the counter reached zero, and warriors shot straight up under the glass dome. They collided there first. Their swords locked between them, and they pushed off, somersaulting in the air to the opposite walls. They rushed each other and plummeted to our level where they separated again. Zephyr landed in the middle of our screen. He whisked his head in my direction and winked before he slipped away right before Mattias's boots hit the screen with an audible thud.

They kept at it, testing each other's strengths and weaknesses until they dropped to the ground and fought with a dexterity and precision I envied. I slid to the edge of my seat, tracing their movements. As quickly as an opportunity arose for a warrior to gain the upper hand, it vanished just as swiftly, leaving no one with an advantage.

Zephyr flew over Mattias only to be kicked in the stomach and nearly hacked in half, but he ducked in time. With a practiced maneuver, he took out Mattias's legs from underneath him and held his sword at the other warrior's throat. For a human, this last sequence would've happened in the blink of an eye. For the first time, I was able to trace all of their movements with ease. That fact fascinated and perturbed me on some levels because I feared losing my humanity at the expense of my new gifts.

I followed Hafthor's example by standing and clapping in celebration of the victor. Zephyr's eyes glowed. He should've been proud of himself. Defeating all twenty-nine elite warriors was an achievement of the highest class. I smiled down at him.

All thirty warriors stepped back into the arena. The platform rose to our level while the transparency dissolved, and the safety screen lifted.

"Congratulations to this year's winner, Zephyr of the Northeast region."

Applause followed.

"Now. As you all must be aware by now, Pure Blair's protector Kolerean has deserted his duty," Hafthor said.

My tongue stuck in my mouth. *Wh-what?!* I forced myself to stand still.

"Powers can be flimsy. It is only appropriate Arien selects a protector from among our best Seraph warriors." He glanced at my confused face.

Choose wisely. Damn it, the Soaz tried to warn me about this.

Someone cleared his throat. Oh, I guess it was my turn to speak. I stepped forward, scanning the proud and confident faces of the warriors. Zephyr smirked, his eyes glinting. I swallowed.

"I, um... You've been all wonderful." I wriggled my hands behind my back, inhaling deeply. "If I must select a new protector, I pick myself. My protector Kolerean has been nothing but loyal to me. So, until I'm provided proof of Kole deserting, I will stand on my own and await his return. I owe him that much, to remain loyal to my protector."

Hafthor's expression hardened. Clapping sounded from behind us. Councilman Elyon approached.

"I say that's an honorable decision."

"I concur. Besides how can she possibly choose from the greatness that's before her," Magister Gavriel said.

"Very well," Hafthor said. "Let us celebrate the victor with a feast at the Grand Hall tonight. Open to all Invicta residents." Cheers and whistles erupted. All Hail Caesar.

The warriors' arena lowered again. Elyon pulled me back by my elbow before I fell on the platform.

"Thank you," I said. He wrapped my arm around his and began walking out.

"It's very brave what you did just now. And honorable. But be careful, Arien. I've known Hafthor for a long time. You can only prod him so many times before he explodes. And he will retaliate."

"I'm aware," I whispered back. Elyon peered at me.

"Then you're braver than I thought." He kissed the top of my hand in the corridor and departed.

The council members each approached me one by one to shake my hand, congratulating me on my choice. Magister Mariola was last. As she shook my hand, she paused and turned our joined hands over so that my wrist was on top.

"That's an unusual bracelet," she said.

"Thank you." After another pause, I tugged my hand free. Mariola strolled past me without another word. Her behavior struck me as odd. I should've tried to engage her in a conversation before, knowing now that Nelia was in her region's research institute. But my instincts told me Magister Mariola was too close to Hafthor to be of any help in this situation.

Hafthor's guards waited for me.

"Where are we going?" I asked one of them in a quiet voice. For a second his brows furrowed.

"We have orders to escort you to your suite," the second guard answered. I nodded and let them guide me.

"If you picked one warrior as your new protector, we wouldn't have to escort you," the first guard grumbled.

"And lose your delightful company? Never."

FORTY-ONE

The guards surprised me by allowing me to return to the infirmary instead of Xavier's suite. I wasn't ready to face him yet. Besides, nothing eases a nasty headache like holding a tiny bundle of joy. I couldn't wait to squeeze those chubby cheeks and let his tiny fingers wrap around my finger.

I halted halfway to Brie's bed. The fact that it was empty wasn't a problem except someone had stripped the bed and taken the bassinet. Someone had tucked away the rocking chair into a corner.

Quiet footsteps approached my side.

"Mandy took the opportunity to relocate Brie and the baby while the gauntlet was taking place to avoid any scrutiny from the Magister's office. He wasn't to be bothered, and since Nelia processed the release, gate guards wouldn't stop them," Zed said.

I nodded.

"She did well," I said with a hardened voice. There was no time for tears or goodbyes. It was better this way. If Damian

was correct—and he insisted on telling the truth—I didn't
have much time left at Invicta myself. At least I wouldn't
have to worry about leaving Brie behind.

I ambled toward the rocking chair and plopped into it. *What
should I do now?* I had only formed a plan to visit my friend but
nothing beyond that. My eye caught a scrap of material sticking
out of the side between the cushion and the armrest. I pulled out
a velvety powder blue blanket, maybe two-by-two feet square,
and brought it to my nose. Ash's baby scent, or more accurately,
baby lotion, lingered on the material. I lowered it to my chest
and began rocking. *I won't fall apart*, I told myself. *I won't!*

A single tear rolled down my cheek.

"God damn it!"

A female medic working in the corner nearest me leaped
out of her chair.

"Is everything all right?" she asked, frowning at me.

"I'm sorry."

"Ignore her, Cindi," Zed said with a lopsided smile. It was
only him and the woman in here now. With no one to take
care of, the staff had resumed work at their other stations.
The infirmary was a dead zone once more. I wondered if they
missed Brie and baby Ash as much as I did. But then she had
been here for only a few days. I closed my eyes and nestled
comfortably into the chair.

My smartwatch buzzed. I reluctantly cracked an eye open.
Xavier wrote: *My suite. Now.*

I turned the screen off and snuggled in deeper. Who
knew nursery chairs were so comfy? Not a minute later, my
smartwatch buzzed again. *Don't look. Don't look.* Ugh. The
curiosity in me won over. I glanced at the screen, and in the
next instant, I was running across the infirmary. I gave Zed a
thumbs-up and kicked it into fifth gear as soon as I turned
the corner.

One word. *Kole.* That was what Mezzo sent me. He was back!

I tore into the door to the suite and ran inside, panting. Xavier, Mezzo, and Anhelm sat on the couches in the living room with morose expressions. I slowed down. An unpleasant realization dawned on me like a stone being cracked on my skull.

"He's not here. Then why? Is he in trouble?" I fixed my eyes on Mezzo. I refused to believe Mezzo would agree to use his name as a ruse to get me over here. Xavier would've done it, but not Mezzo.

"We need to talk," Xavier said. He faced the fireplace with his back to me. I rounded the couch and stood facing him, with Anhelm sitting on the couch behind me.

"Yes, we do." Rage fueled my words. His head lifted, revealing a confused expression. The two warriors ambled to the bar. I guessed they'd pretend not to hear for the next however many minutes.

"I know my behavior earlier—"

I threw my hands in the air. "Is Kole all right?"

"As far as we know."

"Meaning?"

"His access to Invicta was revoked. That's why he hasn't returned yet."

I folded my arms over my chest, shivering from rage. I had no doubt Hafthor was behind it. I lowered my piercing gaze to Xavier.

"Were you aware of your father's plans to use me as his political pawn?"

"What are you talking about?" he asked.

I scoffed. "What about the gauntlet?"

"I was informed of it taking place this morning."

"Before you saw me?" I raised my eyebrows.

Xavier slowly rose to his full height, towering over me. "What are you insinuating?"

I continued to challenge him with an impetuous glare.

His eyes narrowed with understanding. "I'm not your enemy."

"Prove it."

"I sent Anhelm and two other trusted warriors in search of Kolerean."

I glanced over my shoulder at Anhelm, who inclined his head. Some steam seeped out of me. *Was I completely misreading the situation?* The Soaz's words messed with my head.

"Why not tell me?"

"We didn't know what we'd find, and you had enough to worry about with the strict schedule he keeps you on."

I bit my lip, staring at my boots. A minute ago, I was ready to rip his head off. I wasn't ready to admit my mistake yet, though. But I sat down as a peace offering.

"What did you find out about Kole?"

"He hasn't been captured even though the Magister listed him on the dark pages. We have some spies among the users who confirmed it," Anhelm said from the bar.

"We think he's hiding nearby though," Xavier said. "He's waiting to explore a weakness in Invicta's security."

"Can you communicate with him?"

Xavier shook his head. "Too risky."

Why would Hafthor want Kole captured, though? The move would tarnish his reputation. Unless he only wanted Kole out of the way. As in permanently removed... I sank into the couch, chewing on my inner cheek.

"He needs to stay away and forget about me. Is there a way to send a secure message out to him?"

Xavier leaned forward, his forehead furrowing with thought. "You really think it's that easy?"

I closed my eyes with pain I'd tried to hide since he'd left. Xavier wasn't referring to my question, but to Kole being capable of forgetting me. If he felt even a fraction of the emotions I had for him, he would never forget.

FORTY-TWO

My evening schedule opened up. Well, not completely, but Master Pietras didn't need to know I swapped my conditioning in favor of a run to the Invictus Lake. Tomorrow, the council members would travel back to their institutes. The fissure site had been inactive since Bezekah's appearance and the novelty of the new Pure had worn off. They'd return to normal, the status quo for Earthbounder leaders. A nagging roiling in my stomach told me my troubles were only beginning though.

I was hell-bent on removing Kole from my life. I now understood that Hafthor had unsavory plans for me. Plans I'd attempt to avoid but on my own. Any association with Kole and the Soaz's dogs would hunt him. I refused to put him in that situation.

The Invictus Lake was the closest magical source I could access since I couldn't leave Invicta. Perhaps it could remove the protector mark. After all, the Everlake had given him the mark, and water was water, right?

I didn't know much else about the Invictus Lake other

than it was home to the capricious and dangerous nymphs called the Sisters of the Lake, but I was desperate.

I hopped down the trail from the parking area to the basin below. The beach was solemnly empty today. A volleyball net hung to my left and an extinguished bonfire lay in peace in the distance to my right. I trudged across to the sand and the boardwalk until I reached its end and knelt at the edge. Where the Everlake was a clear sheet of water with a pristine transparent quality, the Invictus Lake was dark and opaque. The water constantly rippled across the surface, uneasy.

The sun hid behind the tree-covered hill, weaving beams of yellow light around the trunk and branches as if pointing at something with a laser. A ray of light blinded me momentarily before it skimmed across the boardwalk to the water. It cut through the top layer of murkiness, reflecting surrounding trees and...snow-capped mountains? I swiveled my head around. There were no mountain caps around the lake. I peeked inside the water again, and clearly, mountains stood watch over the water there.

I gasped.

Giggles floated to me on the breeze that swept across the lake. Luminous chartreuse lights from within the lake traveled toward me from different directions as if someone had submerged flashlights and was dragging them around. When they were close, one small face with bulging eyes peered at me from below the surface. The mysterious Sisters of the Lake decided to show themselves to me again.

"Are the lakes connected?" I asked. The nymph's ears flopped with fin-like protrusions, and her thin lips stretched. Was that a *yes*? There was only one way to find out. My mind resisted the idea. The nymphs were capricious and last time I nearly drowned. Donovan had explained they'd judged me worthy then. I crossed my fingers and slipped into the water legs-first.

The lake was even colder than I remembered. Four or five slender figures with gossamer material wrapped around their bodies circled me. I squinted in the murky water, searching for the mountains when bony fingers wrapped around my ankle and dragged me down into absolute darkness. I gulped water in before I forced relative calmness and resisted fighting them. A light source appeared below us, growing brighter. The water transformed into a crystalline state and flung me onto a hard surface. As I lay on a massive stone rock, my lungs burned, and I gulped the air hungrily. Maybe there was an oxygen spell I could learn for the next time I accepted help from wacky nymphs?

I pushed off a stone rock to a sitting position. A puddle of clear water the size of a bathtub glistened next to me. Gray rock rose on all sides of it and above me out toward an opening that revealed snow-capped mountaintops in the distance. I trudged to the opening. The magnificent Everlake lay still as if frozen in time a story below me. I descended by climbing the rock down to a ledge.

"I want... I ask for you to remove Kole's protector mark," I said loud and clear. I squinted across the lake. Surely something should happen, a sign of sorts. Hanging my head low, I sighed. Had I come all this way for nothing?

I dipped a finger into the water to distort the failure staring back at me and pushed to my feet.

"Arien." The urgent whisper reached my ears. I tilted on my feet to peek over the ledge. Like in my dream, a reflection of Sylvan's face stared at me.

"Sylvan?" My legs weakened, and I knelt by the water again. His godlike reflection, or perhaps it wasn't a reflection at all, came in steady. The glacial blue eyes appeared to gaze at me from across a vast window.

"You've not visited lately." I detected a hint of accusation in his tone. Although his serene expression made me question myself.

"I've not needed the stone," I said, shrugging. "Is the Sky Ice there?" Where was there? Neither P6 nor the council knew from what dimension the stone that had saved my life and defeated Bezekah originated. Or why it had assisted me.

"Yes. It's safe and pulsing with more energy ever since it reconnected with you."

"Reconnected?"

"You don't belong there. Your home is here, on Ariada."

Ariada. It finally had a name. And it called to me. Tears welled up in my eyes. I missed it. Somehow, although I'd never been there in this life, my inner being recognized this name and yearned for it. Involuntarily, I lifted off my knees and pressed down above the water calling to me. Promising eternal peace. *Home*.

Sylvan's expression turned gentle and warmth filled me. "Your home is with me," he whispered.

I straightened my elbows, shaking my head. No, that was a lie. My soul rejected his belief. I shouldn't have come here. Kole needed me. Thoughts of him filled my heart with yet another sort of yearning. It felt like home too.

I opened my mouth to say goodbye. Sylvan's eyelids lowered to dangerous slits upon noticing the change in me. A hand breached the surface, sending shards of water around me.

"You must come." His voice boomed on a sudden gust. Steel-cold fingers wrapped around my neck and yanked me down.

FORTY-THREE

T he skin under the anti-allura bracelet heated. Oh no! I yelled for Sylvan to stop, but there was no time to explain. I squeezed my eyes shut, readying for the impact. My cheek connected with the surface first, hitting a solid wall. A force blasted me upward in the air, sending me into a spin. The cave opening sucked me in, causing my back to curve forward. Disoriented, I failed to fill my lungs before the nymphs snatched me and dragged me into the dark water of the Invictus Lake.

I swallowed water and weakness began spreading over me. I'd become weightless.

A hard object pressed into my sternum in equal intervals. I moaned and coughed up fluids. I came to, lying on my side on a boardwalk. I ran a hand over my face and flopped to my back. My arm brushed a pair of shoes. I froze, my eyes wandering up a statue of a warrior with a dissatisfied face.

Donovan loomed above me. His head bent down, eyes scrutinizing. He wore dress pants and a pressed shirt. I propped myself onto my elbows, peering in horror at the white marble mansion—Invicta's form of gentlemen's club.

The council and their advisers were meeting there this evening for their last strategic session. The nymph ladies had it in for me to put me at the mercy of Pures every time I landed in this cursed lake.

"So...you really like the evening swims with clothes on, don't you?" Donovan asked.

I flashed back to the presses on my chest and lingering soreness there.

"Uh...thank you...for the CPR." I forced my wobbly legs to support me upright. "I'm gonna go..." I peered around him for an alternate route. The last time I was here, the only exit was the side garden gate. By the back door, which now stood ajar with bodies milling around near it. I couldn't be spotted by the council and Hafthor. One silhouette strode in our direction, and I sidled closer to Donovan to hide my frame behind his.

He didn't move.

"What're you hiding over there?" a familiar voice asked.

Galadon, son of Magister Aur, neared us. Upon seeing me, a sneer replaced his teasing tone.

"Seriously? I'd think Paulyna would keep your attention longer," he said.

"And I told you, you can have her."

"Did she swim all the way to meet you?"

I stepped away from them. "I'm standing right here, you shit-hole," I said.

Galadon chuckled. "What? He will do, but I won't?" He cocked his head.

"We're not having a secret rendezvous... The nymphs find it funny to dump me on this side of the lake," I said.

Donovan's eyes roamed over the water. He stepped out of his shoes.

"What are you doing?" Galadon asked.

Donovan slapped him on the arm. "Remember when we

used to tempt our fate out here?" He asked. His gaze roamed over the cliffs in the distance.

"Yeah, we were children then."

"You afraid?"

Galadon's features hardened as he stripped his shoes off.

"She's coming with us," he said. I took another step back and nearly tipped into the lake. Donovan gripped my collar and balanced me.

"You want to get out of here unnoticed, don't you?" he asked.

The men slinked their way along the shore. The vegetation here was rough and overgrown, intruding into the water. I weighed my options: the mansion, the lake, or the cliff. Of course, jumping off the cliff was the most logical choice out of the three—I mean, it was me, for god's sake.

"Wait," I whisper-shouted and hurried after them before the darkness camouflaged their shapes. The side of the cliff was steep, and both Donovan and Galadon took turns pulling me up with them.

"Is this safe?" I asked. Invicta's evening lights shone in the distance above the trees, and the roof of the mansion was a small rectangle from this vantage point. The men chuckled.

Below the cliff, the water blended with jagged rocks in the dim sunset filtering through thinner parts of the clouds.

Galadon whooped into my ear, and I shoved him away. He shoved Donovan, and I shook my head. If the excitement was getting to them now, I wondered what they'd been like as children coming out here.

My heart thudded in my chest. There was no turning back.

"Ladies first," Galadon said. Challenge hung heavy in the air. Donovan stood to the side, his expression unreadable. I flicked my wet hair over the shoulder. Drops splashed Galadon's face and he smirked. I took ten steps back, pulled up my elbows with one foot set forward, and rocked back one time before sprinting forward. Blood rushed to my head, and my ears squealed with loud ringing. I pushed off the cliff with an earsplitting scream.

I windmilled my arms profusely, hoping to get farther into the lake and avoid the rock outcroppings. I wasn't confident. But the Earthbounders had been doing it for centuries and survived, so I'd survive it, too.

I straightened my legs and crossed my arms over my chest as I breached the water. I went in like a bullet and, as soon as I could, I swam to the surface. A substantial shadow stuck out of the water about twenty feet away. I scaled the rock and maneuvered my way to the other side where smaller rocks formed a line for the shore. I balanced on the slippery surface with caution.

A splash echoed behind me, chased by another. I bounded into the shallow water and sloshed my way to the rock-lined shore. Wading into the bushes and trees, I finally stopped to catch my breath. I bent forward, resting my hands on my knees. My body shook like a starved adrenaline junkie. In my case, I didn't miss life-threatening situations, though.

"Arien," Donovan called out. "Arien!" The voice carried closer.

"Leave her. I saw her getting out of the water. She's fine."

"She's not dying on my watch," Donovan said brusquely.

I slowed down my breathing and remained perfectly still.

"She's more of a survivalist than any of us. Let's go."

Rocks crunched under determined feet in two directions —one down the coastline and the other toward my hiding spot. Small shrub branches snapped. I slowly slid down the side of the trunk and folded myself into a ball.

"I know you're still here," Donovan said softly. "Listen carefully. Do *not* return to Xavier's suite tonight. Throw your smartwatch in the lake and go to the secondborn wing and your old quarters there. I will meet you there later tonight." Silence. I counted five more seconds.

"If you want to live after tonight, you will do as I say," he said with exasperation.

Tiny rocks crunched beneath feet, the sound fading into the distance.

FORTY-FOUR

I wrapped my arms around my head. What the hell did all that mean?

It was only me and a comforting darkness that remained. After several minutes of numbing indecision, I abandoned my spot and meandered through the vegetation near the lake line. The sun dipped below the horizon while a new moon rose against the night sky. From the Invictus beach, I hiked up the hill to the parking level and jogged on my regular path back to the institute. The outdoors was quiet and empty. Every Earthbounder who wasn't on patrol tonight was participating in the festivities in celebration of the tournament's winner.

Surprisingly, Hafthor didn't send a message directing me to appear tonight. Maybe he'd started taking me for granted, and if that was the case, he would regret it tonight on the last night of the council's stay at Invicta. The tournament earlier today removed any remaining willingness to subjugate myself to the company of the councilmen and their offspring. I used to think gaining some of the councilmen's favor could prove an asset against Hafthor in the future. Now, I doubted any of them would dare stand up to him when it came to me. In their eyes, I was a useful pawn and nothing more.

I rubbed my forehead. Donovan's warning continued to replay in my head.

Should I heed his warning?

I peered at the smartwatch on my wrist. Holding onto it had its cons, such as Hafthor knowing my whereabouts, but he had the face recognition software on his side as well, and it had its pros, such as providing access to most places and communications among others.

I strode to the west wing's staircase, feeling more confident with my decision.

Donovan had shown no interest in my well-being until today, which seemed fake and opportunistic.

I unlocked Xavier's floor security door with my smartwatch.

Donovan had a hidden agenda.

My reasoning insisted I was making the right call. So, why did it feel like I was walking down the plank to my death?

The doorknob to Xavier's receiving office felt warm to the touch. As the door eased open, two Earthbounder silhouettes came into view.

"The Magister wishes for you to join him for dinner," Hafthor's personal guard said.

FORTY-FIVE

I ambled into Hafthor's excessive dining room. The table alone could fit thirty guests. He sat at the head of the table. Xavier stood by his side, both warriors watching me with alike eyes, one pair only a shade darker than the other. The table was set for three. Without being asked to, I rounded the table at the opposite end and stopped by the chair on Hafthor's left side.

"Sit," the Magister said. Out of nowhere, a servant appeared to pull my chair away for me and then scooted it in. Xavier glanced at me from across the table with a hint of confusion. He was letting me know he wasn't clued in as to what this was. My pulse spiked, but I gave away nothing externally.

The servants brought creamy soup and warm fragrant bread. I followed Hafthor's suit by dipping the bread into the liquid. We ate in silence until he finished, and then the servants brought in pork chops, potatoes, and a selection of salads. The well-plated food enticed my eyes, but my stomach hardened with the unspoken tension. I pushed the food around the plate.

"Not hungry?" the Magister asked.

"Not anymore," I said.

He made eye contact with a servant, and the plate disappeared from under my nose, just like that. Xavier's eyebrows furrowed. He took another bite of the meat. I sipped on the water, waiting but not willing to risk Hafthor's wrath by asking questions. I couldn't wait to return to Xavier's quarters and tell him about my suspicions about his brother. The Magister swallowed his last piece and swirled his wine before gulping what remained in his glass.

"It hasn't escaped my notice you've gotten rather comfortable with my son," Hafthor said. I blinked.

"Father—"

"I'm not finished." The Magister placed both palms on the table and instantly appeared taller and mightier. "Invicta is in a politically precarious position. Some declared their undying commitment to our leadership, but others demanded parity. I've been long debating the best approach. I consulted with council members on this point, and I've decided Arien must marry Aur's eldest son to secure a union between our regions. Of course, others are oblivious to Aur's true allegiance to me. The marriage will also shut any accusations of Invicta trying to keep her to ourselves."

"What about her schooling? Everyone agreed she needs to graduate and then the matter will be revisited at the next council meeting twelve months from now." A vein on Xavier's temple engorged and pulsated.

"And today, the council revisited the matter."

"Without the Oath Keeper present."

"What are you insinuating, son?" The men exchanged charged, vehement glares. Xavier's chair scraped the floor, and he rose to his feet.

"I think it's time for Arien to return to the suite." Xavier extended his hand. I rose to unsteady legs, holding Xavier's gaze, when Hafthor clamped my arm.

"Not so fast." His head swiveled toward Xavier. "I've made better arrangements for our guest." Cold seeped into my veins, and I trembled. Xavier's fingers curled into a fist.

"Arien is now Invicta's most precious asset and, as such, deserves the best accommodations in the safest location. I had the staff move her belongings to your mother's suite. I will station my guards outside and throughout the corridor. Absolutely nobody will be able to get to her, and there are no escape routes for her either." Hafthor's dark eyes swept over my shocked face.

"That's a little excessive—"

"It's settled, son. You're dismissed. I expect you to lead a team tonight scouring New Seattle for the rebellion. You've been staying at Invicta far too long, and I think fresh air will make you see things in a clearer light."

Xavier's chest rose and deflated. His eyes paused on my face and resolve set into his expression.

"I think you're right, Father. I need to get out. These walls have been closing in on me."

Hafthor nodded. I tried to get Xavier's attention, but I'd become mute. Hafthor held me in place, and I suspected he had used some compulsion on me. My legs wouldn't budge.

Why was he leaving me? Xavier had sacrificed and rescheduled some of his time for me. I hadn't realized I was such a burden. I rather suspected he'd come to enjoy our banter and me standing up to him. But I was wrong. So devastatingly wrong.

Xavier had left me in the hands of a monster.

Hafthor didn't relent his hold on me. He dragged me

across the hall into a splendid suite across from his, which used to be his wife's sanctuary. He hauled me across a seating area with white posh couches and chairs into a grand master suite with a king-size bed in the middle. White curtains framed the four corners of the canopy above it. Hafthor pushed me forward, and I rolled across a golden duvet.

"Why am I here?" I asked. Not for a second did I believe his story.

Hafthor strolled out of the suite.

"Wait!" I leaped off the bed, my leg catching on a darned curtain. I fell to one knee and tugged on the curtain until it ripped. The door closed and a lock clicked at the entrance. I scampered to the front door, trying the knob. I banged on the door next.

"Let me out!"

A fist blasted the door from the other side. "Shut the fuck up. I don't want to be listening to your whining while we stand here," one of the Magister's guards said.

I took a few steps back and turned around. I ran up to the windows and released the notches only to find the windows permanently shut. I picked up a vase and it shattered against the thick glass. Wrapping arms around my head, I collapsed to my knees and screamed.

FORTY-SIX

I cried myself to a semi-comatose state. Nightmares chased each previous one away—Kole leaving, Nelia's absence, Xavier leaving me with his father. I was unable to keep people I cared about in my life. Cursed.

A blurred shadow came into view in the doorway. I lifted my head, blinking. Hafthor stood there with a satisfied smirk.

"What are you doing here?" I asked. Darkness had not yet lifted outside.

Two of his guards marched in. They circled my arms in a rough hold.

"No!" I tried to punch one guard in the nose but missed. The other one grabbed my ankle and squeezed until I cried out. "I'll do what you want. I will marry whoever you want me to."

Hafthor grunted. "Of course, you'll do as I say. I need one more thing from you."

The guards dragged me to him, restraining my arms behind my back.

"What is it?" I asked. Saltiness dripped into my mouth.

"Did you really think I'd give my competition an advantage over me? While together you may have a child or two, I can have an entire gifted army."

Blood drained from my face, and my legs weakened.

"You want to have children with me?"

His dark laugh resounded all around me until he sobered. He closed the space between us.

"There was a time, I thought, perhaps..." He ran fingers from my temple down to my lips.

"But sadly, your tastes have not refined." He pinched my chin and stared intensely into my eyes.

"I want your eggs." The corners of his mouth slowly curved up, a cunning sneer overtaking his expression. My breathing quickened. Hafthor pushed my chin away, and a cloth covered my mouth and nose. I panicked and kicked forward. But I was too late. I inhaled enough of the substance from the cloth to become lethargic. My eyelids fell as I struggled to hold my breath.

Hafthor's retreating figure became hazy. He stopped in the middle of the living room and turned back.

"Tell the doc, if she's not able to have children after his procedure, then well, things happen..." My head lolled forward, but I could swear his eyes darkened. Then, it was lights out for me.

———

I mumbled incoherent things before I fully awoke. A white sheet covered me from the neck down, but I still had my clothes on and even my boots, which reassured me no one had yet done anything to my body. They tied my forearms to the rails on both sides of the table, and trapped my legs at the end of the bed with thick leather straps. Pounding reverberated through my head. *Ow.* I rested my head back against the table and closed my eyes. Whatever it was I'd inhaled caused a hell of a withdrawal. Footsteps sounded on the other side of the room, and I stiffened. The swiveling door swished open.

"I just arrived," a masculine raspy voice said to a muffled voice from a comms device. "Yes, but—" Pause. "As you wish. I will proceed now. At least she won't need anesthesia since the dose she inhaled will keep her dreaming for another several hours." A few more yeses were said, and he hung up.

"I should've gotten the gig at the Pacific Institute. At least I wouldn't be operating without consent," the surgeon muttered under his breath. Latex slapped against skin. He was getting ready, which meant I had very little time.

I tugged at the bonds, but nothing loosened. So, I tugged harder. A small rip sounded, and I opened my eyes. The surgeon stared at me with disbelief written all over his face. Then he scrambled for a cabinet and got a vial with a syringe out.

"No, wait. You don't have to do this," I said. Beads of sweat gathered on his forehead as he stole anxious glances at me and then the syringe he was filling up with the liquid. I suspected it was an anesthetic agent.

"I swear to tell no one if you release me," I said, pulling and tugging at the bonds. More ripping sounded.

"He will kill me. Now, lie down and I promise to make this entire experience brief and painless." He approached slowly with one hand in front of him and the other holding the syringe upward. Could he see if I'd freed myself?

"Stay back. I have a knife." I pressed the tip of the leather strap to the sheet.

He stopped and began lowering his arm. Then he shook his head.

"You don't understand. My family depends on me," he said as his chin set and gaze sharpened. Determination set in his eyes, and I recognized then I'd lost this battle. Hafthor would have my fertile eggs, and I'd be married off and forced to reproduce if I even could. If my body still worked like one of the human's, the doctor would have to cut my ovaries out to get all the eggs. Hot liquid gathered in my eyes, and I yelled, thrashing left and right, and hoping to free at least one hand before it was too late.

FORTY-SEVEN

The surgeon pulled the sheet off me and threw his weight on my left forearm, pinning it under his rib cage. He angled the needle, tapping my inner elbow vein. I jerked up and headbutted him. My right shoulder popped, and fire erupted in my shoulder blade, but I stunned him. He twisted, his back falling on my legs. I lost sight of the syringe. I thrashed harder, rocking the bed. More leather strings ripped around my ankles and left arm. The right arm turned numb.

The surgeon grunted and slid to the floor, shaking his head. He crawled on all fours and the stupid syringe was still in his right hand. I shrieked and bucked. God, I couldn't allow this to happen. I always knew I was broken, but this would shatter me.

He pulled himself up by the edge of the bed with a crazed look in his eyes.

"A femoral vein will have to do then," he gritted.

He raised his hand in the air, ready to stab me when a knife pierced his neck. Blood sprayed into my face, and I sucked in my lips, afraid to get the blood into my mouth.

Someone cut through the straps, and I flopped off the table, landing on top of a body and liquids everywhere.

"For angel's sake, stop screaming. You will alert other guards." Firm hands wiped my face, and the red film lifted from my vision. Kole's chiseled face with concerned eyes hovered above me. I threw myself at him, squeezing his neck. He pulled me to my feet. The door swiveled as Vex and Talen ran in. Xavier and Mezzo deposited two bodies in the corner. Xavier's hardened eyes connected with mine. He was here. *Kole was here!*

"How—" I asked.

"New unit is on its way," Talen said.

"How many?" Kole asked.

"Five, six, maybe."

"Are they Invicta guards?" Xavier asked. His jaw set as he surveyed the bodies he'd rearranged—Invicta emblems visible on their chests. He'd killed his own men. As the future leader of Invicta, that couldn't sit lightly with him.

"They're not wearing Invicta's guard uniform. Is that common?" Talen said.

"No," Xavier replied.

Pounding footsteps grew louder. The five men formed a line in the middle of the room, with the surgical table and me behind them. I ran up to Kole, who held the right end of the line and withdrew a short sword he had strapped to his pant leg. The enemy paused outside the door, and the distinct sound of a machine gun being loaded echoed. The warriors at once released their wings, turning immune to the human-made weapons. Kole's wing struck me, and I hit the wall, sliding down as bullets penetrated the door and even the wall, ripping into the cabinets and the table. I covered my head and flattened myself against the floor. Shooting stopped and yells, grunts, and the sounds of bodies connecting with one another filled the air. One half of the clinic's door slammed to

the ground. The other hung loosely on one hinge. My five
saviors brought the fight to the men in the corridor.

I crawled to the short sword I'd dropped. A heavy boot
kicked it away from me. I gasped and pushed away, but I hit
the metal base of the table. Fur-covered oversized hands
hauled me up and over a massive shoulder. I kicked him in
the gut, and I got punched in the side, blacking out from pain
for precious seconds. When I came to, we'd crossed the
doorway into the mayhem in the corridor. He turned in the
opposite direction.

"Put. Her. Down." Kole's seething voice stopped my
captor's progress. The rumble in his chest shook my body. He
dropped me like a sack of potatoes to the black stone floor.
The monster cracked his knuckles. He was at least double
Kole's weight, and most of it was muscle.

"I will enjoy ripping those useless wings off one at a time,"
he said in a deep voice. Kole stepped forward. I shouted for
him to stay away. Then the mutant's body thumped to the
floor, blackish blood oozing profusely out of his neck. Kole
sheathed the onyx blade to his bandolier as I stared at him
in awe.

"You killed him," I said. At times, I was queen of the
obvious.

"Arrogance was his downfall." Kole pulled me up to stand.
Xavier dispatched the last of the guards by skewering him
through the stomach. I shifted away from blood spreading
over the floor. Even though blood from the surgeon covered
me from head to toe, I didn't want to step in it. So much
blood. It splattered the walls and parts of the ceiling. It was
darker than any blood I'd seen before and the smell... Burnt
flesh. I covered my nose.

"What are they?" I asked.

"My father's new recruits. From the Fringe," Xavier said.
He scowled at the warriors, pausing on Kole. "I don't know

exactly what's going on here. My father hasn't been forth-coming with me lately. You need to take her now and leave before he realizes she's gone."

"I hacked the security feed for all corridors we took," Anhelm said. "They won't even suspect Xavier was involved. We'll have to blame this on you, as her protector." I didn't recall when he joined the fight, but it made sense for someone to cover their tracks.

Kole nodded, engaging his smartwatch.

"My maps don't show this level. Send me an update."

"There isn't one. This is Hafthor's top secret tunnel. We think there are more," Anhelm said.

"We'll retrace our steps together to a visible point on the maps," Xavier said.

He knelt over the body he'd slain, scrutinizing his features. I stepped forward, and an inkling of recognition fired up my nerves. That face looked familiar. And when Xavier pulled down his collar, I gasped. An unmistakable snake tattoo stretched across his collarbones. The warriors joined us, waiting for an explanation.

"He's not from the Fringe. He attacked us downtown. He's with the rebellion," I said.

Xavier rubbed his chin. "I'm afraid only the attack part is true."

What?

"I don't—"

"He's from the Fringe," Kole said. "The question is why Hafthor uses his new proxies to impersonate rebels."

I glanced up at him and then at Xavier. His head bobbed in affirmation. The snake tattoo on the dead body flashed with glossy green scales. It began pulsating as if it were coming to life. An onyx sword swiped the air and separated the man's head from his dead body. I hid my face in Kole's arm on instinct. More darkish blood sprayed the wall and the floor. My breathing hitched.

Mezzo wiped his sword on his pant leg. "He's a snake shifter. You've got to cut their heads off before they can heal the wounds." I gawked at him.

Talen grunted in agreement. Anhelm and Vex pulled the bodies into the operating room.

"Oh-kay," I said, running my hands through my hair. They trembled.

"Hey." Kole crowded my personal space. I inhaled his sandalwood scent—fresh and spicy. It reminded me of our scarce moments together, and a sense of longing reawakened within my heart.

"You left," I said.

He threaded fingers through the hair on the side of my face, bringing us closer until our foreheads touched together.

"Trust me, that was the dumbest thing I've ever done," he whispered against my mouth.

"So, you regret it?"

"Very much." His eyes hardened.

"Good," I whispered back.

Vex touched Kole's shoulder.

"Come on, Casanova. We're leaving this hellhole. Medical labs give me the creeps."

Kole grabbed my hand, falling into a jog behind Xavier and his men. But before we could round a corner, a high-frequency force swept us off our feet from the ground up. My stomach soared to my throat. As quickly as it started, the wave left us, and our boots thudded to the floor. Xavier's eyes shone with untamed chaos.

FORTY-EIGHT

"What the hell was that?" I asked.

"Invicta's alluron was breached," Xavier said. He fumbled for his tablet, unfolding it and swiping his finger over the content. Anhelm inserted a small comms device into his ear and requested an immediate report from guards nearest to the alluron. His face twisted into a grim expression.

"The Magister called in all units to secure the site," he said.

"We're being invaded." Xavier sneered. He turned the screen around. The corner camera in the alluron room showed beings, most resembling the Earthbounders, appearing inside the alluron and freely stepping out of it without any consequences. Not even the Earthbounders were able to cross the alluron from the inside. Some intruders shifted into their hybrid forms with strange wings I'd never seen before, scaly skin, or claws. Some fully transformed into werewolves. Werewolves...

"They're from the Fringe, aren't they?" I asked.

"Yes," Xavier hissed. His fingers turned white from clenching the screen. "Let's go!"

Mezzo had already sprinted down the corridor to pound on the metal. I started after them when Kole's hand wrapped around my bicep and pulled me back. I gazed at him, my eyes round from adrenaline pumping in my veins. Both Vex and Anhelm remained by his side.

"We don't have to join the fight. This is a perfect time to get you to safety," Kole said. What the hell?

"You're joking, right?" I said with heat. "This isn't just Invicta's fight. These half-demons attacked the strongest Earthbounder institute in the world. If they can do this, what's going to be next? On whose watch? Not on mine." I wriggled my arm out of his hold, but he snatched my wrist before I could blink.

"I never said I wouldn't join the fight," he said. "I was hoping..."

"Oh." I relaxed. "That I wouldn't." I finished his unspoken words. I had little chance against these creatures, but if I could help in any way... If I could do anything to help Invicta defeat the invaders... And I knew I could, or at least I'd try even without the assist from other realms this time around.

"I'm coming with you," I said.

It surprised me when Kole simply jerked his head to the side, as if to say, "Let's go." I expected him to object like he had in the past, but maybe he figured that approach would only push me away.

We reached a small metal door near the elevator shafts. The sound of elevator engines reverberated inside the opening like we'd entered a high-traffic highway. We stepped onto a single-person-wide stairwell running against a rotund multi-elevator shaft and raced down. Light flashed below us from an open entrance similar to where we'd entered the stairwell. The ajar entrance turned into a height-challenging tunnel. The warriors in front of me bent in half to traverse it. Kole held the rear.

We stepped onto a short balcony near the elevated ceiling with no way to descend. Below us, dozens of half-shifted creatures and werewolves fought against scores of Earth-bounders. Some brought the fight to the air. At once, the warriors around me sprang their wings, jumping off one by one. I panicked, reaching for my wings and forcing them to respond. Warm hands framed my face and planted a quick kiss on my lips.

"Find your geek friends and figure out a way to shut the alluron down," Kole said to my stunned face. I didn't have time to react. His charcoal wings spread as he took to the air.

I leaned over the railing. Kole, Vex, and Talen formed a triangle back-to-back that plowed through the demonic spawn. I recognized many of Invicta's warriors. Even Paulyna fought in one corner. The attack called for all capable second-borns to join in the fight. Mezzo used his telesomnia gift to subdue the opponents. I couldn't spot Xavier anywhere.

A man with a spider-like substance on the palms of his hands and the undersides of his bare feet crawled up the wall. His black, pupil-less eyes reflected my terrified face. I calculated my chances of fighting this thing off—which were nonexistent—and ran inside the tunnel, closing the gate behind me. I spun around.

The elevators carried reinforcements down to the alluron level. I sprinted down. The stairwell ended two levels above the ground, with no exit points. I ran my hands over the wall, tapping at different points, and...nothing. I guessed I could make the jump to inspect the bottom, but I'd probably break a leg without my wings to float me to safety, and...I winced as a wave of pain brushed over my shoulder blades. My wings didn't like mentioning getting injured. Oh... I bounded down again with my shoulder blades heating uncomfortably. That's right. *If you don't appear, I might even die*, I directed my thoughts at them. A blast of scorching heat pulsed through my chest, and I stumbled. Pulling myself over the railing, I said one last prayer, closed my eyes, and jumped.

FORTY-NINE

Aquarter of the way down, my breath seized. My wings weren't springing out. I began chopping my arms and legs in the air. Ohmagod. The ground surface was rushing toward me. *Swoosh*. My fall slanted to one side as the right wing erupted, but at least I slowed down. Headed for the wall, I planned to use it to slow myself down further. When the left wing burst outward, it yanked me backward. I concentrated on spreading them out like a parachute. My feet touched the ground, and I fell to my knees as my wings contracted around my back. I swear they did that on purpose. They weren't happy with me at the moment.

I brushed my knees off, inspecting my new surroundings. A two-sided metal door stood in an alcove. I hobbled over to it, pressed the door handle, and peeked out. It opened to a narrow corridor lit with floor-strip fluorescence. At one end, there was a staircase. I scooted the other way as boots thumping on the floor and yelling reached me. That had to be one way warriors reached the alluron chamber. I ran up the opposite way, intent on avoiding the Earthbounders. With my wings out now, I couldn't blend in. And I had no idea whom I could trust not to turn me in to the Magister.

I scaled up the staircase a few levels to reach a corridor I recognized as leading to the infirmary. The room was empty, but that was fine. All I needed was a comms device, and Dez tended to store the latest models as keepsakes—at least, that's what he called them.

At some point between my dinner with Hafthor and waking up in a surgical suite, someone had taken away Nelia's smartwatch from me.

I opened cabinets in haste, finally finding a device I recognized. I strapped it to my wrist and... The sound of the heavy mahogany door sliding to a close alerted me to someone entering. I was still crouching behind a desk. I placed my hands on the floor and lowered my head to peek from under the desk. The space was empty. Huh, I guess I'd misheard something. And yet, the pit of my stomach turned heavier, and I struggled to swallow.

"The cameras didn't lie after all..." a dark voice drawled.

I yelped and flopped over to my butt and hands, feeling more awkward with my wings out. The Soaz leered down at me. I scrambled around the corner of a desk and leaped to my feet. In the next second, he was on me, yanking on my hair. I hit a cabinet and a flat screen above it with my head, leaving a crack behind. Warm liquid pooled above my eyebrow.

"Ahh, that's how I like you the most," he said.

I pulled out a scalpel from an open drawer and faced him.

"How? Scared? I'm not afraid of you." Blood dripped down the side of my face.

The Soaz grinned.

"Bleeding," he said. The way he said that one word made me shiver. He removed his shirt and stepped closer. I pressed my butt into the cabinet, swaying the knife in front of me.

"Go ahead. Cut me." He raised an eyebrow. My forehead wrinkled, but there was no time to decode his message. I swiped the knife across his chest, making a clean, swift cut. He hissed, then trapped my wrist above my head. His other hand circled my waist and brought our bodies together, while his mouth descended on mine. I twisted my head to the side, and he laughed into my ear. An oversized rough tongue ran up my cheek.

"Mmm... You taste so good and feel even better than I've imagined."

I recoiled at the idea of him having been thinking about me. That didn't bode well for me with this psychopath. My wings seemed to agree with me as they shook off his prying hand.

"Your wings are magnificent. A perfect blend of innocence and purity I plan to destroy."

"Too bad the Magister is marrying me off," I said.

His hand pinched the back of my neck, forcing my gaze to meet his.

"He might have plans, but I have plans of my own. And only one of us can succeed." He grinned. "He doesn't even see what's coming."

I narrowed my eyes. "You're behind this invasion," I said.

"I might as well take credit for it, but if you think my father was oblivious to it, you're wrong. His conceited ego craves ruling over the Earthbounders, but the council stands in the way." As he spoke, his eyes began glazing over from the effects of my blood. He lowered his head and nosed my neck.

"And you're happy to do his bidding?"

His head snapped back up, and he was fully alert. He grinned.

"You don't even know half of it," he whispered. "I should thank you for your blood donation. After purifying it and processing it through our lab, we cultivated enough of it to create a potent serum. An allura antidote."

I gasped.

"That's right. You're the reason this attack was even possible." Admiration crossed his features while I gaped at him. I shouldn't have ever given him any of my blood. I was so stupid. Hindsight was such a bitch. I swallowed.

"Then tell me. What's your master plan?" I held my breath. He pried the scalpel out of my hand and tossed it away.

"The day I reveal my plans to you might as well be your last. Now, be an angel and wait here while I deal with my brother." He stepped away from me to reveal Xavier standing in front of the door. How long had he been there?

"You used to always eavesdrop on my private conversations, little brother. That bothered me."

Xavier's calm eyes scanned me up and down.

"She goes free. This is between you and me," he said. He stripped off his sword from his back and tossed it to the floor. Then, he did the same with the throwing knives and tech tools. Damian had no weapons on him that I could tell. But with his mutations, he didn't need them most of the time.

"He's more than a Seraph, X. He's mutated with demons, too," I said.

"X?" Damian wiggled his eyebrows. "Is that your new pet name? What happened to *my little bitch*? Is mother's funeral the last time you cried, or do you still cry yourself to sleep?"

With a roar, Xavier tackled Damian. They crashed through a table and exchanged punches. Then, Xavier hurdled backward with the help of his newly released wings.

He swiveled his head toward me and bellowed, "Get out!"

I hesitated and couldn't leave him. Damian was a monster with powers of both worlds—heaven and hell.

Xavier huffed out a breath. "This is my fight. It's been a long time coming."

Damian chuckled, raising himself up with his bat-like wings. His eyes filled with black ink.

"Brother against brother. How poetic."

"So, it's true. You sold your soul to the devil," Xavier said.

Damian shrugged. "Am I the only one who sees it?" he asked with disdain. "We are the most powerful beings on this planet. We're not here to serve ignorant humans. We're here to rule over them and grow an interplanetary empire." The passion of a godlike complex tinged his words.

"I guess we, the Earthbounders, the chosen ones, have small minds." Xavier's sarcasm imbued his words.

"Exact—" Damian's forehead wrinkled. "I'm gonna enjoy tearing you apart."

"You can try."

They clashed, meeting each other halfway. They fought with brutality and savagery. Blows exchanged with blows. Bloodstained feathers lifted in the air. I winced at the sounds of cracking bones. My eyes stayed magnetized to the fight in front of me, but I forced my legs to move. I gripped the edge of the wooden door, heeding Xavier's words and slipping out.

FIFTY

I skirted around the corner. My skin rippled with electricity each time someone passed through the alluron, even though the walls no longer shook. They continued to come, countless numbers of them. I used voice control on the smartwatch, trying different names and phrases to unlock it. Finally, it buzzed to life after I discovered the passcode etched into the band.

"Call Dez." I plugged in a tiny earbud I'd found next to the watch.

"Who is this?" Dez's strained voice sounded in my ear.

"Dez, it's me—don't mention my name. Where are you?" I purposely avoided mentioning my name in case the security system was "listening."

"Oh?" A pregnant second passed. "We're in the tech lab. I think we may be able to shut Invicta's alluron." My heart skipped a beat. That was what we needed.

"Send me your location." The navigation system opened on my watch and a tiny light blinked to life in the central location, one story above the alluron.

"Warriors are everywhere. Use the vent system I marked in green on your dynamic map. It will guide you to us."

"Thanks, Dez. I'll see you soon."

The map changed to a holographic view and zoomed in on my current location. A green dotted line showed the route Dez recommended. I pinched my lips, sensing my dysfunctional wings. *I need you to hide. Just cooperate with me this one time*, I begged. I cursed when they snapped back in, knocking a breath out of me. That was a first. I kicked in a two-by-two vent cover and began crawling.

After countless turns, I stopped inside a vent the navigation showed to be in the center of the tech room. Except there were no vent openings visible. I put my ear to the metal but couldn't discern any sounds outside. I tentatively tapped a code I remembered from my childhood. It wouldn't mean anything to Dez, but it couldn't be mistaken for random noise either. A square of metal in front of my face ground from friction and fell off. I peeked in. Zed tapped a finger to his mouth and motioned me down. I squeezed through with my upper body, gripping his shoulders. He pulled me out the rest of the way into a partitioned area behind frosted glass. He examined my outfit, and his face twisted.

"Are you bleeding?" he whispered.

"Uh, no, that's demon blood."

His eyebrows rose.

"I probably don't want to know..." he whispered to himself. He picked up a pair of trainee uniforms and a packet of wipes.

"Clean up and change before you come out. There are a couple of other scientists here with us, but they're too busy dealing with this crisis to look closely." He nodded at me and left.

I did as instructed and had to force myself to slow down on my way to the brothers. I needed to know what solution they'd come up with. Zed glanced at me, deep grooves in his forehead revealing he was on to something. Dez and I huddled close. He tapped a stylus on his tablet, opening dynamic 3D graphs.

"That's the frequency the alluron is giving off now. But if I drop the jammer in it..." He dragged another pulsing graph as an overlay, and the alluron responded with an explosion akin to a supernova. After the blast, the frequency registered no more.

"It collapsed. That'll seal off the back door," I said with awe. "You have the jammers, right?"

"Not exactly. I have a weaker version of it. You're wearing it," Zed said.

I inspected my wrist.

"We have to try. Take it off."

Zed shook his head. "The Magister is the only one with the codes to your bracelet," he said. "But I made two other prototypes." Dez ran off while Zed cleaned out his desk and procured tools. He exchanged short words with some of the other scientists, and they scampered around gathering other devices and tools.

Dez arrived with two bracelets similar to mine and laid them out.

"Watch the others as they try to recreate my jammer. We could use at least three more, but do your best," he told Dez.

I shuffled out of the way. Zed worked under a sort of microscope, connecting tiny elements of a chip. My thoughts turned to Kole, Vex, and Talen fighting below this room. I worried about Xavier and whether I'd made the right decision by leaving him alone with his nightmare of a brother. That was his fight and he wouldn't have it any other way. I just hoped he came out alive. I swallowed through a constricted throat.

"It's time to test my theory." Zed's words drew me out of my head.

FIFTY-ONE

I joined a small group of scientists who followed Zed out of the lab. Dez squeezed my elbow to reassure me of his presence. We descended a metal staircase to a room equipped with seats. Four rows of seats faced a black shimmering wall. Dez pressed some keys on a wall console and the blackness turned transparent, revealing the alluron and the mayhem around it. The shifter mutants continued to appear inside the alluron. My heart raced as they crossed the barrier with ease. *Thanks to my stupid blood!*

"Can they see us?" I whispered to Dez.

"No. It's a one-way glass on the inside. This particular technology was merged with allura particles, allowing us to see out but not changing the physical property of the interior wall."

One scientist set a small octopodal robot on a podium. Zed opened a compartment inside the robot and placed both bracelets inside. They uncovered a hidden opening in the floor and let the robot inside. Zed controlled it with a tablet. A small opening appeared in the floor in the alluron chamber, halfway between us and the alluron. I gasped and bit into my

fist when a warrior fell, mighty close to squashing the robot.
Zed navigated it through a maze of moving feet and fallen
items and bodies.

At one point, I was certain a fully shifted werewolf was
going to roll over it. But Zed handled himself well and guided
the little machine to the edge of the alluron. We took a
collective inhale, gnashing teeth from anticipation. I grabbed
Dez's arms and squeezed.

"He's doing it..." I whispered.

One bracelet popped out of the container and landed by a
crystal. The stone fizzled and a wave of smoke traveled up the
alluron. It was working! Further to the left, charcoal wings
dove into the air, and my breath caught. I tried not to think
about him. Or Xavier...

Zed guided the spider robot around the alluron and
deposited the second ring on the alluron border. The alluron
sizzled there as well, and the smoke lifted, connecting with
the smoke from the initial ring. I dug my nails into Dez's arm.
The alluron began cracking with electricity all around its
cylindrical surface, but the beings continued to transport
within it and pass through.

"We need at least one more. How much longer?" Zed
called out.

The scientists shook their heads. "Our lead team is
currently studying your blueprint."

Zed marched out of the room with the group. I tugged at
Dez's sleeve.

"Hack mine," I said. His eyes lowered to my wrist. "You're
one of the best around here. You can do it."

Dez scanned the room around us. He pulled me down to a
chair and took out his collapsible tablet from inside his vest. I
held my arm up as he ran the tablet around my wrist, scanning the jammer device. Then he began studying the compo-
nents and tapping away.

"Urgh," Dez said.

"What?"

"Zed placed safeties in place, so no one could hack the device."

"And the Magister has the controller?"

He nodded. "There is no such thing as an unhackable device, though. It will just require some work, and we might get lucky." *Or we may not*, I silently added. Dez continued to tap away on his device. I strode to the one-way window. Five more brawny Fringe guards arrived via the alluron. I did a rough count of Invicta forces versus the enemy and gulped with a startling realization—the enemy would soon outnumber us two to one. My skin broke into goosebumps, and a spark ignited on the surface of the screen. I stepped back, and the spark dissipated. Testing my suspicion, I outstretched my arm, and tiny electrical currents pulsed to life.

"Dez?"

"Mm-hmm?"

"How confident are you that one more jammer will shut it down?" I continued to wave my hand in front of me. He'd said earlier that the allura's DNA was used to fortify this barrier. The bracelet should have repelled me already, but it didn't.

"About 89 percent."

I pinched my lips. That would have to do. "I'm going in," I said.

"Mmm—*What?*"

FIFTY-TWO

I placed my palm on the screen, white noise and the lack of light temporarily paralyzing my senses. Then I stumbled to the floor. I peered up and shrieked when a man with a split tongue and greenish skin took notice of me and reached down. A Seraph collided with him and knocked him off his course. At once, my hearing returned to me, and the sounds of clashes, roaring, and yelping filled my ears. I leaped to my feet and dashed for the alluron.

I strategically maneuvered over and around bodies until a werewolf cut me off, and I had no other viable route to the alluron. I pressed my hands down in the air like a human would calm a pup. *Shit.* It pounced at me. I crouched and rolled over at that precise moment, positioning myself closer to the alluron. The wolf skidded but loped back up and rushed me again. I glanced at the distance between me and the alluron. It was too far still, but I sprinted for it anyway.

I was no match for a wolf to begin with. His acrid breath ruffled my hair, and I slid to the left, landing under Mezzo's feet. He had beheaded another guard and stopped his sword an inch from my nose.

"Wolf." I pointed at the rushing creature. Mezzo squared with the shifter. I didn't wait. I dove between the legs of a purple giant, picked myself up, and dashed in a straight line with tunnel-like vision toward the alluron. The floor inside of the alluron crackled with energy, announcing new mutants. I tripped over a fallen body by the base and dragged myself up. The outline of a red two-headed creature with a bodybuilder silhouette formed within the alluron. His two sets of eyes shimmered with opalescent clusters of hexagons. They lacked any trace of humanity. I slammed my wrist down on the barrier's line before the monster could cross it.

A torrent of electricity snapped my body into a straight line and fried my vocal cords. The smoke didn't just emanate from the bracelet. My entire palm released billows of the smoky substance as if I was now part of the circuit. Part of the destructive forces. *Collapse, collapse*, I commanded the alluron. The crystals grounding the energy illuminated on a blinding scale and shattered one by one. The red creature within it tore apart, its pieces splattering the floor and walls. The alluron, no longer anchored, lifted off the ground and attached itself to the ceiling. It crawled across it like a semi-transparent plasma. It descended in hollow cylinders, encapsulating all beings with demonic traces. Huh. The alluron turned into dozens of mini versions of itself. The beings hit the barrier, but it no longer gave in. Perhaps the serum made of my blood no longer worked, or maybe the alluron had self-taught itself to adapt.

Satisfied, Invicta warriors dispatched the enemy in a frenzy.

"Arien." Both Kole and Xavier were on me, with Mezzo, Anhelm, Vex, and Talen covering their backs. Their faces showed their concern for me. Xavier's eyes twinkled with pride while Kole's turned multiple shades darker flashing with rage. I tapped my throat, letting them know I couldn't speak.

Xavier attempted to pull my wrist away from the barrier line, but the bracelet was stuck as if someone had welded it in place. I stared at him, relieved to see him here, hoping that meant the Soaz was no more.

When I scanned all the faces crowding, all I noticed were sets of brows pinched together.

"You!" Kole shouted at someone approaching.

"I've hacked two layers of security. I'm working as fast as I can," Dez said. I recognized his voice. The stiffness in my body abated, and I relaxed into a ball with my knees tucked in.

"Hey," I croaked. "Dez is best."

I stared into Kole's beautiful face. I'd missed him. And once I was free of this bracelet, I planned on taking him with me to a safe place and seeing how things could be between us. Without Invicta. Without the bond. Without the protector mark.

The tips of my fingers tickled. Multiple mini allurons rose upward and reunited with the remaining plasma on the ceiling. And the mass appeared to be gliding our way. Pieces of crystals clinked toward the base of the alluron and fused together.

"What's happening?" I asked.

Dez glanced around wildly. "It's rebuilding."

"But the bracelets—" As soon as the words left Kole's mouth, the other two jammers scraped on the ground, getting sucked into the center of the alluron. I gasped when my bracelet yanked me over the edge of the base. Both Xavier and Kole hopped on the base and gripped the bracelet. They immobilized it but couldn't drag it outside the alluron.

The remaining mini allurons joined the mass now.

"Don't let the crystals fuse," Xavier ordered. Warriors caught pieces only to be burned with white fire. The alluron wouldn't be stopped.

"You have to go," I said. Stubbornness set into their features. They tugged at the bracelet with no result. "Leave me!"

"No," they said in unison.

No one knew what would happen once the alluron rearranged itself. Most likely the jammers would get destroyed. And I was attached to one. I cast my beseeching eyes at the four warriors staying close. They all gave a perfunctory nod and stepped onto the base. Relief swept over me. They'd remove the stupid men stuck by my helpless sides.

"Stay where you are." Xavier didn't miss a beat while Kole growled in warning. My eyes filled with hot tears. The plasma above us began reaching down with its tentacles.

"I'll be fine," I fibbed. "But you won't." I scowled at them.

"Liar. You don't know what this device will do to you. Who the fuck put that on you?" Kole seethed.

The first plasma tentacle hovered two feet above the line. All the crystals pulsed with soft light, as if on standby. There was no time to argue. I captured Mezzo's eyes. He ground his teeth, but he owed me one. I didn't relent. He had to do this.

In a flash, Kole and Xavier slumped over from Mezzo's touch. I yelped when my bracelet jostled me closer to the center. The alluron touched the barrier line, causing a chain reaction around the perimeter. The soles of Kole and Xavier's boots outside the alluron were the last things I saw before a bottomless chasm opened up below me.

FIFTY-THREE

s I floated in the air, the bracelets transformed into liquid fire and dissolved into particles. I blinked. Darkness, everywhere I looked. My body hung weightless, and I flowed through the nothingness. In the distance, neon lasers floated in my direction, their luminescence the only source of light in the void. Howling winds descended, updrafts slapping my cheeks. The hit spun me around, and I glimpsed red laser dots far off to one side. I snapped my head to the neon lights. No, not lights. They were my coordinates, the ribbons, and I had to get to them before gollums ripped into me.

I swam for the ribbons, and a gust flipped me backward in the air. Shit, I was even further away. The excited buzzing from gollums spiked my adrenaline. I anticipated the next gust and avoided frontal impact by floating sideways. Still, this process wouldn't get me to the ribbons in time. Below me, horrific red eyes swarmed. After my narrow escape a few weeks back, I had wondered why the gollums weren't susceptible to the gales of the void. As I peered into their eyes now, I grew convinced that they had no fear. They weren't masters of this dimension. Otherwise, they would've escaped long ago. They were masters of themselves.

I closed my eyes, panic rising up and invading all my senses. I breathed slowly, extinguishing the last embers of fear. *Shh, it's okay. I'm okay*. Piece by piece, I plucked fear out of my mind, my heart, and even my soul. The sounds phased into background noise. I became a blank canvas. All I wanted was the blue ribbon. I knew it'd take me to the fae king. It wasn't an ideal solution but better than the unknown destinations other ribbons represented.

I imagined it floating to me. Something prodded my stomach, and I opened my eyes. The blue ribbon, and only the blue ribbon, undulated on gentle air within my reach. Stunned, I reached for it. Before my fingers connected, I glanced over my shoulder. An army of hungry eyes watched me, only a few feet away, their sharp claws outstretched and frozen in space. As if a bubble trapping them had popped, they surged forward, and I screamed.

I whirled in the portal like clothes in a laundromat, howling all the way down. The destination opened, and familiar fae faces filled it. I outstretched my arms, hoping for a chivalrous fae to catch me. I blasted out of the tunnel, passing their stunned faces and plowing into a pile of red sand-like dirt, face-first. I pulled out my halfway-buried head and spit out sand. My hair fared no better.

"Arien." The king's irritation was palpable. "This isn't a good time for a social call." I rolled my eyes, dusting the red powder off. Red. I scanned the ground. Red. I turned around. A red landscape of bare ground, protruding rocks, and rocky hills stretched before my eyes as far as I could see. I gulped.

"Where are we?" I faced the king.

A group of about a dozen fae warriors surrounded us, his own detail. Behind the king, the same landscape unfolded. This wasn't the fae's hidden realm. How had Cygnus transported his warriors with him? How had I gotten here? And where the hell were we?

My eyes fell on a blue electric orb wedged into a rock. A portal. That answered how I was able to track the king to this place. The orb sizzled. King Cygnus's mouth twisted as he plucked the device from the crevice and pocketed it.

"I sensed it grow hot when you initiated your transfer."

"Where are we?"

"You arrived right on time, little angel," one of the king's guards said with a crooked smirk. He ignited a double-edged spear of light out of a foot-long metal cylinder. "Ready to skewer some demons?"

FIFTY-FOUR

I gawked at the fae. Demons? Was I in perpetual hell or something—jumping from one demon battle to another? The fae offered me a similar brass metal cylinder. Foreign writing and symbols wavered on its surface. They pulsated, erratic at first, then in rhythm with my heartbeat. I knew because I felt the pulse acutely in the palm of my right hand. The weapon hummed, and I withdrew my hand, shaking my head.

King Cygnus scanned the land from his perch on a raised rock, his knee bent. We stood well above the ground on a raised dune, giving us a tactical advantage over the enemy. The soil stirred in the distance, sifting red sand pooling into several openings. The suction settled, and single-clawed appendages emerged, dragging the remaining bodies out of the sand. The creatures were a sort of vermilion arachnid with eight legs. Each leg ended in a pointy stinger.

"Spiders?" I asked.

"Cheruse demons. One sting will paralyze you from the neck down and leave you at their mercy."

E. G. SPARKS

"They like to consume their prey alive," another fae chimed in, grinning widely.

I swung my eyes to the threat before us. Several demons rose to standing on their rear two stingers. The three pairs of stingers acted like their arms. Yet, the most bizarre aspect was their heads, resembling spiders with prominent eyes atop them while they were in a crawling stance. The undersides of their heads were visible now, and they contained human eyes and mouths. The caved-in noses were the only non-human characteristic. My face turned ashen. I pulled on the first warrior's sleeve.

"Are you still offering that weapon?"

He handed the cylinder to me, the corners of his mouth rising.

"How do y—?" The weapon activated with a swoosh. My heartbeat drummed in my right hand, feeding into the metal. King Cygnus approached. His face closed off. He lifted my wrist and inspected it.

"Earthbounders can't use our weapons. You're different. Where are your wings?" His eyes narrowed.

"You're asking me about my wings?" I asked, nonplussed. I couldn't hide the tremble in my voice. There were humanoid red spiders with deadly stingers moving our way. King Cygnus raised an eyebrow.

"Cheruse demons are no challenge to us."

"Then why are you here?" *And why am I here?*

"Retribution. Many eons ago now, we set off on an excursion far away from our homeland. When we returned, our homes were rubble and fire. Our women and children were either gone or murdered. No one came forth to claim responsibility for the attack. Many worthless cowards exist in this universe. Absent our homes, wives, and children, we have only one goal left: to annihilate those who wronged us."

This was the most information I'd ever gotten from the

king. The fae used to have families, a place to call home, and it had all come crashing down overnight. The story pulled on a string in my heart.

"Is that why you needed to create a portal?"

He nodded. "Your life force is potent. When I created Arana, the portal was but the size of a pearl. I've cultivated it ever since, but your essence triggered exponential growth, activating it."

"Oh." *Well, you're welcome.* But then I remembered how the king had deceived and used me to obtain my life force. Knowing his goal all this time was to exact justice for the innocent fae slaughtered by demons softened the blow a little. I didn't know which was worse—not having a family to call your own all your life or having one and losing it in the most macabre way.

My thoughts sidelined to Kole, Rae, Zaira, Vex, and Talen. And Nelia. I had my own people now, and they felt like family to me. A family of crazy badass demon hunters, but who was I to complain?

Shouts erupted from scores of fae warriors I hadn't seen blending with the terrain. They raced toward the cheruse demons who now each stood erect on two of their stingers, the other three pairs of stingers at the ready. I squeezed my fist around the fae weapon, taking a long breath in.

"You must return now. You're not ready to engage with cheruse demons." The king withdrew his own spear cylinder, his mouth set in an angry line. His eyes zeroed in on his enemy. I swallowed. "My men will escort you to an allura not far from here."

"Can't I use your portal?"

"The portal's power is finite. Each use strips it of its charge. So, unless you're willing to power it up with your essence again, I suggest you use an allura." His tone dripped with condescension. The king was not a man of patience. I inclined my head. At least we agreed on one point—no one would be using my essence today. No one but me.

Two fae warriors nudged me down the side of the rock plateau. The red sand reverberated with clashes between the fae and the demons nearby. It rattled and shifted, almost as if it were alive itself. The fae flanked me, watchful. We jogged up to another rock and stopped to assess our surroundings again. We repeated these steps multiple times.

"That's it," one warrior said. He brushed away dirt from one side of a rock, revealing a symbol. He pushed a square-shaped block in, and the rock popped open in the middle. The warrior grabbed the split and separated the two sides far enough for us to enter. A carved tunnel led to an opening with a reservoir of still-red water in the center. I inched closer. This had to be it, the allura. A lively shimmer on the surface reflected my face and some interesting focal points near the ceiling. Statues of some sort. I gazed upward and shrieked when one statue craned its head.

"Cheruse demons," the fae said in unison. I counted five spider-like creatures.

"Jump," the warrior demanded.

"There are two of you and five of them."

The fae snickered. One grabbed my arm and slowly backed me to the edge. The demons slid down their velvety webs, like riding a zip line, all at once. I drew my spear up at the ready. But the fae beat me to each strike. They blocked and attacked with practiced stealth and inborn grace. The demons stayed away from the water, but when the warriors shifted to the left with three demons furiously throwing their stingers around, I found myself exposed and facing one of them. Putting the spear in front of me, I noticed the demon wincing and backing off. He didn't like the light. But then he swung a right hook at me, and I leaped back. Still holding the spear in front of me, I hoped to buy time so the backup could dispatch this loner as well. I had no training with a spear.

"Guys, how is it going over there?" All I heard was grunts in response. *Okay, don't panic.*

"Good spider," I mumbled. Another stinger flew at me, and I ducked. "Damn it, bad spider." As if the creature understood me, it released an assault of stingers at me. I sprang, ducked, and rolled on the ground. Frustration got the better of me eventually, and I aimed and then threw my spear at it. Shit, big mistake. The spear grazed its shoulder, but now, I was weaponless and alone with a pissed-off giant eight-legged freak. Its almond-shaped eyes gave away no emotion, but the human-like lips thinned out in grim dissatisfaction. I abandoned any hope of defeating the creature and darted away. The fae warriors had dispatched one demon and had the other two cornered near the entrance to the tunnel.

"Help!" My boots kicked red sand with each sinking step. I pumped my arms. One of the fae detached from the confrontation and ran toward me.

"On my mark, duck left," he yelled.

I was within twenty feet of him now.

"My left or your left?" I croaked breathlessly. The demon had no trouble keeping up with me.

"Duck!"

I hesitated before throwing myself to my right. I saw in slow motion the fae's spear flying in the air, right on the target. It hit my left bicep first, sending a burning sensation down my arm, then lodged itself into the demon's chest. The creature let out a shrill and convulsed to the ground, where the sand buried it.

The spear deactivated, and the metal cylinder fell to the ground. I grabbed my arm, expecting to see a gash there. The spear hadn't even breached the skin. It hurt like a thousand volts had grazed my arm. I sucked in a breath.

The fae scooped up his weapon.

"Fae weapons don't affect us."

"I am not fae," I said through gritted teeth.

"True. Yet, you ignited the spear. We enchanted our weapons to only respond to us and never to harm us. Ergo, the spear shouldn't have harmed you even though it went through you."

I clutched the arm to my chest, schooling my eyes.

"So, what you're saying is you weren't sure—"

"The demon was about to impale you." The fae hiked both eyebrows for emphasis. His companion strode over and inspected my arm. I gritted my teeth when he applied pressure. My bicep felt tender, and I wouldn't have been surprised if a purple bruise appeared later.

"It's fine," I said. I plucked the fae's fingers off my arm, one by one. These men had a skewed understanding of boundaries. "Thank you for saving my life."

"We must return to the king now," the closest fae said.

I nodded. We retraced our steps to the edge of the red lake.

"Any idea how to activate this allura?"

The fae crouched beside me, gliding his fingers through the water.

"This isn't an allura. The barrier is at the bottom of the reservoir."

"You know how to swim, right?" The second warrior eyed me suspiciously.

"Enough to not drown." I closed my eyes and inhaled deeply. My thoughts swirled around Kole of their own volition. When I opened my eyes a few seconds later, a small smile graced my lips. I had my coordinates—the closest portal to Kole's position. Now, the not-so-fun part of diving to the bottom of the red lake.

"Here goes nothing," I whispered.

I strolled in, sighing at the pleasant warmth emanating from the lake. Before I could second-guess it, I gulped in the brisk air and dove under. The bright red hue gradually darkened, and I fought the oncoming panic. Slick, long leaves and fronds stymied my progress to the lake's floor. They entangled my legs and torso. My lungs begged for oxygen as I tore at the weeds and pushed them out of my way. I was nearly out of time. A thick curtain of flora hung all around me, and I persevered through sheer determination.

There was no sign of the floor. Only endless water. Fear crept in. Was I going to die here? On a different planet? Away from Kole and my friends? My limbs weakened and refused to move.

Childlike giggles filled my eardrum, and I jerked awake. Water nymphs dragged me from my tomb. On the other side of the floral wall, bright light illuminated the lake's floor. The nymphs let go, and I hurled like a billiard ball into the bright slot.

FIFTY-FIVE

The allura sucked me out of the water and into a tunnel of fluorescent rings. *Kole. Take me to Kole*, I commanded this interplanetary expressway. The speed at which I traveled vaulted to unimaginable levels, the rings blending into a tube and the light intensifying. I cried out from the blinding exposure and squeezed my eyes shut.

I breached the allura's endpoint with a splash. Another body of water connected with it. The force of the entry cata-pulted me through the water and over its surface, the sandy shore greeting me.

A black-clad figure stood at the water's edge. Masculine with broad shoulders. I zeroed in on his sculpted face set in astonishment. Kole remained still as I torpedoed toward him. The trajectory arced downward, and I readied myself for a rough landing. My protector jogged over to meet me and plucked me out of the air.

Oof. Kole cushioned my fall by taking the brunt of the impact. Although, I suspected packed sand would've been softer than Kole. I lay on top of him, relief warming me. My chest heaved from labored breaths coming in and out, but that didn't stop me from smiling down at him.

My lungs burned, and I tasted the brackish water of the red lake. Had I just been on a different planet? I rested my forehead on Kole's shoulder. His touch shifted from self-affirming to nostalgic as he drew slow circles on my back. I scrutinized the glassy film on the Everlake's surface.

"What are you doing here?" I wheezed.

Kole chuckled.

"Praying. I wasn't expecting much, but here you are. An embodiment of a miracle."

I lifted my head and grinned at him.

"What?" he asked.

"I've never heard of an angel who doesn't believe in miracles."

Kole swept wet strands behind my ear. "I like to stand out."

"So you do." My chest vibrated from laughter and residual hypoxia.

Too soon, laughter extinguished between us. Kole's eyes darkened, and mine held onto them like a lifesaver. If he rejected me—us—again, I wouldn't know how to be around him anymore. He was the only man my soul craved. I pushed up and lay by his side, stargazing.

"I'm short on wishing dust. Can you lend me some?" I asked.

"No." Kole propped himself up on one elbow, gazing skyward. "But I might be able to make one of your wishes come true."

I watched with anticipation as his head slowly swiveled downward, meeting my flushed face. There was only one wish on my mind now, and I prayed Kole knew precisely which one. Galaxies sparkled in his eyes around a reflection—a face with round expectant eyes and parted lips. They drifted closer. Closer...

I closed my eyes as thousands of pleasure points on my lips exploded on contact. Kole's robust lips took mine hostage, pliable and demanding. Coaxing heat to the surface only he could ignite and quench. I was lost to him. He didn't take more than what I was ready for, satisfied with the slow tempo. As if he feared I'd disappear.

If only I could can this moment and store it on a "forever" shelf.

Kole withdrew first, placing a sweet kiss on the tip of my nose.

"I can safely say, now, I believe in miracles," Kole said. I ran a hand through his unruly dark locks.

"You look so...peaceful," I said. I struggled with how to describe the new Kole. He radiated an intense aura whenever he was near me, and I soon discovered that intensity was his constant state. Always chasing after the next demon, protecting humanity. Never stopping. Here and now, with me, I glimpsed his turmoil giving in to contentment for the first time.

"You are my calm. My peace. My sunrises and my sunsets. You complete my days."

I stared at him, speechless. For a man who professed he was poor with words, well, that was a pretty damn good attempt. I pushed up and kissed him tenderly, trailing kisses across his cheek.

"What happened after I jumped? Did the alluron shut down?" I whispered against his skin.

Kole's brows drew together. He pulled me to a sitting position with him.

"About that... I'm angry with you again. I thought..." He shook his head as if to clear it. "Your plan worked. We dispatched all the remaining demons and hybrids. Do you know how long it's been since you disappeared?" His eyes found mine again. Anguish marred their edges.

"How long?" The last time I transported to Arana, a day there cost me two weeks of Earth's time. How long could an interplanetary jump last in Earth's terms?

"Four days."

"Oh. That's not long," I said, confused at Kole's reaction.

"That's an eternity." He took my hand and gave it a gentle squeeze. I swallowed, not knowing how to respond. Could I really mean this much to him? I squeezed his hand in return.

An image of Daria skittered across my vision and a pang of pain shot down my back, making me curl into a ball.

"What's wrong?"

I drew in a breath as I tried to straighten.

"Daria's calling me. I gifted her a feather to alert me when she learns Paulie's loc—*Oww*." The exit points for my wings heated. "Why does it hurt so much?" I didn't see Mezzo being this affected when I called upon his favor.

"It's intense when the message is urgent. With time, you'll learn to shield yourself."

My mind hung on one word: *urgent*. "Paulie's in trouble," I said.

"I'll take you. I'm parked near."

Daria's face filled my vision again. "Hurry," she whispered, turning to something over her shoulder. "There isn't time." I stopped, pulling my hand out of Kole's grasp.

"No," he said, dominating my space. We both knew the fastest way for me to get to Daria was to jump through the Everlake. I couldn't carry him with me while this pain ricocheted through my body.

"Kole, I have to go. Now." I placed a hand on his chest. I trembled as a wave of pain wracked my back again, reminding me of the call. I gritted my teeth. He registered all of it.

"I don't like this. Where are you meeting her?"

I concentrated on the pull between myself and Daria. A vision of Daria sitting in her uncle's office overlapped my sight.

"The dry cleaning shop in Chinatown." The next wave of pain weakened my legs, and I fell against Kole's chest. He scooped me up and rushed into the water, waist-deep.

"Go. I will be right behind you." His muscles strained, hesitant to release me. He set me on my feet and placed a chaste kiss on my lips. A wane grin curled my lips.

"I'll see you soon," I promised. Quickly, I turned away from him and waded deeper into the water, ducking under.

FIFTY-SIX

I surrendered to the magic of allura. White light signaled the endpoint, and I readied my body. I soared out of the corridor to a seasoned warrior-worthy crouch. The pain abated immediately. I smiled to myself because I finally did it —I was becoming a worthy warrior. The stars aligned for me this one time.

I landed in Paulie's friend's secret room filled with magic paraphernalia, but absent anyone's presence. The place was dark. The only light filtering into the office was through a cracked door. My heart picked a faster tempo as my intuition told me something was off. Slowly, I headed for the door when I hit an invisible wall. I tapped it with my shoulder and felt around it with my hands. Breathing heavily, I took a step back. The invisible barrier encircled me, anchored by white rotund candles stationed on the floor. *No!*

"Daria!" I pounded my fists on the barrier and rammed my shoulder into it in desperation. The candles flickered at once. Malcolm's room flaked away, and a new backdrop came into focus—a grassy clearing in a forest. Candles puffed out in unison, and I leaped out of the vicious transportation circle, fearing it'd trap me again.

"Here you are." Fallen branches cracked underneath Daria's boots. I took a step toward her, questions written all over my face, when a dark, bulky shadow filled the space behind her.

"Watch out!" I sprinted for her and stalled halfway as giggles carried to me. Eyes widening, I took in the warrior with a hideous scar blemishing one side of his jaw and neck, but with an otherwise angelic face.

"You should've seen your face." Daria held her belly, unable to break her laughing spell.

I ignored her, my gaze fixed on Damian's contorted smirk. Shivers ran down my spine, my body having an unsolicited reaction to Damian's presence. His presence spelled out trouble, brute actions, pain... I'd seen Damian's true nature—the psychological one—and his true physical form. They had called me a monster, a demon-spawn, oblivious to demon hybrids among their own. As if reading my mind, Damian raised his eyebrows.

"Let me guess, Bezekah's soleil wasn't a mistake?" I asked, returning my attention to the foolish girl before me.

"When Paulie first pitched the idea to me, I thought he was insane. Who's stupid enough to break into the Emporium? I knew I only had one chance to do it, so I weighed my options." She juggled an imaginary scale in her hands. "Do I get a soleil for an old inane druid, or do the heist of a century? I posted a listing on the black site and guess what happened next?" She squealed, "The Soaz himself contacted me."

Of course. Why hadn't I seen this coming? Why hadn't Paulie?

Damian rested a palm on Daria's shoulder, with a pinch of pride in his expression. But, if he was proud of anything, that'd be for beguiling this young girl, and not for her own merit. His plan had worked perfectly. Until me... I'd sent Bezekah to the hells he'd come from.

Daria's eyes glistened with adoration as she glanced upwards. Damian lowered his head, gliding his fingers into the hair at her nape. My stomach churned, but I couldn't take my eyes away from the two deceivers even when they were about to make out right in front of me.

Snap.

Daria's bliss-struck face fell slack, following her body to the ground. I watched, transfixed, as Daria's body crumpled to the grass, lifeless. I wouldn't have put it past Damian to kill with bare hands and show no emotion doing it. But to witness it? That does something to your psyche.

Only a veritable monster was capable of that.

"What? You didn't think I'd let her go free and blabber about what happened?"

I bristled. Daria had her flaws, but she was also young and naive. She didn't deserve to go out that way. Wrong time, wrong place, and one wrong Earthbounder.

"She wouldn't have told a soul. She was madly in love with you."

Damian scoured Daria's body and shrugged. "Teenagers. They change their mind—"

Before he could finish, I dashed for the spelled circle. I had no idea how that magic worked exactly, but it was my best bet at getting away. A few candles flickered when I crossed the barrier. A body like a bulldozer ran me over and pressed my face into the dirt. I struggled to breathe when he wouldn't let up. Blindly, I found his arm and dug my nails into it, drawing welts in the skin. Strength drained out of me faster without air, slowing my movements.

Damian hoisted me up and tossed me in the air. I landed in a heap several feet away, greedily sucking in air. Scrambling to all fours, Damian's fist grabbed my hair and hauled me to my feet. My scalp burned, but I wouldn't give him the satisfaction of seeing my pain. I let hatred for him shine in my eyes instead. A storm of emotions brewed around his pupils, yellow swerving in the rich brown. His eyes lit up with a yellow hue before he sank his teeth into my neck.

Bam. The venom in his teeth lulled me into compliance, chipping at any remaining mental barriers. *Get out of there, Arien. You must get out.* My skin heated.

"Not this time," Damian whispered into my ear. He quit draining me right before my power reservoirs got hypercharged. My legs shook, and I couldn't hold my weight. He left me wilted like a flower deprived of light.

The winds picked up, and their roaring canceled out all nature sounds. Strands of my hair blasted my face. I shut my eyes, fighting the urge to lay my head on Damian's shoulder and rest. No, he might have won this standoff, but it went against my grain to give in. The winds shifted downward, and I realized these were no ordinary winds. A helicopter landed near us. I squinted. A female figure emerged—a button-down shirt and a long skirt with heels. Her face was blurry, but the voice betrayed her identity.

"I need her alive," said Mariola, the Magister of the Northern region. She lifted my limp hand and ran her fingers over my mother's bracelet. "I knew my sister was stupid, but what cretin gives her child the only item tying her to the institution she so abhorrently despised?" She didn't wait for an answer. Mariola dropped my arm and turned around. Damian followed with me in his arms. She was talking about my mother. Her sister?

The hopelessness of my situation set in. I gulped for air, setting my face in a harsh scowl, afraid to spill a single tear. Damian set me in his lap for the journey, and I prayed I'd get sick and throw up all over him before we got to our destination.

He rubbed his chin in my hair, and nausea set in. "You tried to warn them, and they didn't listen. You see, they are all inferior to you and I."

"There isn't a place in this universe where *you and I* are a thing," I said through gritted teeth.

"Pardon me, I shall clarify your place."

"Which is?" I swallowed, hesitant to find out the answer.

"Beneath me."

Did he mean it literally or metaphorically? My eyes bored into his.

I choked on a scream as Damian drove a long needle into my neck. I grabbed his arm. Cold liquid like antifreeze seeped into a major vein and flooded through my body. Black spots danced in front of my eyes. My hands fell away. My head lolled, falling into the crook of his neck. Damian purred with pleasure.

"I...hate...you..." I breathed before I tumbled off the cliff of consciousness.

DEAR READER

I am eternally grateful for your continued support! If you enjoyed this second installment in Arien's journey, please consider leaving a review. Reviews help authors reach more wonderful readers like you.

Arien's story concludes in the last book in this trilogy MARBLE SUN. You can order here: https://amzn.to/ 3D8NuL8.

May you soar high always!

www.egsparks.com

ABOUT THE AUTHOR

E. G. Sparks is an award-winning dark fantasy romance author. Her debut novel, "Sky Ice," won the Silver/2nd Place award in the 2024 Feathered Quill Book Awards for the Fantasy category and was a Finalist in the 2024 Wishing Shelf Book Awards.

She delights in sharing fantasy worlds and making her heroines' lives difficult. When not in her writing cave, E. G. can be found hanging out with family and friends, traveling, gardening, doing yoga, and (you guessed it!) reading.

E. G. resides in sunny Florida with her husband, three beautiful daughters, two dogs, and a cat.

She invites readers to get first looks, bonuses, and more by subscribing to her newsletter at: www.egsparks.com

Made in the USA
Columbia, SC
18 March 2025

55321464R00178